TILLIE

was born in Nebraska in 1912
for most of her life. The necessit
children through 'everyday jobs
Public libraries were her college. Her publications include *Tell Me a Riddle* (1962) whose title novella received the O. Henry Award as the best American story of 1961; *Yonnondio: From the Thirties* (1974); *Silences* (1978); and *Mother to Daughter, Daughter to Mother* (1984).

Among the colleges where Tillie Olsen has taught or been writer-in-residence are Amherst College, Stanford University, MIT, and Kenyon College. She is the recipient of five Honorary Degrees; grants from the National Endowment for the Arts and the Ford Foundation; Radcliffe Institute and Guggenheim Fellowships; and an award from the National Institute of Arts and Letters. In conjunction with their issuance of stamps commemorating Emily Brontë, Charlotte Brontë, George Eliot and Elizabeth Gaskell, the British Post Office in 1980 selected Tillie Olsen for a special award as 'the American woman writer best exemplifying in our time their ideals and literary excellence.'

Tillie Olsen's work has been much anthologised, has been translated into thirteen languages, and adapted into three films and various staged productions. She lives in San Francisco.

VIRAGO
MODERN
CLASSIC
NUMBER
363

By the same author

Silences

Mother to Daughter, Daughter to Mother

Tell Me A Riddle

&

Yonnondio

Tillie Olsen

With Introductions by
Cora Kaplan

Virago

Tell Me A Riddle

Published by VIRAGO PRESS Limited 1980

First published in Great Britain
by Faber and Faber Limited 1964

Yonnondio

First published in Great Britain
by Faber and Faber Limited 1975

This edition first published in Great Britain
by VIRAGO PRESS Limited 1990
20–23 Mandela Street, Camden Town, London NW1 0HQ

*A CIP catalogue record for this book
is available from the British Library*

Printed in Great Britain by
Cox & Wyman Limited, Reading, Berks

Tell Me A Riddle

For my mother
1885–1956

INTRODUCTION

Tillie Olsen's fiction speaks on behalf of the unnumbered, voiceless working men and women, especially women, whose needs and aspirations went unfulfilled, stifled by depression, world war and a poverty which still flourished in boom years. Her art too suffered in those long decades when "the simplest circumstances for creation did not exist". Her writing put by, she bore and raised children and worked at everyday jobs, while involving herself in workers' struggles. These were years of artistic frustration, of "conscious storing" and "secret . . . reconnaissance" that eventually formed these extraordinary stories. In her work she explores the multiple causes and effects of "silences", and in doing so retrieves for the reader not only the peculiar sufferings and triumphs of individuals but the meaning of whole decades of American experience, intensely lived but barely recorded. Each of the four stories in this collection gives the effect, so concentrated is her prose, of a much longer work. In particular the title story, "Tell Me a Riddle" has the density and force of a novel, as if the author's own long silence had pressed its subject, the life and death of an immigrant woman, into an economic and powerful form, giving off fiercer light and heat than great fiction may times its length.

Written and published in the fifties and early sixties, the stories first appeared as a collection in 1962 when their author was fifty. For American readers they have become classics of short fiction, known and prized for over a generation. *Tell Me a Riddle* was, and continues to be, a transforming book for feminism, countering the too dominant emphases on middle-class concerns in the movement's early theoretical writing. In 1962, when the new movement was not yet born, Tillie Olsen spoke from an earlier, almost forgotten feminist tradition, in the first of two talks which form the core of her critical work, *Silences* (1978). These essays explore literary silences, "the unnatural thwarting of what struggles to come into being, but cannot . . . It is concerned with the relationships of circumstances–including class, color, sex; the times, climate into which one is born–to the creation of literature." Believing imaginative literature to be the "incomparable medium" of culture, linked to all creative acts of consciousness, she states her "hatred for all that, societally rooted, unnecessarily lessens and denies it; slows, impairs, silences writers." Limited production, cut off or late flowering like her own, requires explanation not apology. In the last twenty years she has devoted much of her time and energy to the rediscovery of the forgotten women writers, as well as the promotion of new and unknown female talent. In her fiction the same hatred is mobilised to understand the particular circumstances which stunt all forms of human growth. Writing well and living fully, with the material and psychological conditions in which to do both, are never separated. A passionate rage at maiming circumstance provides the energy and argument of Tillie Olsen's fiction. It is the substance of her imaginative and critical project–and the force behind change.

All these stories written during the relative affluence of the 1950s concern themselves with harsher times, harder material conditions coupled with something lost and priceless, a collective political idealism and involvement.

The mother in "I Stand Here Ironing" explains that they were poor and "could not afford for her the soil of easy growth . . . she [Emily] . . . was a miracle to me [but had to grow into a world] where she was no miracle at all . . . She is a child of her age, of depression, of war, of fear." Mother and daughter are equally but differently damaged; Emily internalises depression, expresses casually despair, fear: "We'll all be atom dead . . ." she tells her mother. The mother must suffer that "all that is in her will not bloom–but in how many does it?", but asks for her daughter what she has won for herself, "enough to live by", and the will to fight the searing pressure of the iron.

Printed in the order in which they were written, the stories build on each other. The mother/speaker of the first story is both character and author; there is no commentary outside the questions and answers which move with the "tormented" passage of the iron across fabric and time. The mother's refusal to "total" her daughter's life, "all that life that has happened outside of me, beyond me", is the author's refusal of too absolute or simple a determinism. The narrative seeks to expose, not resolve the contradictory relations between social forces and individual history, and resists its own symbolisation of women's work or being, as iron, ironer or dress. The story points to what is beyond it, to a future altered by its reading, lived by the reader.

In the last three stories the authorial voice is only one of many that compete for our attention and understanding. Whitey's seaman's slang dominates "Hey Sailor, What Ship?", slurred with alcohol, as he "lurches through the past", his health and hopes smashed as much by his recognition of the "death of brotherhood" as by booze. His old political comrades and friends, Lennie and Helen, see him as a tie to a long gone part of their lives. In their now different lives, the eldest daughter sees Whitey as an "old wino" who they exploit and despise, forbidden the house unless he is sober, "because of the children".

Whitey wants the remnants of brotherhood in the present, acceptance of what he has become, and why, rather than Lennie's sentimental evocations of a fraternal past. Tillie Olsen reminds us elsewhere that in our society "any person who is lucky enough to achieve recognition does so at the expense of those who do not get the chance". Lennie's survival in a world where men "eat each other" is built on Whitey's refusal to take on and profit by the values of such a world. Deepening with the narrative, the seaman's comradely salutation–"Hey Sailor, What Ship?"–is a highly charged question, personal and political, by the end.

Moving along a few years with Lennie and Helen's family, "O Yes" describes another kind of broken loyalty across racial as well as class divides. Two girl friends, Carol and Parialee, are "sorted" at puberty; peer groups and teachers separate the new middle-class from the black and white working-class children. The solidarity of the black community is represented in the store-front church where Carol attends, but cannot cope with, Parialee's baptism. Parialee's mother Alva tries to explain to Carol the shouting and singing that frightened her: "church is home . . . maybe the only place they can feel how they feel and maybe let it come out". Jeannie, at seventeen, knows from her own experience that Carol must "run with" her own crowd. "O Yes" ends with Helen's mourning her own lack of community to sustain her, mourning her powerlessness to give Carol the courage to act on "having to care".

The crucial limits of mothering, and the near impossible task of transmitting political values from one generation to the next are recurrent themes in Tillie Olsen's work; so also is the revision of American ideas of progress. Eva, the heroine of "Tell Me a Riddle", has suffered forty-seven years of subordination in marriage–long, anxious years of poverty and child-rearing. Once in childhood, part of a great movement for change, she had known "transport, meaning, community". Now formed, deformed by the isolation that a traditional domestic life has forced on her, she does not "need others to enjoy". She has had to live "for" not "with" people and only asks that she be able to use the freedom of the empty house, the minimal domestic tasks "to journey on". Her husband, panicked by the absence of social relations, appalled by the solitude Eva craves, wants to sell up and retire to a "Haven" for pensioners. The story illuminates, as no polemic can, the real cost of the sexual division of labour in our culture. David has lived "with" people; accepting modern America, he has lost the "holiest dreams" he and Eva shared in their Russian radical youth. Eva stored her dreams as if "for seventy years she had hidden a tape recorder, infinitely microscopic, within her, . . . trapping every song, every melody, every word read, heard, and spoken. . ." Too buried in making do, her children under different influences from their world, she has not been able to "teach" her children the revolutionary message "not to go back, not to go back". Sickened, she watches one child practice an orthodoxy she despises, "a Religion that stifled and said: in Paradise, woman, you will be the footstool of your husband. . ."; watches, with complex emotions, another re-enact her exhausted multiple motherhood. More and more she articulates her pain and anger against waste of human potentiality, the threat of nuclear destruction of all life.

At last, dying, the damned speech is released: philosophy, politics, poetry, song, fragmented and interrupted by the words that were spoken–scolding a child, requests for cheaper meat. David listens, helpless, raging, as her delirium taunts him with all that she has withheld and he has lost. The broken up prose of the last section of the story mimes Eva's disordered recapitulation, reorders her living, giving us her words as a concrete poetic testament, a lifeline to real human progress. Her granddaughter Jeannie, reacting against the subtler new oppression of her time catches and holds Eva's message. Each painful turn of the story releases Eva to us, towards death.

No piece of women's experience is trashed or discarded in Tillie Olsen's fiction, but the traditional "gifts"–mothering, love, sexual pleasure–are not falsely celebrated, since their practice, in our society, limits other liberating activities, silences other creative expression. The forced "discontinuities" of job, child care, and housework cost the author decades of what ought to have been her writing life. Yet in these stories, produced during years of frightening political reaction in the United States, when it must have seemed as if the collective struggles and achievements of her non-writing decades might also be lost, belief always surfaces. Written from, rather than just about working women's lives, the unique, wrenching angle of vision, the wonderful concentration of the writing which can catch in a phrase a whole lifetime's lost possibility, has been lived and worked for.

In praising the pleasures and uses of written literature, Tillie Olsen has always tried to demystify the circumstances which allow it to happen at all. In describing herself as "fortunate" she makes a further comment on the ironies of the American dream. "How can I be personally bitter," she asks "when I have been able to do what so few of my sex and class have had the chance to do? But I am bitter, do not forgive, their silencing and the enormous loss of what they had to give."

Cora Kaplan, 1980

CONTENTS

These are printed in the order of their having been written.

The contents of this collection appeared originally, in slightly different form, as follows:

"I Stand Here Ironing" copyright 1956 by the Pacific Coast Committee for the Humanities of the American Council of Learned Societies, in *Pacific Spectator*.

"Hey Sailor, What Ship?" copyright © 1957 by Bantam Books, Inc., reprinted from *New Campus Writing No.* 2 with permission of Bantam Books, Inc., New York.

"O Yes" copyright 1957 by the University of Nebraska Press, in *Prairie Schooner* (under the title "Baptism").

"Tell Me a Riddle" in NEW WORLD WRITING 16.

I

I STAND HERE IRONING

I stand here ironing, and what you asked me moves tormented back and forth with the iron.

"I wish you would manage the time to come in and talk with me about your daughter. I'm sure you can help me understand her. She's a youngster who needs help and whom I'm deeply interested in helping."

"Who needs help. . . ." Even if I came, what good would it do? You think because I am her mother I have a key, or that in some way you could use me as a key? She has lived for nineteen years. There is all that life that has happened outside of me, beyond me.

And when is there time to remember, to sift, to weigh, to estimate, to total? I will start and there will be an interruption and I will have to gather it all together again. Or I will become engulfed with all I did or did not do, with what should have been and what cannot be helped.

She was a beautiful baby. The first and only one of our five that was beautiful at birth. You do not guess how new and uneasy her tenancy in her now-loveliness. You did not know her all those years she was thought homely, or see her poring over her baby pictures, making me tell her over and over how beautiful she had been—and would be, I would tell her—and was now, to the seeing eye. But the seeing eyes were few or non-existent. Including mine.

I nursed her. They feel that's important nowadays. I nursed all the children, but with her, with all the fierce rigidity of first motherhood, I did like the books then said. Though her cries battered me to trembling and my breasts ached with swollenness, I waited till the clock decreed.

Why do I put that first? I do not even know if it matters, or if it explains anything.

She was a beautiful baby. She blew shining bubbles of sound. She loved motion, loved light, loved colour and music and textures. She would lie on the floor in her blue overalls patting the surface so hard in ecstasy her hands and feet would blur. She was a miracle to me, but when she was eight months old I had to leave her daytimes with the woman downstairs to whom she was no miracle at all, for I worked or looked for work and for Emily's father, who "could no longer endure" (he wrote in his good-bye note) "sharing want with us."

I was nineteen. It was the pre-relief, pre-WPA world of the depression. I would start running as soon as I got off the streetcar, running up the stairs, the place smelling sour, and awake or asleep to startle awake, when she saw me she would break into a clogged weeping that could not be comforted, a weeping I can yet hear.

After a while I found a job hashing at night so I could be with her days, and it was better. But it came to where I had to bring her to his family and leave her.

It took a long time to raise the money for her fare back. Then she got chicken pox and I had to wait longer. When she finally came, I hardly knew her, walking quick and nervous like her father, looking like her father, thin, and dressed in a shoddy red that yellowed her skin and glared at the pock marks. All the baby loveliness gone.

She was two. Old enough for nursery school they said, and I did not know then what I know now—the fatigue of the long day, and the lacerations of group life in the kinds of nurseries that are only parking places for children.

Except that it would have made no difference if I had known. It was the only place there was. It was the only way we could be together, the only way I could hold a job.

And even without knowing, I knew. I knew the teacher that was evil because all these years it has curdled into my memory, the little boy hunched in the corner, her rasp, "why aren't you outside, because Alvin hits you? that's no reason, go out, scaredy." I knew Emily hated it even if she did not clutch and implore "don't go Mommy" like the other children, mornings.

She always had a reason why we should stay home. Momma, you look sick. Momma, I feel sick. Momma, the teachers aren't there today, they're sick. Momma, we can't go, there was a fire there last night. Momma, it's a holiday today, no school, they told me.

But never a direct protest, never rebellion. I think of our others in their three-, four-year-oldness—the explosions, the tempers, the denunciations, the demands—and I feel suddenly ill. I put the iron down. What in me demanded that goodness in her? And what was the cost, the cost to her of such goodness?

The old man living in the back once said in his gentle way: "You should smile at Emily more when you look at her." What *was* in my face when I looked at her? I loved her. There were all the acts of love.

It was only with the others I remembered what he said, and it was the face of joy, and not of care or tightness or worry I turned to them—too late for Emily. She does not smile easily, let alone almost always as her brothers and sisters do. Her face is closed and sombre, but when she wants, how fluid. You must have seen it in her pantomimes, you spoke of her rare gift for comedy on the stage that rouses a laughter out of the audience so dear they applaud and applaud and do not want to let her go.

Where does it come from, that comedy? There was none of it in her when she came back to me that second time, after I had had to send her away again. She had a new daddy now to learn to love, and I think perhaps it was a better time. Except when we left her alone nights, telling ourselves she was old enough.

"Can't you go some other time, Mommy, like tomorrow?" she would ask. "Will it be just a little while you'll be gone? Do you promise?"

The time we came back, the front door open, the clock on the floor in the hall. She rigid awake. "It wasn't just a little while. I didn't cry. Three times I called you, just three times, and then I ran downstairs to open the door so you could come faster. The clock talked loud. I threw it away, it scared me what it talked."

She said the clock talked loud again that night I went to the hospital to have Susan. She was delirious with the fever that comes before red measles, but she was fully conscious all the week I was gone and the week after we were home when she could not come near the new baby or me.

She did not get well. She stayed skeleton thin, not wanting to eat, and night after night she had nightmares. She would call for me, and I would rouse from exhaustion to sleepily call back: "You're all right, darling, go to sleep, it's just a dream," and if she still called, in a sterner voice, "now go to sleep, Emily, there's nothing to hurt you." Twice, only twice, when I had to get up for Susan anyhow, I went in to sit with her.

Now when it is too late (as if she would let me hold and comfort her like I do the others) I get up and go to her at once at her moan or restless stirring. "Are you awake, Emily? Can I get you something, dear?" And the answer is always the same: "No, I'm all right, go back to sleep, Mother."

They persuaded me at the clinic to send her away to

a convalescent home in the country where "she can have the kind of food and care you can't manage for her, and you'll be free to concentrate on the new baby." They still send children to that place. I see pictures on the society page of sleek young women planning affairs to raise money for it, or dancing at the affairs, or decorating Easter eggs or filling Christmas stockings for the children.

They never have a picture of the children so I do not know if the girls still wear those gigantic red bows and the ravaged looks on the every other Sunday when parents can come to visit "unless otherwise notified"—as we were notified the first six weeks.

Oh it is a handsome place, green lawns and tall trees and fluted flower beds. High up on the balconies of each cottage the children stand, the girls in their red bows and white dresses, the boys in white suits and giant red ties. The parents stand below shrieking up to be heard and the children shriek down to be heard, and between them the invisible wall "Not To Be Contaminated by Parental Germs or Physical Affection."

There was a tiny girl who always stood hand in hand with Emily. Her parents never came. One visit she was gone. "They moved her to Rose Cottage," Emily shouted in explanation. "They don't like you to love anybody here."

She wrote once a week, the laboured writing of a seven-year-old. "I am fine. How is the baby. If I write my leter nicly I will have a star. Love." There never was a star. We wrote every other day, letters she could never hold or keep but only hear read—once. "We simply do not have room for children to keep any personal possessions," they patiently explained when we pieced one Sunday's shrieking together to plead how much it would mean to Emily, who loved so to keep things, to be allowed to keep her letters and cards.

Each visit she looked frailer. "She isn't eating," they told us.

(They had runny eggs for breakfast or mush with lumps, Emily said later, I'd hold it in my mouth and not swallow. Nothing ever tasted good, just when they had chicken.)

It took us eight months to get her released home, and only the fact that she gained back so little of her seven lost pounds convinced the social worker.

I used to try to hold and love her after she came back, but her body would stay stiff, and after a while she'd push away. She ate little. Food sickened her, and I think much of life too. Oh she had physical lightness and brightness, twinkling by on skates, bouncing like a ball up and down up and down over the jump rope, skimming over the hill; but these were momentary.

She fretted about her appearance, thin and dark and foreign-looking at a time when every little girl was supposed to look or thought she should look a chubby blonde replica of Shirley Temple. The door-bell sometimes rang for her, but no one seemed to come and play in the house or be a best friend. Maybe because we moved so much.

There was a boy she loved painfully through two school semesters. Months later she told me how she had taken pennies from my purse to buy him candy. "Liquorice was his favourite and I brought him some every day, but he still liked Jennifer better'n me. Why, Mommy?" The kind of question for which there is no answer.

School was a worry to her. She was not glib or quick in a world where glibness and quickness were easily confused with ability to learn. To her overworked and exasperated teachers she was an overconscientious "slow learner" who kept trying to catch up and was absent entirely too often.

I let her be absent, though sometimes the illness was imaginary. How different from my now-strictness about attendance with the others. I wasn't working. We had a new baby, I was home anyhow. Sometimes, after Susan grew old enough, I would keep her home from school, too, to have them all together.

Mostly Emily had asthma, and her breathing, harsh and laboured, would fill the house with a curiously tranquil sound. I would bring the two old dresser mirrors and her boxes of collections to her bed. She would select beads and single ear-rings, bottle tops and shells, dried flowers and pebbles, old postcards and scraps, all sorts of oddments; then she and Susan would play Kingdom, setting up landscapes and furniture, peopling them with action.

Those were the only times of peaceful companionship between her and Susan. I have edged away from it, that poisonous feeling between them, that terrible balancing of hurts and needs I had to do between the two, and did so badly, those earlier years.

Oh there are conflicts between the others too, each one human, needing, demanding, hurting, taking—but only between Emily and Susan, no, Emily toward Susan that corroding resentment. It seems so obvious on the surface, yet it is not obvious. Susan, the second child, Susan, golden- and curly-haired and chubby, quick and articulate and assured, everything in appearance and manner Emily was not; Susan, not able to resist Emily's precious things, losing or sometimes clumsily breaking them; Susan telling jokes and riddles to company for applause while Emily sat silent (to say to me later: that was *my* riddle, Mother, I told it to Susan); Susan, who for all the five years' difference in age was just a year behind Emily in developing physically.

I am glad for that slow physical development that widened the difference between her and her contemporaries, though she suffered over it. She was too vulnerable for that terrible world of youthful competition, of preening and parading, of constant measuring of yourself against every other, of envy, "If I had that copper hair," or "If I had that skin. . . ." She tormented herself enough about not looking like the others, there was enough of the unsureness, the having to be conscious of words before you speak, the constant caring—what are they thinking of me? What kind of an impression am I making?—there was enough without having it all magnified by the merciless physical drives.

Ronnie is calling. He is wet and I change him. It is rare there is such a cry now. That time of motherhood is almost behind me when the ear is not one's own but must always be racked and listening for the child cry, the child call. We sit for a while and I hold him, looking out over the city spread in charcoal with its soft aisles of light. "*Shoogily*," he breathes and curls closer. I carry him back to bed, asleep. *Shoogily*. A funny word, a family word, inherited from Emily, invented by her to say: *comfort*.

In this and other ways she leaves her seal, I say aloud. And startle at my saying it. What do I mean? What did I start to gather together, to try and make coherent? I was at the terrible, growing years. War years. I do not remember them well. I was working, there were four smaller ones now, there was not time for her. She had to help be a mother, and housekeeper, and shopper. She had to set her seal. Mornings of crisis and near hysteria trying to get lunches packed, hair combed, coats and shoes found, everyone to school or Child Care on time, the baby ready for transportation. And always the paper scribbled on by a smaller one, the book looked at by Susan then mislaid, the homework not done. Running out to that huge school where she was one, she was lost, she was a drop; suffering over her unpreparedness, stammering and unsure in her classes.

There was so little time left at night after the kids were bedded down. She would struggle over books, always eating (it was in those years she developed her enormous appetite that is legendary in our family) and I would be ironing, or preparing food for the next day, or writing V-mail to Bill, or tending the baby. Sometimes, to make me laugh, or out of her despair, she would imitate happenings or types at school.

I think I said once: "Why don't you do something like this in the school amateur show?" One morning she phoned me at work, hardly understandable through the weeping: "Mother, I did it. I won, I won; they gave me first prize; they clapped and clapped and wouldn't let me go."

Now suddenly she was Somebody, and as imprisoned in her difference as she had been in her anonymity.

She began to be asked to perform at other high schools, even in colleges, then at city and state-wide affairs. The first one we went to, I only recognized her that first moment when thin, shy, she almost drowned herself into the curtains. Then: Was this Emily? The control, the command, the convulsing and deadly clowning, the spell, then the roaring, stamping audience, unwilling to let this rare and precious laughter out of their lives.

Afterwards: You ought to do something about her with a gift like that—but without money or knowing how, what does one do? We have left it all to her, and the gift has as often eddied inside, clogged and clotted, as been used and growing.

She is coming. She runs up the stairs two at a time with her light graceful step, and I know she is happy tonight. Whatever it was that occasioned your call did not happen today.

"Aren't you ever going to finish the ironing, Mother? Whistler painted his mother in a rocker. I'd have to paint mine standing over an ironing-board."

I STAND HERE IRONING

This is one of her communicative nights and she tells me everything and nothing as she fixes herself a plate of food out of the icebox.

She is so lovely. Why did you want me to come in at all? Why were you concerned? She will find her way.

She starts up the stairs to bed. "Don't get me up with the rest in the morning." "But I thought you were having midterms." "Oh, those," she comes back in, kisses me, and says quite lightly, "in a couple of years when we'll all be atom-dead they won't matter a bit."

She has said it before. She *believes* it. But because I have been dredging the past, and all that compounds a human being is so heavy and meaningful in me, I cannot endure it tonight.

I will never total it all. I will never come in to say: She was a child seldom smiled at. Her father left me before she was a year old. I had to work her first six years when there was work, or I sent her home and to his relatives. There were years she had care she hated. She was dark and thin and foreign-looking in a world where the prestige went to blondeness and curly hair and dimples, she was slow where glibness was prized. She was a child of anxious, not proud, love. We were poor and could not afford for her the soil of easy growth. I was a young mother, I was a distracted mother. There were the other children pushing up, demanding. Her younger sister seemed all that she was not. There were years she did not let me touch her. She kept too much in herself, her life was such that she had to keep too much in herself. My wisdom came too late. She has much to her and probably little will come of it. She is a child of her age, of depression, of war, of fear.

Let her be. So all that is in her will not bloom—but in how many does it? There is still enough left to live by. Only help her to know—help make it so there is cause for her to know that she is more than this dress on the ironing-board, helpless before the iron.

1953–1954

2

HEY SAILOR, WHAT SHIP?

I

The grimy light; the congealing smell of cigarettes that had been smoked long ago and of liquor that had been drunk long ago; the boasting, cursing, wheedling, cringing voices, and the greasy feel of the bar as he gropes for his glass.

Hey Sailor, what ship?

His face flaring in the smoky mirror. The veined gnawing. Wha's it so quiet for? Hey, hit the tune-box. (*Lennie and Helen and the kids.*) Wha time's it anyway? Gotta . . .

Gotta something. Stand watch? No, din't show last night, ain't gonna show tonight, gonna sign off. Out loud: Hell with ship. You got any friends, ship? then hell with your friends. That right, Deeck? And he turns to Deeck for approval, but Deeck is gone. Where's Deeck? Givim five bucks and he blows.

All right, says a nameless one, you're loaded. How's about a buck?

Less one buck. Company. But he too is gone.

And he digs into his pockets to see how much he has left.

Right breast pocket, a crumpled five. Left pants pocket, three, no, four collapsed one-ers. Left jacket pocket, pawn ticket, Manila; card, "When in Managua it's Marie's for Hospitality"; union book; I.D. stuff; trip card; two ones, one five, accordion-pleated together. Right pants pocket, jingle money. Seventeen bucks. And the hands tremble.

Where'd it all go? and he lurches through the past. One hundred and fifty draw yesterday. No, day before, maybe even day 'fore that. Seven for a bottle when cashed the cheque, 20 to Blackie, 33 back to Goldballs, cab to Frisco, 38, 39 for the jacket and the kicks (new jacket, new kicks, look good to see Lennie and Helen and the kids), 24 smackers dues and 10-dollar fine. That fine. . . .

Hey, to the barkeep, one comin' up. And he swizzles it down, pronto. Twenty and 7 and 33 and 39. Ten-dollar fine and 5 to Frenchy at the hall and drinkin' all night with Johnson, don't know how much, and on the way to the paymaster. . . .

The PAYmaster. Out loud, in angry mimicry, with a slight scandihoovian accent, to nobody, nobody at all: Whaddaya think of that? Hafta be able to sign your name or we can't give you your cheque. Too stewed to sign your name, he says, no cheque.

Only seventeen bucks. Hey, to the barkeep, how 'bout advancing me fifty? Hunching over the bar, confidential, so he sees the bottles glistening in the depths. See? and he ruffles in his pockets for the voucher, P.F.E., Michael Jackson, thass me, five hundred and twenty-seven and eleven cents. You don' know me? Been here all night, all day. Bell knows me. Get Bell. Been drinkin' here twenty-three years, every time hit Frisco. Ask Bell.

But Bell sold. Forgot, forgot. Took his cushion and moved to Petaluma to raise chickens. Well hell with you. Got any friends? then hell with your friends. Go to Pearl's. (*Not Lennie and Helen and the kids?*) See what's new, or old. Got 'nuf lettuce for *them* babies. But the idea is visual, not physical. Get a bottle first. An he waits for the feeling good that should be there, but there is none, only a sickness lurking.

THE BULKHEAD sign bile green in the rain. Rain and the street clogged with cars, going home from work cars. Screw 'em all. He starts across. Screech, screech, screech. Brakes jammed on for a block back. M. Norbert Jacklebaum makes 'em stop, said without glee. On to Pearl's. But someone is calling. Whitey, Whitey, get in here you stumblebum. And it is Lennie, a worn likeness of Lennie, so changed he gets in all right, but does not ask questions or answer them. (Are you on a ship or on the beach? How long was the trip? You sick, man, or just stewed? Only three or four days and you're feeling like this? *No*, no stopping for a bottle or to buy presents.

He only sits while the sickness crouches underneath, waiting to spring, and it muddles in his head, *going to see Lennie and Helen and the kids, no presents for 'em, an' don't even feel good.*

HEY SAILOR, WHAT SHIP?

Hey Sailor, what ship?

2

And so he gets there after all, four days and everything else too late. It is an old peaked house on a hill and he has imaged and entered it over and over again, in a thousand various places a thousand various times: on watch and over chow, lying on his bunk or breezing with the guys; from sidewalk beds and doorway shelters, in flophouses and jails; sitting silent at union meetings or waiting in the places one waits, or listening to the Come to Jesus boys.

The stairs are innumerable and he barely makes it to the top. Helen (Helen? so . . . greyed?), Carol, Allie, surging upon him. A fever of hugging and kissing. 'Sabout time, shrills Carol over and over again. 'Sabout time.

Who is real and who is not? Jeannie, taller than Helen suddenly, just standing there, watching. I'm in first grade now, yells Allie, now you can fix my dolly crib, Whitey, it's smashted.

You hit it just right. We've got stew, pressure cooker stuff, but your favourite anyway. How long since you've eaten? And Helen looks at him, kisses him again, and begins to cry.

Mother! orders Jeannie, and marches her into the kitchen.

Whassmatter Helen? One look at me, she begins to cry.

She's glad to see you, you S.O.B.

Whassmatter her? She don't look so good.

You don't look so good either, Lennie says grimly. Better sit for a while.

Mommy oughta quit work, volunteers Carol; she's tired. All the time.

Whirl me round like you always do, Whitey, whirl me round, begs Allie.

Where did you go this time, Whitey? asks Carol. Thought you were going to send me stamps for my collection. Why didn't you come Christmas? Can you help me make a puppet stage?

Cut it, kids, not so many questions, orders Lennie, going up the stairs to wash. Whitey's got to take it easy. We'll hear about everything after dinner.

Your shoes are shiny, says Allie. Becky in my class got new shoes too, Mary Janes, but they're fuzzy. And she kneels down to pat his shoes.

Forgotten, how big the living-room was. (And is he really here?) Carol reads the funnies on the floor, her can up in the air. Allie inspects him gravely. You got a new hurt on your face, Whitey. Sing a song, or say Thou Crown 'n Deep. And after dinner can I bounce on you?

Not so many questions, repeats Carol.

Whitey's just gonna sit here. . . . Should go in the kitchen. Help your mommy.

Angry from the kitchen: Well, I don't care. I'm calling Marilyn and tell her not to come; we'll do our homework over there. I'm certainly not going to take a chance and let her come over here.

Shhh, Jeannie, shhh. He beg that, or Helen? The

windows are blind with steam, all hidden behind them the city, the bay, the ships. And is it chow time already? He starts up to go, but it seems he lurched and fell, for the sickness springs at last and consumes him. And now Allie is sitting with him. C'mon, sit up and eat, Whitey, Mommy says you have to eat; I'll eat too. Perched beside him, pretty as you please. I'll take a forkful and you take a forkful. You're sloppy, Whitey—for it trickles down his chin. It does not taste; the inside of him burns. She chatters and then the plate is gone and now the city sparkles at him through the windows. Helen and Lennie are sitting there and somebody who looks like somebody he knows.

Chris, reminds Lennie. Don't you remember Chris, the grocery boy when we lived on Aerial way? We told you he's a M.D. now. Fat and a poppa and smug; aren't you smug, Chris?

I almost shipped with you once, Whitey. Don't you remember?

(Long ago. Oh yes, oh yes, but there was no permit to be had; and even if there had been, by that time I didn't have no drag.) Aloud: I remember. You still got the itch? That's why you came round, to get fixed up with a trip card?

I came around to look at you. But that was all he was doing, just sitting there and looking.

Whassmatter? Don't like my looks? Get too beautiful since you last saw me? Handsome new nose 'n everything.

You got too beautiful. Where can I take him, Helen?

Can't take me no place. M. Norbert Jacklebaum's fine.

You've got to get up anyhow, Whitey, so I can make up the couch. Go on, go upstairs with Chris. You're in luck, I even found a clean sheet.

He settles back down on the couch, the lean scarred arms bent under his head for a pillow, the muscles ridged like rope.

He's a lousy doc, affectionately. Gives me a shot of B-1, sleeping pills, and some bum advice. Whaddaya think of that, he remembered me. Thirteen years and he remembers me.

How could he help remembering you with all the hell his father used to raise cause he'd forget his deliveries listening to your lousy stories? You were his he-ro. . . . How do you like the fire?

Your wood, Whitey, says Helen. Still the stuff you chopped three years back. Needs restacking though.

Get right up and do it. . . . Whadja call him for?

You scared us. Don't forget, your last trip up here was for five weeks in Marine Hospital.

We never saw it hit you like this before, says Lennie. After a five-, six-week tear maybe, but you say this was a couple days. You were really out.

Just catching up on my sleep, tha's all.

There is a new picture over the lamp. Bleached hills, a fresh-ploughed field, red horses and a blue-overalled figure.

I got a draw coming. More'n five hundred. How's financial situation round here?

We're eating.

Allie say she want me to fix something? Or was it Carol? Those kids are sure. . . . A year'n a half. . . . An effort to talk, for the sleeping pills are already gripping him, and the languid fire, and the rain that has started up again and cannot pierce the windows. How *you* feeling, Helen? She looks more like Helen now.

Keeping my head above water. She would tell him later. She always told him later, when he would be helping in the kitchen maybe, and suddenly it would come out, how she really was and what was really happening, sometimes things she wouldn't even tell Lennie. And this time, the way she looked, the way Lennie looked. . . .

Allie is on the stairs: I had a bad dream, Mommy. Let me stay here till Jeannie comes to bed with me, Mommy, please. By Whitey.

What was your bad dream, sweetheart?

Lovingly she puts her arms around his neck, curls up. I was losted, she whispers, and instantly is asleep.

He starts as if he had been burned, and quick lest he wake her, begins stroking her soft hair. It is destroying, dissolving him utterly, this helpless warmth against him, this lovely feel of a child—lost country to him and unattainable.

Sure were a lot of kids begging, he says aloud. I think it's worse.

Korea? asks Len.

Never got ashore in Korea. Yokohama, Cebu, Manila. (The begging children and the lost, the thieving children and the children who were sold.)

And he strokes, strokes Allie's soft hair as if the strokes would solidify, dense into a protection.

We lay around Pusan six weeks. Forty-three days on that tub no bigger'n this house and they wouldn't give us no leave ashore. Forty-three days. Len, I never had a drop, you believe me, Len?

Felt good most of this trip, Len, just glad to be sailing again, after Pedro. Always a argument. Somebody says, Christ it's cold, colder'n a whore's heart, and somebody jumps right in and says, coldern'n a whore's heart, hell, you ever in Kobe and broke and Kumi didn't give you five yen? And then it starts. Both sides.

Len and Helen like those stories. Tell another. Effort.

You should hear this Stover. Ask him, was you ever in England? and he claps his hands to his head and says, was I ever in England, Oh boy, was I ever in England, those limeys, they beat you with bottles. Ask him, was you ever in Marseilles and he claps his hands to his head and says, was I ever in Marseilles, Oh boy, was I ever in Marseilles, them frogs, they kick you with spikes in their shoes. Ask him, was you ever in Shanghai, and he says, was I ever in Shanghai, was I ever in Shanghai, man, they throw the crockery and the stools at you. Thass everyplace you mention, a different kind of beating.

There was this kid on board, Howie Adams. Gotta bring him up here. Told him 'bout you. Best people in the world, I says, always open house. Best kid. Not like those scenery bums and cherry pickers we got sailing nowadays. Guess what, they made me ship's delegate.

Well, why not? asks Helen; you were probably the best man on board.

A tide of peaceful drowsiness washes over the tumult in him; he is almost asleep, though the veined brown hand still tremblingly strokes, strokes Allie's soft pale hair.

Is that Helen? No, it is Jeannie, so much like Helen of years ago, suddenly there under the hall light, looking in at them all, her cheeks glistening from the rain.

Never saw so many peaceful wrecks in my life. Her look is loving. That's what I want to be when I grow up, just a peaceful wreck holding hands with other peaceful wrecks. For Len and Helen are holding hands. We really fixed Mr. Nickerson. Marilyn did my English, I did her algebra, and her brother Tommy, wrote for us "I will not" 500 times; then we just tagged on "talk in class, talk in class, talk in class".

She drops her books, kneels down beside Whitey, and using his long ago greeting asks softly, "Hey Sailor, what ship?", then turns to her parents. Study in contrasts, Allie's face and Whitey's, where's my camera? Did you tell Whitey I'm graduating in three weeks, do you think you'll be here then, Whitey, and be . . . all right? I'll give you my diploma and write in your name so you can pretend you got through junior high, too. Allie's sure glad you came.

And without warning, with a touch so light, so faint, it seems to breathe against his cheek, she traces a scar. That's a new one, isn't it? Allie noticed. She asked me, does it hurt? Does it?

He stops stroking Allie's hair a moment, starts up again desperately, looks so ill, Helen says sharply: It's late. Better go to bed, Jeannie, there's school tomorrow.

It's late, it's early. Kissing him, Helen, Lennie. Good night. Shall I take my stinky little sister upstairs to bed with me whatever she's doing down here, or shall I leave her for one of you strong men to carry?

Leaning from the middle stair, didn't know you were sick, Whitey, thought you were like . . . some of the other times. From the top stair, see you later, alligators.

Most he wants alone now, alone and a drink, perhaps sleep. And they know. We're going to bed now too. Six comes awful early.

So he endures Helen's kiss too, and Len's affectionate poke. And as Len carries Allie up the stairs, the fire leaps up, kindles Len's shadow so that it seems a dozen bent men cradle a child up endless stairs, while the rain traces on the windows, beseechingly, ceaselessly, like seeking fingers of the blind.

Hey Sailor, what ship? Hey Sailor, what ship?

3

In his sleep he speaks often and loudly, sometimes moans, and toward morning begins the trembling. He wakes into an unshared silence he does not recognize, accustomed so to the various voices of the sea, the multipitch of those with whom sleep as well as work and food is shared; the throb of engines, churn of the propeller; or hazed through drink the noises of the street or the thin walls like ears—magnifying into lives as senseless as one's own.

Here there is only the whisper of the clock (motor by which this house runs now) and the sounds of oneself.

The trembling will not cease. In the kitchen there is a note:

> *Bacon and eggs in the icebox and coffee's made. The kids are coming straight home from school to be with you. DON'T go down to the front, Lennie'll take you tomorrow. Love.*

Love.

The row of cans on the cupboard shelves is thin. So things are still bad, he thinks, no money for stocking up. He opens all the doors hopefully, but if there is a bottle, it is hidden. A long time he stares at the floor, goes out into the yard where fallen rain beads the grasses that will be weeds soon enough, comes back, stares at his dampened feet, stares at the floor some more (needs scrubbing, and the woodwork can stand some too; well, maybe after I feel better), but there are no dishes in the sink, it is all cleaner than he expected.

Upstairs, incredibly, the beds are made, no clothes crumpled on the floor. Except in Jeannie's and Allie's room: there, as remembered, the dust feathers in the corners and dolls sprawl with books, records, and underwear. Guess she'll never get it clean. And up rises his old vision, his favourite vision, of how he will return here, laden with groceries, no one in the littered house, and quickly, before they come, straighten the upstairs (the grime in the wash-basin), clean the downstairs, scrub the kitchen floor, wash the hills of dishes, put potatoes in and light the oven, and when they finally troop in say, calmly, Helen, the house is clean, and there's steak for dinner.

Whether it is this that hurts in his stomach or the burning chill that will not stop, he dresses himself hastily, arguing with the new shoes that glint with a life all their own. On his way out, he stops for a minute to gloss his hand over the bookcase. Damn good paint job, he says out loud, if I say so myself. Still stands up after fourteen years. Real good that red backing Helen liked so much 'cause it shows above the books.

Hey Sailor, what ship?

4

It is five days before he comes again. A cabbie precedes him up the stairs, loaded with bundles. Right through, right into the kitchen, man, directs Whitey, feeling good, oh quite obviously feeling good. The shoes are spotted now, he wears a torn Melton in place of the new jacket. Groceries, he announces heavily, indicating the packages plopped down. Steak. Whatever you're eating, throw it out.

Didn't I tell you they're a good-looking bunch? triumphantly indicating around the table. 'Cept that Lennie hyena over there. Go on, man, take the whole five smackers.

Don't let him go, Whitey, I wanta ride in the cab, screams Allie.

To the top of the next hill and back, it's a windy curly round and round road, yells Carol.

I'll go too, says Jeannie.

Shut up, Lennie explodes, let the man go, he's working. Sit down, kids. Sit down, Whitey.

Set another plate, Jeannie, says Helen.

An' bring glasses. Got coke for the kids. We gonna have a drink.

I want a cab ride, Allie insists.

Wait till your mean old bastard father's not lookin'. Then we'll go.

Watch the language, Whitey, there's a gentleman present, says Helen. Finish your plate, Allie.

Thass right. Know who the gen'lmun is? I'm the gen'lmun. The world, says Marx, is divided into two classes. . . .

Seafaring gen'lmun and shoreside bastards, choruses Lennie with him.

Why, Daddy! says Jeannie.

You're a mean ole bassard father, says Allie.

Thass right, tell him off, urges Whitey. Hell with waitin' for glasses. Down the ol' hatch.

My class is divided by marks, says Carol, giggling helplessly at her own joke, and anyway what about ladies? Where's my drink? Down the hatch.

I got presents, kids. In the kitchen.

Where they'll stay, warns Helen, till after dinner. Just keep sitting.

Course Jeannie over there doesn't care 'bout a

present. She's too grown up. Royal highness doesn't even kiss old Whitey, just slams a plate at him.

Fork, knife, spoon too, says Jeannie, why don't you use them?

Good chow, Helen. But he hardly eats, and as they clear the table, he lays down a tenner.

All right, sailor, says Lennie, put your money back.

I'll take it, says Carol, if it's an orphan.

If you get into the front room quick, says Lennie, you won't have to do the dishes.

Who gives a shit about the dishes?

Watch it, says Helen.

Whenja start doin' dishes in this house after dinner anyways?

Since we got organized, says Lennie, always get things done when they're supposed to be. Organized the life out of ourselves. That's what's the matter with Helen.

Well, when you work, Helen starts to explain.

Lookit Daddy kiss Mommy.

Give me my present and whirl me, Whitey, whirl me, demands Allie.

No whirling. Jus' sat down, honey. How'd it be if I bounce you? Lef' my ol' lady in New Orleans with twenty-four kids and a can of beans.

Guess you think 'cause I'm ten I'm too big to bounce any more, says Carol.

Bounce everybody. Jeannie. Your mom. Even Lennie.

HEY SAILOR, WHAT SHIP?

What is life
Without a wife (bounce)
And a home (bounce bounce)
Without a baby?

Hey, Helen, bring in those presents. Tell Jeannie, don't come in here, don't get a present. Jeannie, play those marimba records. Want marimba. Feel good, sure feel good. Hey, Lennie, get your wild ass in here, got things to tell you. Leave the women do the work.

Wild ass, giggles Allie.

Jeannie gets mad when you talk like that, says Carol. Give us our presents and let's have a cab ride and tell us about the time you were torpedoed.

Tell us Crown 'n Deep.

Go tell yourself. I'm gonner have a drink.

Down the hatch, Whitey.

Down the hatch.

Better taper off, guy, says Lennie, coming in. We want to have an evening.

Tell Helen bring the presents. She don't hafta be jealous. I got money for her. Helen likes money.

Upstairs, says Helen, they'll get their presents upstairs. After they're ready for bed. There's school tomorrow.

First we'll get them after dinner and now after we're ready for bed. That's not fair, wails Allie.

I never showed him my album yet, says Carol. He never said Crown n' Deep yet.

It isn't fair. We never had our cab ride.

HEY SAILOR, WHAT SHIP?

Whitey'll be here tomorrow, says Helen.

Maybe he won't, says Carol. He's got a room rented, he told me. Six weeks' rent in advance and furnished with eighteen cans of beans and thirty-six cans of sardines. All shored up, says Whitey. Somebody called Deeck stays there too.

Lef' my wile ass in New Orleans, twenty-four kids and a present of beans, chants Allie, bouncing herself up and down on the couch. And it's not *fair*.

Say good night to them, Whitey, they'll come down in their nightgowns for a good-night kiss later.

Go on, kids. Mind your momma, don't be like me. An' here's a dollar for you an' a dollar for you. An' a drink for me.

But Lennie has taken the bottle. Whass matter, doncha like to see me feelin' good? Well, screw you, brother, I'm supplied, and he pulls a pint out of his pocket.

Listen, Whitey, says Jeannie, I've got some friends coming over and . . . Whitey, please, they're not used to your kind of language.

That so? 'Scuse me, your royal highness. Here's ten dollars, your royal highness. Help you forgive?

Please go sit in the kitchen. Please, Daddy, take him in the kitchen with you.

Jeannie, says Lennie, give him back the money.

He gave it to me, it's mine.

Give it back.

All right. Flinging it down, running up the stairs.

Quit it, Whitey, says Lennie.

Quit what?

Throwing your goddam money around. Where do you think you are, down on the front?

'S better down on the front. You're gettin' holier than the dago pope.

I mean it, guy. And tone down that language. Let's have the bottle.

No. Into the pocket. Do *you* good to feel good for a change. You 'n Helen look like you been through the meat grinder.

Silence.

Gently: Tell me about the trip, Whitey.

Good trip. Most of the time. 'Lected me ship's delegate.

You told us.

Tell you 'bout that kid, Howie? Best kid. Got my gear off the ship and lef' it down at the hall for me. Whaddaya think of that?

(Oh feeling good, come back, come back.)

Jeannie in her hat and coat. Thank you for the ear-rings, Whitey. Stiffly.

Real crystals. Best . . . Lennie, 'm gonna give her ten dollars. For treat her friends. After all, ain't she my wife?

Whitey, do I have to hear that story again? I was four years old.

Again? (He had told the story so often, as often as anyone would listen, whenever he felt good, and always as he told it, the same shy happiness would wing through him, how when she was four, she had crawled into bed beside him one morning, announcing triumphantly to her mother: I'm married to Whitey now, I don't have to sleep by myself any more.) Sorry, royal highness, won't mention it. How's watch I gave you, remember?

(Not what he means to say at all. Remember the love I gave you, the worship offered, the toys I mended and made, the questions answered, the care for you, the pride in you?)

I lost the watch, remember? "I was too young for such expensive presents". You keep talking about it because that's the only reason you give presents, to buy people to be nice to you and to yak about the presents when you're drunk. Here's your ear-rings too. I'm going outside to wait for my friends.

Jeannie! It is Helen, back down with the kids. Jeannie, come into the kitchen with me.

Jeannie's gonna get heck, says Carol. Geeeee, down the hatch. Wish I could swallow so long. Is my dresser set solid gold like it looks?

Kiss the dolly you gave me, says Allie. She's your grandchild now. You kiss her too, Daddy. I bet she was the biggest dolly in the store.

Your dolly can't talk. Thass good, honey, that she can't talk.

Here's my album, Whitey. It's got a picture of you. Is that really you, Whitey? It don't look like. . . .

Don't look, he says to himself, closing his eyes. Don't look. But it is indelible. Under the joyful sun, proud sea, proud ship as background, the proud young man, glistening hair and eyes, joyful body, face open to life, unlined. Sixteen? Seventeen? Close it up, he says, M. Norbert Jacklebaum never saw the guy. Quit punchin' me.

HEY SAILOR, WHAT SHIP?

Nobody's punchin' you Whitey, says Allie. You're feeling your face.

Tracing the scars, the pits and lines, the battered nose; seeking to find.

Your name's Michael Jackson, Whitey, why do you always say Jacklebaum? marvels Allie.

Tell Crown 'n Deep. I try to remember it and I never can, Carol says, very softly. Neither can Jeannie. Tell Crown 'n Deep, tell how you learnt it. If you feel like. Please.

Oh yes, he feels like. *When there is November in my soul*, he begins. No, wrong one.

Taking the old proud position. The Valedictory, written the dawn 'fore he was executed, by Jose Rizal, national hero of the Philippines. Taught me by Li'l Joe Roco, not much taller'n you, Jeannie, my first shipmate.

I'm Carol, not Jeannie.

Li'l Joe. Never got back home, they were puttin' the hatch covers on and . . . I only tell it when it's special. El Ultimo Adios. Known as The Valedictory, 1896.

Land I adore, farewell. . . .
Our forfeited garden of Eden,
Joyous I yield up for thee my sad life
And were it far brighter,
Young or rose-strewn, still would I give it.

Vision I followed from afar,
Desire that spurred on and consumed me,

Beautiful it is to fall,
That the vision may rise to fulfillment.

Go on, Whitey.

Little will matter, my country,
That thou shouldst forget me.
I shall be speech in they ears, fragrance and colour,
Light and shout and loved song. . . .

Inaudible.

O crown and deep of my sorrows,
I am leaving all with thee, my friends, my love,
Where I go are no tyrants. . . .

He stands there, swaying. Say good night, says Lennie. Whitey'll tell it all some other time. . . . Here, guy, sit down.

And in the kitchen.

You know how he talks. How can you let him? In front of the little kids.

They don't hear the words, they hear what's behind them. There are worse words than swear words, there are words that hurt. When Whitey talks like that, it's everyday words; the men he lives with talk like that, that's all.

Well, not the kind of men I want to know. I don't go over to anybody's house and hear words like that.

Jeannie, who are you kidding? You kids use all those words at school.

That's different, that's being grown-up, like smoking. And he's so drunk. Why didn't Daddy let me keep the ten dollars? It would mean a lot to me, and it doesn't mean anything to him.

It's his money. He worked for it, it's the only power he has. We don't take Whitey's money.

Oh no. Except when he gives it to you.

When he was staying with us, when they were rocking chair, unemployment cheques, it was different. He was sober. It was his share.

He's just a Howard Street wino now—why don't you and Daddy kick him out of the house? He doesn't belong here.

Of course he belongs here, he's a part of us. Jeannie, this is the only house in the world he can come into and be around people without having to pay.

Somebody who brings presents and whirls you around and expects you to jump for his old money.

Remember how good he's been to you. To us. Jeannie, he was only a few years older than you when he started going to sea.

I know. Now you're going to tell me the one about how he saved Daddy's life in the strike in 1934.

He knows more about people and places than almost anyone I've ever known. You can learn from him.

When's he like that any more? He's just a Howard Street wino, that's all.

Jeannie, I care you should understand. You think Mr. Norris is a tragedy, you feel sorry for him because he talks so intelligent and lives in a nice house and has quiet drunks. You've got to understand.

Just a wino. Even if it's whisky when he's got the money. Which isn't for long.

To understand.

In the beginning there had been youth and the joy of raising hell and that curious inability to take a whore unless he were high with drink.

And later there were memories to forget, dreams to be stifled, hopes to be murdered.

Know who was the ol' man on the ship? Blackie Karns, Kissass Karns hisself.

Started right when you did, Whitey.

Oh yes. (A few had nimbly, limberly clambered up.) Remember in the war he was the only one of us would wear his braid uptown? That one year I made mate? Know how to deal with you, he says. No place for you on the ships any more, he says. My asshole still know more than all you put together, I says.

What was it all about, Whitey?

Don' remember. Rotten feed. Bring him up a plate and say, eat it yourself. Nobody gonna do much till we get better. We got better.

This kid, overtime comin' to him. Didn't even wanta beef about it. I did it anyway. Got fined by the union for takin' it up. M. Norbert Jacklebaum fined by the union, "conduct unbefitting ship's delegate" says the Patrolman, "not taking it up through proper channels." (His old fine talent for mimicry jutting through the blurred-together words.)

These kids, these cherry pickers, they don't realize how we got what we got. Beginnin' to lose it, too.

Think anybody backed me up, Len? Just this Howie and a scenery bum, Goldballs, gonna write a book. Have you in it, Jackson, he says, you're a real salt.

Understand. The death of the brotherhood. Once, once an injury to one is an injury to all. Once, once they had to live for each other. And whoever came off the ship fat shared, because that was the only way of survival for all of them, the easy sharing, the knowing that when you needed, waiting for a trip card to come up, you'd be staked.

Now it was a dwindling few, and more and more of them winos, who shipped sometimes or had long ago irrevocably lost their book for nonpayment of dues.

Hey, came here to feel good. Down the hatch. Hell with you. You got any friends? Hell with your friends.

Helen is back. So you still remember El Ultimo, Whitey. Remember when we first heard Joe recite it?

I remember.

Remember too much, too goddam much. For twenty-three years, the watery shifting: many faces, many places, many voices.

But more and more, certain things the same. The gin mills and the cathouses. The calabozas and jails and stockades. More and more New York and Norfolk and New Orleans and Pedro and Frisco and Seattle like the foreign ports: docks, clip joints, hockshops, cathouses, skid rows, the Law and the Wall: only so far shall you go and no further, uptown forbidden, not your language, not your people, not your country.

Added sometimes now, the hospital.

What's going to happen with you, Whitey?

What I care? Nobody hasta care what happens to M. Jacklebaum.

How can we help caring, Whitey? Jesus, man, you're a chunk of our lives.

Shove it, Lennie. So you're a chunk of my life. So?

Understand. Once they had been young together.

To Lennie he remained a tie to adventure and a world in which men had not eaten each other; and the pleasure, when the mind was clear, of chewing over with that tough mind the happenings of the times or the queernesses of people, or laughing over the mimicry.

To Helen he was the compound of much help given, much support: the ear to hear, the hand that understands how much a scrubbed floor, or a washed dish, or a child taken care of for a while, can mean.

They had believed in his salvation, once. Get him away from the front where he has to drink for company and for a woman. The torn-out-of-him confession, the drunken end of his eight-months-sober try to make a go of it on the beach—don't you see, I can't go near a whore unless I'm lit?

If they could know what it is like now, so casual as if it were after thirty years of marriage.

Later, the times he had left money with them for plans: fix his teeth, buy a car, get into the Ship Painters, go see his family in Chi. But soon enough the demands for the money when the drunken need was on him, so that after a few tries they gave up trying to keep it for him.

Later still, the first time it became too much and

Lennie forbade the house to him unless he were "O.K."—"because of the children".

Now the decaying body, the body that was betraying him. And the memories to forget, the dreams to be stifled, the hopeless hopes to be murdered.

What's going to happen with you, Whitey? Helen repeats. I never know if you'll be back. If you'll be able to be back.

He tips the bottle to the end. Thirstily he thinks: Deeck and his room where he can yell or sing or pound and Deeck will look on without reproach or pity or anguish.

I'm goin' now. Good-bye.

Wait, Whitey. We'll drive you. Want to know where you're shacked, anyways.

Go own steam. Send you a card.

By Jeannie, silent and shrunken into her coat. He passes no one in the streets. They are inside, each in his slab of house, watching the flickering light of television. The sullen fog is on his face, but by the time he has walked to the third hill, it has lifted so he can see the city below him, wave after wave, and there, at the crest of the third hill, the tiny house he has left, its eyes unshaded. After a while they blur with the myriad others that stare at him so blindly.

Then he goes down.

Hey Sailor, what ship?
Hey Marinero, what ship? (San Francisco 1953, 1955

For Jack Eggan, Seaman. 1915–1938
Killed in the retreat across the Ebro, Spain

3

O YES

I

They are the only white people there, sitting in the dimness of the Negro church that had once been a corner store, and all through the bubbling, swelling, seething of before the services, twelve-year-old Carol clenches tight her mother's hand, the other resting lightly on her friend, Parialee Phillips, for whose baptism she has come.

The white-gloved ushers hurry up and down the aisle, beckoning people to their seats. A jostle of people. To the chairs angled to the left for the youth choir, to the chairs angled to the right for the ladies' choir, even up to the platform, where behind the place for the dignitaries and the mixed choir, the new baptismal tank gleams—and as if pouring into it from the ceiling, the blue-painted River of Jordan, God standing in the waters, embracing a brown man in a leopard skin and pointing to the letters of gold:

O YES

REJOICE

GOD IS LOVE

I AM THE WAY THE TRUTH THE LIFE

At the clear window, the crucified Christ embroidered on the starched white curtain leaps in the wind of the sudden singing. And the choirs march in. Robes of wine, of blue, of red.

"We stand and sings too," says Parialee's mother, Alva, to Helen; though already Parialee has pulled Carol up. Singing, little Lucinda Phillips fluffs out her many petticoats; singing, little Bubbie bounces up and down on his heels.

Any day now I'll reach that land of freedom,
Yes, o yes
Any day now, know that promised land

The youth choir claps and taps to accent the swing of it. Beginning to tap, Carol stiffens. "Parry, look. Somebody from school."

"Once more once," says Parialee, in the new way she likes to talk now.

"Eddie Garlin's up there. He's in my math."

"Couple cats from Franklin Jr. chirps in the choir. No harm or alarm."

Anxiously Carol scans the faces to see who else she might know, who else might know her, but looks quickly down to Lucinda's wide skirts, for it seems Eddie looks back at her, sullen or troubled, though it is hard to tell, faced as she is into the window of curtained sunblaze.

I know my robe will fit me well
I tried it on at the gates of hell

If it were a record she would play it over and over, Carol thought, to untwine the intertwined voices, to search how the many rhythms rock apart and yet are one glad rhythm.

When I get to heaven gonna sing and shout
Nobody be able to turn me out

"That's Mr. Chairback Evans going to invocate," Lucinda leans across Parry to explain. "He don't invoke good like Momma."

"Shhhh."

"Momma's the only lady in the church that invocates. She made the prayer last week. (Last month, Lucy.) I made the children's 'nouncement last time. (That was way back Thanksgiving.) And Bubbie's 'nounced too. Lots of times."

"Lucy-inda. SIT!"

Bible study announcements and mixed-choir practice announcements and Teen Age Hearts meeting announcements.

If Eddie said something to her about being there, worried Carol, if he talked to her right in front of somebody at school.

Messengers of Faith announcements and Mamboettes announcement and Committee for the Musical Tea.

Parry's arm so warm. Not realizing, starting up the old game from grade school, drumming a rhythm on the other's arm to see if the song could be guessed. "Parry, guess."

But Parry is pondering the platform.

The baptismal tank? "Parry, are you scared . . . the baptizing?"

"This cat? No." Shaking her head so slow and scornful, the barrette in her hair, sun fired, strikes a long rail of light. And still ponders the platform.

New Strangers Baptist Church invited you and Canaan Fair Singers announcements and Battle of Song and Cosmopolites meet. "O Lord, I couldn't find no ease," a solo. The ladies' choir:

O what you say seekers, o what you say seekers,
Will you never turn back no more?

The mixed choir sings:

Ezekiel saw that wheel of time
Every spoke was of humankind . . .

And the slim worn man in the pin-stripe suit starts his sermon On the Nature of God. How God is long-suffering. Oh, how long he has suffered. Calling the roll of the mighty nations, that rose and fell and now are dust for grinding the face of Man.

O voice of drowsiness and dream to which Carol does not need to listen. As long ago. Parry warm beside her too, as it used to be, there in the classroom at Mann Elementary, and the feel of drenched in sun and dimness and dream. Smell and sound of the chalk wearing itself away to nothing, rustle of books, drumming tattoo of Parry's fingers on her arm: *Guess.*

And as the preacher's voice spins happy and free, it is the used-to-be play-yard. Tag. Thump of the volley ball. Ecstasy of the jump rope. Parry, do pepper. Carol, do pepper. Parry's bettern Carol, Carol's bettern Parry. They're both. . . .

Did someone scream?

It seemed someone screamed—but all were sitting as before, though the sun no longer blared through the window. She tried to see up where Eddie was, but the ushers were standing at the head of the aisle now, the ladies in white dresses like nurses or waitresses wear, the men holding their white-gloved hands up so one could see their palms.

"And God is Powerful," the preacher was chanting. "Nothing for him to scoop out the oceans and pat up the mountains. Nothing for him to scoop up the miry clay and create man. Man, I said, create Man."

The lady in front of her moaned "*O yes*" and others were moaning "*O yes*".

"And when the earth mourned the Lord said, Weep not, for all will be returned to you, every dust, every atom. And the tired dust settles back, goes back. Until that Judgment Day. That great day."

"*O yes.*"

The ushers were giving out fans. Carol reached for one and Parry said: "What *you* need one for?" but she took it anyway.

"You think Satchmo can blow; you think Muggsy can blow; you think Dizzy can blow?" He was straining to an imaginary trumpet now, his head far back and his voice coming out like a trumpet.

"Oh Parry, he's so good."

"Well. Jelly jelly."

"Nothing to Gabriel on that great getting-up morning. And the horn wakes up Adam, and Adam runs to wake up Eve, and Eve moans; Just one more minute, let me sleep, and Adam yells, Great Day, woman, don't you know it's the Great Day?"

"*Great Day, Great Day,*" the mixed choir behind the preacher rejoices:

When our cares are past
when we're home at last . . .

"And Eve runs to wake up Cain." Running round the platform, stooping and shaking imaginary sleepers, "and Cain runs to wake up Abel." Looping, scalloping his voice—"Grea-aaa-aat Daaaay." All the choirs thundering:

Great Day
When the battle's fought
And the victory's won

Exultant spirals of sound. And Carol caught into it (Eddie forgotten, the game forgotten) chanting with Lucy and Bubbie: "*Great Day.*"

"Ohhhhhhhhh," his voice like a trumpet again, "the re-unioning. Ohhhhhhhh, the rejoicing. After the ages immemorial of longing."

Someone *was* screaming. And an awful thrumming

sound with it, like feet and hands thrashing around, like a giant jumping of a rope.

"*Great Day.*" And no one stirred or stared as the ushers brought a little woman out into the aisle, screaming and shaking, just a little shrunk-up woman not much taller than Carol, the biggest thing about her her swollen hands and the cascades of tears wearing her face.

The shaking inside Carol too. Turning and trembling to ask. "What? . . . that lady?" But Parry still ponders the platform; little Lucy loops the chain of her bracelet round and round; and Bubbie sits placidly, dreamily. Alva Phillips is up fanning a lady in front of her; two lady ushers are fanning other people Carol cannot see. And her mother, her mother looks in a sleep.

Yes. He raised up the dead from the grave. He made old death behave.

Yes. Yes. From all over, hushed. *O Yes*

He was your mother's rock. Your father's mighty tower. And he gave us a little baby. A little baby to love.

I am so glad

Yes, your friend, when you're friendless. Your father when you're fatherless. Way maker. Door opener.

O Yes

When it seems you can't go on any longer, he's there. You can, he says, you can

Yes

And that burden you been carrying—ohhhhh that burden—not for always will it be. No, not for always.

O YES

I will put my Word in you and it is power. I will put my Truth in you and it is power.

O Yes

Out of your suffering I will make you to stand as a stone. A tried stone. Hewn out of the mountains of ages eternal.
Ohhhhhhhhhhh. Out of the mire I will lift your feet. Your tired feet from so much wandering. From so much work and wear and hard times.

Stay with me

From so much journeying—and never the promised land. And I'll wash them in the well your tears made. And I'll shod them in the gospel of peace, and of feeling good. Ohhhhhhhhh.

O Yes.

Behind Carol, a trembling wavering scream. Then the thrashing. Up above, the singing:

They taken my blessed Jesus and flogged him to the woods
And they made him hew out his cross and they dragged him to Calvary

Shout brother, Shout shout shout. He never cried a word.

Powerful throbbing voices. Calling and answering to each other.

They taken my blessed Jesus and whipped him up the hill
With a knotty whip and a raggedy thorn he never cried a word

Shout, sister. Shout shout shout. He never cried a word.

Go tell the people the Saviour has risen
Has risen from the dead and will live forevermore
And won't have to die no more.
Halleloo.
Shout, brother, shout
We won't have to die no more!

A single exultant lunge of shriek. Then the thrashing. All around a clapping. Shouts with it. The piano whipping, whipping air to a froth. Singing now.

I once was lost who now am found
Was blind who now can see

On Carol's fan, a little Jesus walked on wondrously blue waters to where bearded disciples spread nets out of a fishing boat. If she studied the fan—became it—it might make a wall around her. If she could make what was happening (*what* was happening?) into a record small and round to listen to far and far as if into a seashell—the stamp and rills and spirals all tiny (but never any screaming).

wade wade in the water

Jordan's water is chilly and wild
I've got to get home to the other side
God's going to trouble the waters

The music leaps and prowls. Ladders of screamings.

The drumming feet of ushers running. And still little Lucy fluffs her skirts, loops the chain on her bracelet; still Bubbie sits and rocks dreamily; and only eyes turn for an instant to the aisle as if nothing were happening. "Mother, come away," Carol begs, but her mother holds her so tight. Alva Phillips, strong Alva, rocking too and chanting, *O Yes*. No, do not look.

Wade,
Sea of trouble all mingled with fire
Come on my brethren it's time to go higher
Wade wade

The voices in great humming waves, slow, slow (when did it become the humming?), everyone swaying with it too, moving like in slow waves and singing, and up where Eddie is, a new cry, wild and open, "O help me, Jesus," and when Carol opens her eyes she closes them again, quick, but still can see the new known face from school (not Eddie), the thrashing writhing body, struggling against the ushers with the look of grave and loving support on their faces, and hear the torn, tearing cry: 'Don't take me away life everlasting, don't take me away."

And now the rhinestones in Parry's hair glitter wicked; the white hands of the ushers, fanning, foam in the air; the blue-painted waters of Jordan swell and thunder; Christ spirals on his cross in the window– and she is drowned under the sluice of the slow singing and the sway.

So high up and forgotten the waves and the world, so stirless the deep cool green and the wrecks of what had been. Here now Hostess Foods, where Alva Phillips works her nights—but different from that time Alva had taken them through before work, for it is all sunken under water, the creaking loading platform where they had left the night behind; the closet room where Alva's swaddles of sweaters, boots and cap hung, the long hall lined with pickle barrels, the sharp-freezer door swinging open.

Bubbles of breath that swell. A gulp of numbing air. She swims into the chill room where the huge wheels of cheese stand, and Alva swims too, deftly oiling each machine: slicers and wedgers and the convey, that at her touch start to roll and grind. The light of day blazes up and Alva is holding a cup, saying: Drink this, baby.

"DRINK IT." Her mother's voice and the numbing air demanding her to pay attention. Up through the waters and into the car.

"That's right, lambie, now lie back." Her mother's lap.

"Mother."

"Shhhhh. You almost fainted, lambie."

Alva's voice. "You gonna be all right, Carol . . . Lucy, I'm telling you for the last time, you and Buford get back into that church. Carol is *fine*."

"Lucyinda, if I had all your petticoats I could float." Crying. "Why didn't you let me wear my full skirt with the petticoats, Mother."

"Shhhhh, lamb." Smoothing her cheek. "Just breathe, take long deep breaths."

". . . How you doing now, you little ol' consolation prize?" It is Parry, but she does not come in the car or reach to Carol through the open window: "No need to cuss and fuss. You going to be sharp as a tack, Jack."

Answering automatically: "And cool as a fool."

Quick, they look at each other.

"Parry, we have to go home now, don't we, Mother? I almost fainted, didn't I, Mother? . . . Parry, I'm sorry I got sick and have to miss your baptism."

"Don't feel sorry. I'll feel better you not there to watch. It was our mommas wanted you to be there, not me."

"Parry!" Three voices.

"Maybe I'll come over to play kickball after. If you feeling better. Or bring the pogo." Old shared joys in her voice. "Or any little thing."

In just a whisper: "Or any little thing. Parry. Good-bye, Parry."

And why does Alva have to talk now?

"You all right? You breathin deep like your momma said? Was it too close 'n hot in there? Did something scare you, Carrie?"

Shaking her head to lie, "No."

"I blame myself for not paying attention. You not used to people letting go that way. Lucy and Bubbie, Parialee, they used to it. They been coming since they lap babies."

"Alva, that's all right. Alva, Mrs. Phillips."

"You *was* scared. Carol it's something to study about. You'll feel better if you understand."

Trying not to listen.

"You not used to hearing what people keeps inside, Carol. You know how music can make you feel things? Glad or sad or like you can't sit still? That was religion music, Carol."

"I have to breathe deep, Mother said."

"Not everybody feels religion the same way. Some it's in their mouth, but some it's like a hope in their blood, their bones. And they singing songs every word that's real to them, Carol, every word out of they own life. And the preaching finding lodgment in their hearts."

The screaming was tuning up in her ears again, high above Alva's patient voice and the waves lapping and fretting.

"Maybe somebody's had a hard week, Carol, and they locked up with it. Maybe a lot of hard weeks bearing down."

"Mother, my head hurts."

"And they're home, Carol, church is home. Maybe the only place they can feel how they feel and maybe let it come out. So they can go on. And it's all right."

"Please, Alva. Mother, tell Alva my head hurts."

"Get Happy, we call it, and most it's a good feeling, Carol. When you got all that locked up inside you."

"Tell her we have to go home. It's all right, Alva. Please, Mother. Say good-bye. Good-bye."

O YES

When I was carrying Parry and her father left me, and I fifteen years old, one thousand miles away from home, sin-sick and never really believing, as still I don't believe all, scorning, for what have it done to help, waiting there in the clinic and maybe sleeping, a voice called: Alva, Alva. So mournful and so sweet: Alva. Fear not, I have loved you from the foundation of the universe. And a little small child tugged on my dress. He was carrying a parade stick, on the end of it a star that outshined the sun. Follow me, he said. And the real sun went down and he hidden his stick. How dark it was, how dark. I could feel the darkness with my hands. And when I could see, I screamed. Dump trucks run, dumping bodies in hell, and a convey line run, never ceasing with souls, weary ones having to stamp and shove them along, and the air like fire. Oh I never want to hear such screaming. Then the little child jumped on a motorbike making a path no bigger than my little finger. But first he greased my feet with the hands of my mother when I was a knee baby. They shined like the sun was on them. Eyes he placed all around my head, and as I journeyed upward after him, it seemed I heard a mourning: "Mama Mama you must help carry the world." The rise and fall of nations I saw. And the voice called again Alva Alva, and I flew into a world of light, multitudes singing, Free, free, I am so glad.

2

Helen began to cry, telling her husband about it. "You and Alva ought to have your heads examined, taking her there cold like that," Len said. "All right, wreck my best handkerchief. Anyway, now that she's had a bath, her Sunday dinner. . . ."

"And been fussed over," seventeen-year-old Jeannie put in.

"She seems good as new. Now *you* forget it, Helen."

"I can't. Something . . . deep happened. If only I or Alva had told her what it would be like. . . . But I didn't realize."

You don't realize a lot of things, Mother, Jeannie said, but not aloud.

"So Alva talked about it after instead of before. Maybe it meant more that way."

"Oh Len, she didn't listen."

"You don't know if she did or not. Or what there was in the experience for her. . . ."

Enough to pull that kid apart two ways even more, Jeannie said, but still not aloud.

"I was so glad she and Parry were going someplace together again. Now that'll be between them too. Len, they really need, miss each other. What happened in a few months? When I think of how close they were, the hours of makebelieve and dressup and playing ball and collecting. . . ."

"Grow up, Mother." Jeannie's voice was harsh. "Parialee's collecting something else now. Like her own crowd. Like jivetalk and rhythmandblues. Like teachers who treat her like a dummy and white kids who treat her like dirt; boys who think she's really something and chicks who. . . ."

"Jeannie, I know. It hurts."

"Well, maybe it hurts Parry too. Maybe. At least

she's got a crowd. Just don't let it hurt Carol though, 'cause there's nothing she can do about it. That's all through, her and Parialee Phillips, put away with their paper dolls."

"No, Jeannie, no."

"It's like Ginger and me. Remember Ginger, my best friend in Horace Mann. But you hardly noticed when it happened to us, did you . . . because she was white? Yes, Ginger, who's got two kids now, who quit school year before last. Parry's never going to finish either. What's she got to do with Carrie any more? They're going different places. Different places, different crowds. And they're sorting. . . ."

"Now wait, Jeannie. Parry's just as bright, just as capable."

"They're in junior high, Mother. Don't you know about junior high? How they sort? And it's all where you're going. Yes and Parry's coloured and Carrie's white. And you have to watch everything, what you wear and how you wear it and who you eat lunch with and how much homework you do and how you act to the teacher and what you laugh at. . . . And run with your crowd."

"It's that final?" asked Len. "Don't you think kids like Carol and Parry can show it doesn't *have* to be that way."

"They can't. They can't. They don't let you."

"No need to shout," he said mildly. "And who do you mean by 'they' and what do you mean by 'sorting'?"

How they sort. A foreboding of comprehension whirled within Helen. What was it Carol had told her of the Welcome Assembly the first day in junior high? The models showing How to Dress and How Not to Dress and half the girls in their loved new clothes watching their counterparts up on the stage—*their* straight skirt, their sweater, their ear-rings, lipstick, hairdo—"How Not to Dress," "a bad reputation for your school." It was nowhere in Carol's description, yet picturing it now, it seemed to Helen that a mute cry of violated dignity hung in the air. Later there had been a story of going to another Low 7 homeroom on an errand and seeing a teacher trying to wipe the forbidden lipstick off a girl who was fighting back and cursing. Helen could hear Carol's frightened, self-righteous tones: ". . . and I hope they expel her; she's the kind that gives Franklin Jr. a bad rep; she's tough and she smokes and doesn't care about anything and always gets into fights." Yet there was nothing in these incidents to touch the heavy comprehension that waited. . . . Homework, the wonderings those times Jeannie and Carol needed help: "What if there's no one at home to give the help, and the teachers with their 240 kids a day can't or don't or the kids don't ask and they fall hopelessly behind, what then?"—but this too was unrelated. And what had it been that time about Parry? "Mother, Melanie and Sharon won't go if they know Parry's coming." Then of course you'll go with Parry, she's been your friend longer, she had answered, but where was it they were going and what had finally happened? Len, my head hurts, she felt like saying, in Carol's voice in the car, but Len's eyes were grave on Jeannie who was saying passionately:

"If you think it's so goddam important why do we have to live here where it's for real; why don't we move to Ivy like Betsy (yes, I know, money), where it's the deal to be buddies, in school anyway, three coloured kids and their father's a doctor or judge or something big wheel and one always gets elected President or head song girl or something to prove how we're democratic. . . . What do you want of that poor kid anyway? Make up your mind. Stay friends with Parry—but be one of the kids. Sure. Be a brain—but not a square. Rise on up, college prep, but don't get separated. Yes, stay one of the kids but. . . ."

"Jeannie. You're not talking about Carol at all, are you, Jeannie? Say it again. I wasn't listening. I was trying to think."

"She will not say it again," Len said firmly, "you look about ready to pull a Carol. One a day's our quota. And you, Jeannie, we'd better cool it. Too much to talk about for one session. . . . Here, come to the window and watch the Carol and Parry you're both all worked up about."

In the wind and the shimmering sunset light, half the children of the block are playing down the street. Leaping, bouncing, hallooing, tugging the kites of spring. In the old synchronized understanding, Carol and Parry kick, catch, kick, catch. And now Parry jumps on her pogo stick (the last time), Carol shadowing her, and Bubbie, arching his body in a semicircle of joy, bounding after them, high, higher, higher.

And the months go by and supposedly it is forgotten,

except for the now and then when, self-important, Carol will say: I really truly did nearly faint, didn't I, Mother, that time I went to church with Parry?

And now seldom Parry and Carol walk the hill together. Melanie's mother drives by to pick up Carol, and the several times Helen has suggested Parry, too, Carol is quick to explain: "She's already left" or "She isn't ready; she'll make us late."

And after school? Carol is off to club or skating or library or someone's house, and Parry can stay for kickball only on the rare afternoons when she does not have to hurry home where Lucy, Bubbie and the cousins wait to be cared for, now Alva works the four to twelve-thirty shift.

No more the bending together over the homework. All semester the teachers have been different, and rarely Parry brings her books home, for where is there space or time and what is the sense? And the phone never rings with: what you going to wear tomorrow, are you bringing your lunch, or come on over, let's design some clothes for the Katy Keane comic-book contest. And Parry never drops by with Alva for Saturday snack to or from grocery shopping.

And the months go by and the sorting goes on and seemingly it is over until that morning when Helen must stay home from work, so swollen and feverish is Carol with mumps.

The afternoon before, Parry had come by, skimming up the stairs, spilling books and binders on the bed: Hey frail, lookahere and wail, your momma askin for homework, what she got against YOU? . . . looking quickly once then not looking again and talking fast. . . . Hey, you bloomed. You gonna be your own pumpkin, hallowe'en? Your momma know yet its mu-umps? And lumps. Momma says: no distress, she'll be by tomorrow morning see do you need anything while your momma's to work. . . . (Singing: *whole lotta shakin goin on.*) All your 'signments is inside; Miss Rockface says the teachers to write 'em cause I mightn't get it right all right.

But did not tell: Does your mother work for Carol's mother? Oh, you're neighbours! Very well, I'll send along a monitor to open Carol's locker but you're only to take these things I'm writing down, nothing else. Now say after me: Miss Campbell is trusting me to be. A good responsible girl. And go right to Carol's house. After school. Not stop anywhere on the way. Not lose anything. And only take what's written on the list. And remember not to loiter. On the way.

You really gonna mess with that book stuff? Sign on *mine* says do-not-open-until-eX-mas. . . . That Mrs. Fernandez doll she didn't send nothin, she was the only, says feel better and read a book to report if you feel like and I'm the most for takin care for you; she's my most, wish I could get her but she only teaches 'celerated. . . . Flicking the old read books on the shelf but not opening to mock-declaim as once she used to . . . Vicky, Eddie's g.f. in Rockface office, she's on suspended for sure, yellin to

Rockface: you bitchkitty don't you give me no more bad shit. That Vicky she can sure sling-ating-ring it. Staring out the window as if the tree not there in which they had hid out and rocked so often. . . . For sure. (*Keep mo-o-vin.*) Got me a new pink top and lilac skirt. Look sharp with this purple? Cinching in the wide belt as if delighted with what newly swelled above and swelled below. Wear it Saturday night to Sweet's, Modernaires Sounds of Joy, Leroy and Ginny and me goin if Momma'll stay home. IF. (*Shake my baby shake.*) How come old folks still likes to party? Huh? Asking of Rembrandt's weary old face looking from the wall. How come (softly) you long-gone you. Touching her face to his quickly, lightly. NEXT mumps is your buddybud Melanie's turn to tote your stuff. I'm gettin the hoovus goovus. Hey you so un-neat, don't care what you bed with. Removing the books and binders, ranging them on the dresser one by one, marking lipstick faces—bemused or mocking or amazed—on each paper jacket. Better. Fluffing out smoothing the quilt with exaggerated energy. Any little thing I can get, cause I gotta blow. Tossing up and catching their year-ago, arm-in-arm graduation picture, replacing it deftly, upside down, into its mirror crevice. Joe. Bring you joy juice or fizz water or kickapoo? Adding a frown line to one bookface. Twanging the paper fishkite, the Japanese windbell overhead, setting the mobile they had once made of painted eggshells and decorated straws to twirling and rocking. And is gone.

She talked to the lipstick faces after, in her fever, tried to stand on her head to match the picture, twirled and twanged with the violent overhead.

Sleeping at last after the disordered night. Having surrounded herself with the furnishings of that world of childhood she no sooner learned to live in comfortably, than had to leave.

The dollhouse stands there to arrange and rearrange; the shell and picture card collections to resort and remember; the population of dolls given away to little sister, borrowed back, propped all around to dress and undress and caress.

She has thrown off her nightgown because of the fever, and her just budding breast is exposed where she reaches to hold the floppy plush dog that had been her childhood pillow.

Not for anything would Helen have disturbed her. Except that in the unaccustomedness of a morning at home, in the bruised restlessness after the sleepless night, she clicks on the radio—and the storm of the singing whirls into the room:

. . . of trouble all mingled with fire
Come on my brethern we've got to go higher
Wade, wade. . . .

And Carol runs down the stairs, shrieking and shrieking. "Turn it off, Mother, turn it off." Hurling herself at the dial and wrenching it so it comes off in her hand.

"Ohhhhh," choked and convulsive, while Helen tries to hold her, to quiet.

"Mother, why did they sing and scream like that?"

"At Parry's church?"

"Yes." Rocking and strangling the cries. "I hear it all the time." Clinging and beseeching. ". . . What was it, Mother? Why?"

Emotion, Helen thought of explaining, *a characteristic of the religion of all oppressed peoples, yes your very own great-grandparents*—thought of saying. And discarded.

Aren't you now, haven't you had feelings in yourself so strong they had to come out some way? ("what howls restrained by decorum")—thought of saying. And discarded.

Repeat Alva: *hope . . . every word out of their own life. A place to let go. And church is home.* And discarded.

The special history of the Negro people—history?—just you try living what must be lived every day—thought of saying. And discarded.

And said nothing.

And said nothing.

And soothed and held.

"Mother, some of the teachers and kids don't like Parry when they don't even know what she's like. Just because . . ." Rocking again, convulsive and shamed. "And I'm not really her friend any more."

No news. Betrayal and shame. Who betrayed? Whose shame? Brought herself to say aloud: "But may be friends again. As Alva and I are." And soothed.

The sobbing a whisper. "That girl Vicky who got that way when I fainted, she's in school. She's the one keeps wearing the lipstick and they wipe it off and she's always in trouble and now maybe she's suspended. Mother."

"Yes, lambie."

"She acts so awful outside but I remember how she was in church and whenever I see her now I have to wonder. And hear . . . like I'm her, Mother, like I'm her." Clinging and trembling. "Oh why do I have to feel it's happening to me too?

"Mother, I want to forget about it all and not care. Why can't I forget? Oh why is it like it is and why do I have to care?"

Caressing, quieting.

Thinking: *caring asks doing. It is a long baptism into the seas of humankind, my daughter. Better immersion than to live untouched. . . . Yet how will you sustain?*

Why is it like it is?

Sheltering her daughter close, mourning the illusion of the embrace.

And why do I have to care?

While in her, her own need leapt and plunged for the place of strength that was not—where one could scream or sorrow while all knew and accepted, and gloved and loving hands waited to support and understand.

For Margaret Heaton, who always taught

1956

4

TELL ME A RIDDLE

"These Things Shall Be"

I.

For forty-seven years they had been married. How deep back the stubborn, gnarled roots of the quarrel reached, no one could say—but only now, when tending to the needs of others no longer shackled them together, the roots swelled up visible, split the earth between them, and the tearing shook even to the children, long since grown.

Why now, why now? wailed Hannah.

As if when we grew up weren't enough, said Paul.

Poor Ma. Poor Dad. It hurts so for both of them, said Vivi. They never had very much; at least in old age they should be happy.

Knock their heads together, insisted Sammy; tell 'em: you're too old for this kind of thing; no reason not to get along now.

Lennie wrote to Clara: They've lived over so much together; what could possibly tear them apart?

Something tangible enough.

Arthritic hands, and such work as he got, occasional. Poverty all his life, and there was little breath left for running. He could not, could not turn away from this desire: to have the troubling of responsibility, the fretting with money, over and done with; to be free, to be *care*free where success was not measured by accumulation, and there was use for the vitality still in him.

There was a way. They could sell the house, and with the money join his lodge's Haven, co-operative for the aged. Happy communal life, and was he not already an official; had he not helped organize it, raise funds, served as a trustee?

But she—would not consider it.

"What do we need all this for?" he would ask loudly, for her hearing aid was turned down and the vacuum was shrilling. "Five rooms" (pushing the sofa so she could get into the corner) "furniture" (smoothing down the rug) "floors and surfaces to make work. Tell me, why do we need it?" And he was glad he could ask in a scream.

"Because I'm use't."

"Because you're use't. This is a reason, Mrs. Word Miser? Used to can get unused!"

"Enough unused I have to get used to already. . . . Not enough words?" turning off the vacuum a moment to hear herself answer. "Because soon enough we'll need only a little closet, no windows, no furniture, nothing to make work for but worms. Because now I want room. . . . Screech and blow like you're doing, you'll need that closet even sooner. . . . Ha, again!" for the vacuum bag wailed, puffed half up, hung stubbornly limp. "This time fix it so it stays; quick before the phone rings and you get too important-busy."

But while he struggled with the motor, it seethed in him. Why fix it? Why have to bother? And if it can't be fixed, have to wring the mind with how to pay the repair? At the Haven they come in with their own machines to clean your room or your cottage; you fish, or play cards, or make jokes in the sun, not with knotty fingers fight to mend vacuums.

Over the dishes, coaxingly: "For once in your life, to be free, to have everything done for you, like a queen."

"I never liked queens."

"No dishes, no garbage, no towel to sop, no worry what to buy, what to eat."

"And what else would I do with my empty hands? Better to eat at my own table when I want, and to cook and eat how I want."

"In the cottages they buy what you ask, and cook it how you like. *You* are the one who always used to say: better humankind born without mouths and stomachs than always to worry for money to buy, to shop, to fix, to cook, to wash, to clean."

"How cleverly you hid that you heard. I said it then because eighteen hours a day I ran. And you never scraped a carrot or knew a dish towel sops. Now—for you and me—who cares? A herring out of a jar is enough. But when *I* want, and nobody to bother."

And she turned off her ear button, so she would not have to hear.

But as *he* had no peace, juggling and rejuggling the money to figure: how will I pay for this now?; prying out the storm windows (there they take care of this); jolting in the streetcar on errands (there I would not have to ride to take care of this or that); fending the patronizing relatives just back from Florida (there it matters what one is, not what one can afford), he gave *her* no peace.

"Look! In their bulletin. A reading circle. Twice a week it meets."

"Haumm," her answer of not listening.

"A reading circle. Chekhov they read that you like, and Peretz. Cultured people at the Haven that you would enjoy."

"Enjoy!" She tasted the word. "Now, when it pleases you, you find a reading circle for me. And forty years ago when the children were morsels and there was a Circle, did you stay home with them once so I could go? Even once? You trained me well. I do not need others to enjoy. Others!" Her voice trembled. "Because *you* want to be there with others. Already it makes me sick to think of you always around others. Clown, grimacer, floormat, yesman, entertainer, whatever they want of you."

And now it was he who turned on the television loud so he need not hear.

Old scar tissue ruptured and the wounds festered anew. Chekhov indeed. She thought without softness of that young wife, who in the deep night hours while she nursed the current baby, and perhaps held another in her lap, would try to stay awake for the only time there was to read. She would feel again the weather of the outside on his cheek when, coming late from a meeting, he would find her so, and stimulated and ardent, sniffing her skin, coax: "I'll put the baby to bed, and you—put the book away, don't read, don't read."

That had been the most beguiling of all the "don't read, put your book away" her life had been. Chekhov indeed!

"Money?" She shrugged him off. "Could we get poorer than once we were? And in America, who starves?"

But as still he pressed:

"Let me alone about money. Was there ever enough? Seven little ones—for every penny I had to ask—and sometimes, remember, there was nothing. But always *I* had to manage. Now *you* manage. Rub your nose in it good."

But from those years she had had to manage, old humiliations and terrors rose up, lived again, and forced her to relive them. The children's needings; that grocer's face or this merchant's wife she had had to beg credit from when credit was a disgrace, the scenery of the long blocks walked around when she could not pay; school coming, and the desperate going over the old to see what could yet be remade; the soups of meat bones begged "for-the-dog" one winter. . . .

Enough. Now they had no children. Let *him* wrack

his head for how they would live. She would not exchange her solitude for anything. *Never again to be forced to move to the rhythms of others.*

For in this solitude she had won to a reconciled peace.

Tranquillity from having the empty house no longer an enemy, for it stayed clean—not as in the days when it was her family, the life in it, that had seemed the enemy: tracking, smudging, littering, dirtying, engaging her in endless defeating battle—and on whom her endless defeat had been spewed.

The few old books, memorized from rereading; the pictures to ponder (the magnifying glass superimposed on her heavy eyeglasses). Or if she wishes, when he is gone, the phonograph, that if she turns up very loud and strains, she can hear: the ordered sounds and the struggling.

Out in the garden, growing things to nurture. Birds to be kept out of the pear tree, and when the pears are heavy and ripe, the old fury of work, for all must be canned, nothing wasted.

And her one social duty (for she will not go to luncheons or meetings) the boxes of old clothes left with her, as with a life-practised eye for finding what is still wearable within the worn (again the magnifying glass superimposed on the heavy glasses) she scans and sorts—this for rag or rummage, that for mending and cleaning, and this for sending abroad.

Being able at last to live within, and not move to the rhythms of others, as life had forced her to: denying;

removing; isolating; taking the children one by one; then deafening, half-blinding—and at last, presenting her solitude.

And in it she had won to a reconciled peace.

Now he was violating it with his constant campaigning: *Sell the house and move to the Haven.* (You sit, you sit—there too you could sit like a stone.) He was making of her a battleground where old grievances tore. (Turn on your ear button—I am talking.) And stubbornly she resisted—so that from wheedling, reasoning, manipulation, it was bitterness he now started with.

And it came to where every happening lashed up a quarrel.

"I will sell the house anyway," he flung at her one night. "I am putting it up for sale. There will be a way to make you sign."

The television blared, as always it did on the evenings he stayed home, and as always it reached her only as noise. She did not know if the tumult was in her or outside. Snap! she turned the sound off. "Shadows," she whispered to him, pointing to the screen, "look, it is only shadows." And in a scream: "Did you say that you will sell the house? Look at me, not at that. I am no shadow. You cannot sell without me."

"Leave on the television. I am watching."

"Like Paulie, like Jenny, a four-year-old. Staring at shadows. *You cannot sell the house.*"

"I will. We are going to the Haven. There you would not hear the television when you do not want it. I could sit in the social room and watch. You could lock yourself up to smell your unpleasantness in a room by yourself—for who would want to come near you?"

"No, no selling." A whisper now.

"The television is shadows. Mrs. Enlightened! Mrs. Cultured! A world comes into your house—and it is shadows. People you would never meet in a thousand lifetimes. Wonders. When you were four years old, yes, like Paulie, like Jenny, did you know of Indian dances, alligators, how they use bamboo in Malaya? No, you scratched in your dirt with the chickens and thought Olshana was the world. Yes, Mrs. Unpleasant, I will sell the house, for there better can we be rid of each other than here."

She did not know if the tumult was outside, or in her. Always a ravening inside, a pull to the bed, to lie down, to succumb.

"Have you thought maybe Ma should let a doctor have a look at her?" asked their son Paul after Sunday dinner, regarding his mother crumpled on the couch, instead of, as was her custom, busying herself in Nancy's kitchen.

"Why not the President too?"

"Seriously, Dad. This is the third Sunday she's lain down like that after dinner. Is she that way at home?"

"A regular love affair with the bed. Every time I start to talk to her."

Good protective reaction, observed Nancy to herself. The workings of hos-til-ity.

"Nancy could take her. I just don't like how she looks. Let's have Nancy arrange an appointment."

"You think she'll go?" regarding his wife gloomily. "All right, we have to have doctor bills, we have to have doctor bills." Loudly: "Something hurts you?"

She startled, looked to his lips. He repeated: "Mrs. Take It Easy, something hurts?"

"Nothing. . . . Only you."

"A woman of honey. That's why you're lying down?"

"Soon I'll get up to do the dishes, Nancy."

"Leave them, Mother, I like it better this way."

"Mrs. Take It Easy, Paul says you should start ballet. You should go to see a doctor and ask: how soon can you start ballet?"

"A doctor?" she begged. "Ballet?"

"We were talking, Ma," explained Paul, "you don't seem any too well. It would be a good idea for you to see a doctor for a checkup."

"I get up now to do the kitchen. Doctors are bills and foolishness, my son. I need no doctors."

"At the Haven," he could not resist pointing out, "a doctor is *not* bills. He lives beside you. You start to sneeze, he is there before you open up a Kleenex. You can be sick there for free, all you want."

"Diarrhoea of the mouth, is there a doctor to make you dumb?"

"Ma. Promise me you'll go. Nancy will arrange it."

"It's all of a piece when you think of it," said Nancy, "the way she attacks my kitchen, scrubbing under every cup hook, doing the inside of the oven so I can't enjoy Sunday dinner, knowing that half-blind or not, she's going to find every speck of dirt. . . ."

"Don't, Nancy, I've told you—it's the only way she knows to be useful. What did the *doctor* say?"

"A real fatherly lecture. Sixty-nine is young these days. Go out, enjoy life, find interests. Get a new hearing aid, this one is antiquated. Old age is sickness only if one makes it so. Geriatrics, Inc."

"So there was nothing physical."

"Of course there was. How can you live to yourself like she does without there being? Evidence of a kidney disorder, and her blood count is low. He gave her a diet, and she's to come back for follow-up and lab work. . . . But he was clear enough: Number One prescription—start living like a human being. When I think of your dad, who could really play the invalid with that arthritis of his as active as a teenager, and twice as much fun. . . ."

"You didn't tell me the doctor says your sickness is in you, how you live." He pushed his advantage. "Life and enjoyments you need better than medicine. And this diet, how can you keep it? To weigh each morsel and scrape away the bits of fat to make this soup, that pudding. There, at the Haven, they have a dietician, they would do it for you."

She is silent.

"You would feel better there, I know it," he says gently. "There there is life and enjoyments all around."

"What is the matter, Mr. Importantbusy, you have no card game or meeting you can go to?"—turning her face to the pillow.

For a while he cut his meetings and going out,

fussed over her diet, tried to wheedle her into leaving the house, brought in visitors:

"I should come to a fashion tea. I should sit and look at pretty babies in clothes I cannot buy. This is pleasure?"

"Always you are better than everyone else. The doctor said you should go out. Mrs. Brem comes to you with goodness and you turn her away."

"Because *you* asked her to, she asked me."

"They won't come back. People you need, the doctor said. Your own cousins I asked; they were willing to come and make peace as if nothing had happened. . . ."

"No more crushers of people, pushers, hypocrites, around me. No more in *my* house. You go to them if you like."

"Kind he is to visit. And you, like ice."

"A babbler. All my life around babblers. Enough!"

"She's even worse, Dad? Then let her stew a while," advised Nancy. "You can't let it destroy you; it's a psychological thing, maybe too far gone for any of us to help."

So he let her stew. More and more she lay silent in bed, and sometimes did not even get up to make the meals. No longer was the tongue-lashing inevitable if he left the coffee cup where it did not belong, or forgot to take out the garbage or mislaid the broom. The birds grew bold that summer and for once pocked the pears, undisturbed.

A bellyful of bitterness and every day the same quarrel in a new way and a different old grievance the quarrel forced her to enter and relive. And the new torment: I am not really sick, the doctor said it, then why do I feel so sick?

One night she asked him: "You have a meeting tonight? Do not go. Stay . . . with me."

He had planned to watch "This Is Your Life" anyway, but half sick himself from the heavy heat, and sickening therefore the more after the brooks and woods of the Haven, with satisfaction he grated:

"Hah, Mrs. Live Alone And Like It wants company all of a sudden. It doesn't seem so good the time of solitary when she was a girl exile in Siberia. 'Do not go. Stay with me.' A new song for Mrs. Free As A Bird. Yes, I am going out, and while I am gone chew this aloneness good, and think how you keep us both from where if you want people you do not need to be alone."

"Go, go. All your life you have gone without me."

After him she sobbed curses he had not heard in years, old-country curses from their childhood: Grow, oh shall you grow like an onion, with your head in the ground. Like the hide of a drum shall you be, beaten in life, beaten in death. Oh shall you be like a chandelier, to hang, and to burn. . . .

She was not in their bed when he came back. She lay on the cot on the sun-porch. All week she did not speak or come near him; nor did he try to make peace or care for her.

He slept badly, so used to her next to him. After all the years, old harmonies and dependencies deep in their bodies; she curled to him, or he coiled to her each warmed, warming, turning as the other turned, the nights a long embrace.

It was not the empty bed or the storm that woke him, but a faint singing. *She* was singing. Shaking off the drops of rain, the lightning riving her lifted face, he saw her so; the cot covers on the floor.

"This is a private concert?" he asked. "Come in, you are wet."

"I can breathe now," she answered; "my lungs are rich." Though indeed the sound was hardly a breath.

"Come in, come in." Loosing the bamboo shades.

"Look how wet you are." Half helping, half carrying her, still faint-breathing her song.

A Russian love song of fifty years ago.

He had found a buyer, but before he told her, he called together those children who were close enough to come. Paul, of course, Sammy from New Jersey, Hannah from Connecticut, Vivi from Ohio.

With a kindling of energy for her beloved visitors, she arrayed the house, cooked and baked. She was not prepared for the solemn after-dinner conclave, they too probing in and tearing. Her frightened eyes watched from mouth to mouth as each spoke.

His stories were eloquent and funny of her refusal to go back to the doctor; of the scorned invitations; of her stubborn silences or the bile "like a Niagara"; of her contrariness: "If I clean it's no good how I cleaned;

if I don't clean, I'm still a master who thinks he has a slave."

("Vinegar he poured on me all his life; I am well marinated; how can I be honey now?")

Deftly he marched in the rightness for moving to the Haven; their money from social security free for visiting the children, not sucked into daily needs and into the house; the activities in the Haven for him; but mostly the Haven for *her*: her health, her need of care, distraction, amusement, friends who shared her interests.

"This does offer an outlet for Dad," said Paul; "he's always been an active person. And economic peace of mind isn't to be sneezed at, either. I could use a little of that myself."

But when they asked: "And you, Ma, how do you feel about it?" could only whisper:

"For him it is good. It is not for me. I can no longer live between people."

"You lived all your life *for* people," Vivi cried.

"Not with." Suffering doubly for the unhappiness on her children's faces.

"You have to find some compromise," Sammy insisted. "Maybe sell the house and buy a trailer. After forty-seven years there's surely some way you can find to live in peace."

"There is no help, my children. Different things we need."

"Then live alone!" He could control himself no longer. "I have a buyer for the house. Half the money for you, half for me. Either alone or with me to the

Haven. You think I can live any longer as we are doing now?"

"Ma doesn't have to make a decision this minute, however you feel, Dad," Paul said quickly, "and you wouldn't want her to. Let's let it lay a few months, and then talk some more."

"I think I can work it out to take Mother home with me for a while," Hannah said. "You both look terrible, but especially you, Mother. I'm going to ask Phil to have a look at you."

"Sure," cracked Sammy. "What's the use of a doctor husband if you can't get free service out of him once in a while for the family? And absence might make the heart . . . you know."

"There was something after all," Paul told Nancy in a colourless voice. "That was Hannah's Phil calling. Her gall bladder. . . . Surgery."

"Her *gall* bladder. If that isn't classic. 'Bitter as gall'—talk of psychosom——"

He stepped closer, put his hand over her mouth and said in the same colourless, plodding voice. "We have to get Dad. They operated at once. The cancer was everywhere, surrounding the liver, everywhere. They did what they could . . . at best she has a year. Dad . . . we have to tell him."

2

Honest in his weakness when they told him, and that she was not to know. "I'm not an actor. She'll know right away by how I am. Oh that poor woman.

I am old too, it will break me into pieces. Oh that poor woman. She will spit on me: 'So my sickness was how I live.' Oh Paulie, how she will be, that poor woman. Only she should not suffer. . . . I can't stand sickness, Paulie, I can't go with you."

But went. And play-acted.

"A grand opening and you did not even wait for me. . . . A good thing Hannah took you with her."

"Fashion teas I needed. They cut out what tore in me; just in my throat something hurts yet. . . . Look! so many flowers, like a funeral. Vivi called, did Hannah tell you? And Lennie from San Francisco, and Clara; and Sammy is coming." Her gnome's face pressed happily into the flowers.

It is impossible to predict in these cases, but once over the immediate effects of the operation, she should have several months of comparative well-being.

The money, where will come the money?

Travel with her, Dad. Don't take her home to the old associations. The other children will want to see her.

The money, where will I wring the money?

Whatever happens, she is not to know. No, you can't ask her to sign papers to sell the house; nothing to upset her. Borrow instead, then after. . . .

I had wanted to leave you each a few dollars to make life easier, as other fathers do. There will be nothing left now. (Failure! you and your "business is exploitation". Why didn't you make it when it could be made?—Is that what you're thinking of me, Sammy?)

Sure she's unreasonable, Dad—but you have to stay with her; if there's to be any happiness in what's left of her life, it depends on you.

Prop me up, children, think of me, too. Shuffled, chained with her, bitter woman. No Haven, and the little money going. . . . How happy she looks, poor creature.

The look of excitement. The straining to hear everything (the new hearing aid turned full). Why are you so happy, dying woman?

How the petals are, fold on fold, and the gladioli colour. The autumn air.

Stranger grandsons, tall above the little gnome grandmother, the little spry grandfather. Paul in a frenzy of picture-taking before going.

She, wandering the great house. Feeling the books; laughing at the maple shoemaker's bench of a hundred years ago used as a table. The ear turned to music.

"Let us go home. See how good I walk now." "One step from the hospital," he answers, "and she wants to fly. Wait till Doctor Phil says."

"Look—the birds too are flying home. Very good Phil is and will not show it, but he is sick of sickness by the time he comes home."

"Mrs. Telepathy, to read minds," he answers; "read mine what it says: when the trunks of medicines become a suitcase, then we will go."

The grandboys, they do not know what to say to us. . . . Hannah, she runs around here, there, when is there time for herself?

Let us go home. Let us go home.

Musing; gentleness—*but for the incidents of the rabbi in the hospital, and of the candles of benediction.*

Of the rabbi in the hospital:

Now tell me what happened, Mother.

From the sleep I awoke, Hannah's Phil, and he stands there like a devil in a dream and calls me by name. I cannot hear. I think he prays. Go away, please, I tell him, I am not a believer. Still he stands, while my heart knocks with fright.

You scared *him*, Mother. He thought you were delirious.

Who sent him? Why did he come to me?

It is a custom. The men of God come to visit those of their religion they might help. The hospital makes up the list for them—race, religion—and you are on the Jewish list.

Not for rabbis. At once go and make them change.

Tell them to write: Race, human; Religion, none.

And of the candles of benediction:

Look how you have upset yourself, Mrs. Excited Over Nothing. Pleasant memories you should leave.

Go in, go back to Hannah and the lights. Two weeks I saw candles and said nothing. But she asked me.

So what was so terrible? She forgets you never did, she asks you to light the Friday candles and say the benediction like Phil's mother when she visits. If the candles give her pleasure, why shouldn't she have the pleasure?

Not for pleasure she does it. For emptiness. Because his family does. Because all around her do.

That is not a good reason too? But you did not hear her. For heritage, she told you. For the boys, from the past they should have tradition.

Superstition! From our ancestors, savages, afraid of the dark, of themselves: mumbo words and magic lights to scare away ghosts.

She told you: how it started does not take away the goodness. For centuries, peace in the house it means.

Swindler! does she look back on the dark centuries? Candles bought instead of bread and stuck into a potato for a candlestick? Religion that stifled and said: in Paradise, woman, you will be the footstool of your husband, and in life—poor chosen Jew—ground under, despised, trembling in cellars. And cremated. And cremated.

This is religion's fault? You think you are still an orator of the 1905 revolution? Where are the pills for quieting? Which are they?

Heritage. How have we come from our savage past, how no longer to be savages—this to teach. To look back and learn what humanizes—this to teach. To smash all ghettos that divide man—not to go back, not to go back—this to teach. Learned books in the house, will man live or die, and she gives to her boys—superstition.

Hannah that is so good to you. Take your pill, Mrs. Excited For Nothing, swallow.

Heritage! But when did I have time to teach? Of Hannah I asked only hands to help.

Swallow.

Otherwise—musing; gentleness.

Not to travel. To go home.

The children want to see you. We have to show them you are as thorny a flower as ever.

Not to travel.

Vivi wants you should see her new baby. She sent the tickets—aeroplane tickets—a Mrs. Roosevelt she wants to make of you. To Vivi's we have to go.

A new baby. How many warm, seductive babies. She holds him stiffly, *away* from her, so that he wails. And a long shudder begins, and the sweat beads on her forehead.

"Hush, shush," croons the grandfather, lifting him back. "You should forgive your grandmamma, little prince, she has never held a baby before, only seen them in glass cases. Hush, shush."

"You're tired, Ma," says Vivi. "The travel and the noisy dinner. I'll take you to lie down."

(*A long travel from, to, what the feel of a baby evokes*)

In the aeroplane, cunningly designed to encase from motion (no wind, no feel of flight), she had sat severely and still, her face turned to the sky through which they cleaved and left no scar.

So this was how it looked, the determining, the crucial sky, and this was how man moved through it, remote above the dwindled earth, the concealed human life. Vulnerable life, that could scar.

There was a steerage ship of memory that shook across a great, circular sea: clustered, ill human beings; and through the thick-stained air, tiny fretting waters in a window round like the aeroplane's—sun round, moon round. (The round thatched roofs of Olshana.) Eye round—like the smaller window that framed distance the solitary year of exile when only her eyes could travel, and no voice spoke. And the polar winds hurled themselves across snows trackless and endless and white—like the clouds which had closed together below and hidden the earth.

Now they put a baby in her lap. Do not ask me, she would have liked to beg. Enough the worn face of Vivi, the remembered grandchildren. I cannot, cannot. . . .

Cannot what? Unnatural grandmother, not able to make herself embrace a baby.

She lay there in the bed of the two little girls, her new hearing aid turned full, listening to the sound of the children going to sleep, the baby's fretful crying and hushing, the clatter of dishes being washed and put away. They thought she slept. Still she rode on.

It was not that she had not loved her babies, her children. The love—the passion of tending—had risen with the need like a torrent; and like a torrent drowned and immolated all else. But when the need was done—oh the power that was lost in the painful damming back and drying up of what still surged, but had nowhere to go. Only the thin pulsing left that could not quiet, suffering over lives one felt, but could no longer hold nor help.

On that torrent she had borne them to their own lives, and the river-bed was desert long years now. Not there would she dwell, a memoried wraith. Surely that was not all, surely there was more. Still the springs, the springs were in her seeking. Somewhere an older power that beat for life. Somewhere coherence, transport, meaning, community. If they would but leave her in the air now stilled of clamour, in the reconciled solitude, to journey on.

And they put a baby in her lap. Immediacy to embrace, and the breath of *that* past: warm flesh like this that had claims and nuzzled away all else and with lovely mouths devoured; hot-living like an animal—intensely and now; the turning maze; the long drunkenness; the drowning into needing and being needed. Severely she looked back—and the shudder seized her again, and the sweat. Not that way. Not there, not now could she, not yet. . . .

And all that visit, she could not touch the baby.

"Daddy, is it the . . . sickness she's like that?" asked Vivi. "I was so glad to be having the baby—for her. I told Tim, it'll give her more happiness than anything, being around a baby again. And she hasn't played with him once."

He was not listening, "Aahh little seed of life, little charmer," he crooned, "Hollywood should see you. A heart of ice you would melt. Kick, kick. The future you'll have for a ball. In 2050 still kick. Kick for your grandaddy then."

Attentive with the older children; sat through their performances (command performance; we command you to be the audience); helped Ann sort autumn leaves to find the best for a school programme; listened gravely to Richard tell about his rock collection, while her lips mutely formed the words to remember: *igneous*, *sedimentary*, *metamorphic;* looked for missing socks, books and bus tickets; watched the children whoop after their grandfather who knew how to tickle, chuck, lift, toss, do tricks, tell secrets, make jokes, match riddle for riddle. (Tell me a riddle, Grammy. I know no riddles, child.) Scrubbed sills and woodwork and furniture in every room; folded the laundry; straightened drawers; emptied the heaped baskets waiting for ironing (while he or Vivi or Tim nagged: You're supposed to rest here, you've been sick) but to none tended or gave food—and could not touch the baby.

After a week she said: "Let us go home. Today call about the tickets."

"You have important business, Mrs. Inahurry? The President waits to consult with you?" He shouted, for the fear of the future raced in him. "The clothes are still warm from the suitcase, your children cannot show enough how glad they are to see you, and you want home. There is plenty of time for home. We cannot be with the children at home."

"Blind to around you as always: the little ones sleep four in a room because we take their bed. We are two more people in a house with a new baby, and no help."

"Vivi is happy so. The children should have their grandparents a while, she told to me. I should have my mommy and daddy. . . ."

"Babbler and blind. Do you look at her so tired? How she starts to talk and she cries? I am not strong enough yet to help. Let us go home."

TELL ME A RIDDLE

(To reconciled solitude.)

For it seemed to her the crowded noisy house was listening to her, listening for *her. She could feel it like a great ear pressed under her heart. And everything knocked: quick constant raps: let me in, let me in.*

How was it that soft reaching tendrils also became blows that knocked?

C'mon, Grandma, I want to show you. . . .

Tell me a riddle, Grandma. (*I know no riddles*)

Look, Grammy, he's so dumb he can't even find his hands. (Dody and the baby on a blanket over the fermenting autumn mould)

I made them—for you. (Flat paper dolls with aprons that lifted on scalloped skirts that lifted on flowered pants; hair of yarn and great ringed questioning eyes) (Ann)

Watch me, Grandma. (Richard snaking up the tree, hanging exultant, free, with one hand at the top. Below Dody hunching over in pretend-cooking.) (*Climb too, Dody, climb and look*)

Be my nap bed, Grammy. (The "No!" too late.) Morty's abandoned heaviness, while his fingers ladder up and down her hearing-aid cord to his drowsy chant: eentsiebeentsiespider.

(*Children trust.*)

It's to start off your own rock collection, Grandma. That's a trilobite fossil, 200 million years old (millions of years on a boy's mouth) and that one's obsidian, black glass.

Knocked and knocked.

Mother, I *told* you the teacher said we had to bring it back all filled out this morning. Didn't you even ask Daddy? Then tell *me* which plan and I'll check it: evacuate or stay in the city or wait for you to come and take me away. (Seeing the look of straining to hear.) It's for Disaster, Grandma. (*Children trust*)

Vivi in the maze of the long, the lovely drunkenness. The old old noises: baby sounds; screaming of a mother flayed to exasperation; children quarrelling; children playing; singing; laughter.

And Vivi's tears and memories, spilling so fast, half the words not understood.

She had started remembering out loud deliberately, so her mother would know the past was cherished, still lived in her.

Nursing the baby: My friends marvel, and I tell them, oh it's easy to be such a cow. I remember how beautiful my mother seemed nursing my brother, and the milk just flows. . . . Was that Davy? It must have been Davy. . . .

Lowering a hem: How did you ever . . . when I think how you made everything we wore . . . Tim, just think, seven kids and Mommy sewed everything . . . do I remember you sang while you sewed? That white dress with the red apples on the skirt you fixed over for me, was it Hannah's or Clara's before it was mine?

Washing sweaters: Ma, I'll never forget, one of those days so nice you washed clothes outside; one of the first spring days it must have been. The bubbles just danced up and down while you scrubbed, and we chased after, and you stopped to show us how to blow our own bubbles with green onion stalks . . . you always. . . .

"Strong onion, to still make you cry after so many years," her father said, to turn the tears into laughter.

While Richard bent over his homework: Where is it now, do we still have it, the Book of the Martyrs? It always seemed so, well—exalted, when you'd put it on the round table and we'd all look at it together; there was even a halo from the lamp. The lamp with the beaded fringe you could move up and down; they're in style again, pulley lamps like that, but without the fringe. You know the book I'm talking about, Daddy, the Book of the Martyrs, the first picture was a bust of Spartacus . . . Socrates? I wish there was something like that for the children, Mommy, to give them what you. . . . (And the tears splashed again)

(What I intended and did not? Stop it, daughter, stop it, leave that time. And he, the hypocrite, sitting there with tears in his eyes—it was nothing to you then, nothing.)

. . . The time you came to school and I almost died of shame because of your accent and because I knew you knew I was ashamed; how could I? . . . Sammy's harmonica and you danced to it once, yes you did, you and Davy squealing in your arms. . . . That time you bundled us up and walked us down to the railway station to stay the night 'cause it was heated and we didn't have any coal, that winter of the strike, you didn't think I remembered that, did you, Mommy? . . . How you'd call us out to see the sunsets. . . .

Day after day, the spilling memories. Worse now, questions, too. Even the grandchildren: Grandma, in the olden days, when you were little. . . .

It was the afternoons that saved.

While they thought she napped, she would leave the mosaic on the wall (of children's drawings, maps, calendars, pictures, Ann's cardboard dolls with their great ringed questioning eyes) and hunch in the girls' cupboard, on the low shelf where the shoes stood, and the girls' dresses covered.

For that while she would painfully sheathe against the listening house, the tendrils and noises that knocked, and Vivi's spilling memories. Sometimes it helped to braid and unbraid the sashes that dangled, or to trace the pattern on the hoop slips.

Today she had jacks and children under jet trails to forget. Last night, Ann and Dody silhouetted in the window against a sunset of flaming man-made clouds of jet trail, their jacks ball accenting the peaceful noise of dinner being made. Had she told them, yes she had told them of how they played jacks in her village though there was no ball, no jacks. Six stones, round and flat, toss them out, the seventh on the back of the hand, toss, catch and swoop up as many as possible, toss again. . . .

Of stones (repeating Richard) there are three kinds: earth's fire jetting; rock of layered centuries; crucibled new out of the old (*igneous*, *sedimentary*, *metamorphic*).

But there was that other—frozen to black glass, never to transform or hold the fossil memory . . . (let not my seed fall on stone). There was an ancient man who fought to heights a great rock that crashed back down eternally—eternal labour, freedom, labour . . . (stone will perish, but the word remain). And you, David, who with a stone slew, screaming: Lord, take my heart of stone and give me flesh

Who was screaming? Why was she back in the common room of the prison, the sun motes dancing in the shafts of light, and the informer being brought in, a prisoner now, like themselves. And Lisa leaping, yes, Lisa, the gentle and tender, biting at the betrayer's jugular. Screaming and screaming.

No, it is the children screaming. Another of Paul and Sammy's terrible fights?

In Vivi's house. Severely: you are in Vivi's house.

Blows, screams, a call: "Grandma!" For her? Oh please not for her. Hide, hunch behind the dresses deeper. But a trembling little body hurls itself beside her—surprised, smothered laughter, arms surround her neck, tears rub dry on her cheek, and words too soft to understand whisper into her ear (Is this where you hide too, Grammy? It's my secret place, we have a secret now).

And the sweat beads, and the long shudder seizes.

It seemed the great ear pressed inside now, and the knocking. "We have to go home," she told him, "I grow ill here."

"It is your own fault, Mrs. Bodybusy, you do not

rest, you do too much." He raged, but the fear was in his eyes. "It was a serious operation, they told you to take care. . . . All right, we will go to where you can rest."

But where? Not home to death, not yet. He had thought to Lennie's, to Clara's; beautiful visits with each of the children. She would have to rest first, be stronger. If they could but go to Florida—it glittered before him, the never-realized promise of Florida. California: of course. (The money, the money, dwindling!) Los Angeles first for sun and rest, then to Lennie's in San Francisco.

He told her the next day. "You saw what Nancy wrote: snow and wind back home, a terrible winter. And look at you—all bones and a swollen belly. I called Phil: he said: 'A prescription, Los Angeles sun and rest.' "

She watched the words on his lips. "You have sold the house," she cried, "that is why we do not go home. That is why you talk no more of the Haven. Why there is money for travel. After the children you will drag me to the Haven."

"The Haven! Who thinks of the Haven any more? Tell her, Vivi, tell Mrs. Suspicious: a prescription, sun and rest, to make you healthy. . . . And how could I sell the house without *you*?"

At the place of farewells and greetings, of winds of coming and winds of going, they say their good-byes.

They look back at her with the eyes of others before them: Richard with her own blue blaze; Ann with the

Nordic eyes of Tim; Morty's dreaming brown of a great-grandmother he will never know; Dody with the laughing eyes of him who had been her springtide love (who stands beside her now); Vivi's, all tears.

The baby's eyes are closed in sleep.

Good-bye, my children.

3

It is to the back of the great city he brought her, to the dwelling places of the cast-off old. Bounded by two lines of amusement piers to the north and to the south, and between a long straight paving rimmed with black benches facing the sand—sands so wide the ocean is only a far fluting.

In the brief vacation season, some of the boarded stores fronting the sands open, and families, young people and children, may be seen. A little tasselled tram shuttles between the piers, and the lights of roller coasters prink and tweak over those who come to have sensation made in them.

The rest of the year it is abandoned to the old, all else boarded up and still; seemingly empty, except the occasional days and hours when the sun, like a tide, sucks them out of the low rooming houses, casts them on to the benches and sandy rim of the walk—and sweeps them into decaying enclosures back again.

A few newer apartments glint among the low bleached squares. It is in one of these Lennie's Jeannie has arranged their rooms. "Only a few miles north and south people pay hundreds of dollars a month for just this gorgeous air, Grandaddy, just this ocean closeness."

She had been ill on the plane, lay ill for days in the unfamiliar room. Several times the doctor came by—left medicine she would not take. Several times Jeannie drove in the twenty miles from work, still in her Visiting Nurse uniform, the lightness and brightness of her like a healing.

"Who can believe it is winter?" he asked one morning. "Beautiful it is outside like an ad. Come, Mrs. Invalid, come to taste it. You are well enough to sit in here, you are well enough to sit outside. The doctor said it too."

But the benches were encrusted with people, and the sands at the sidewalk's edge. Besides, she had seen the far ruffle of the sea: "there take me," and though she leaned against him, it was she who led.

Plodding and plodding, sitting often to rest, he grumbling. Patting the sand so warm. Once she scooped up a handful, cradling it close to her better eye; peered, and flung it back. And as they came almost to the brink and she could see the glistening wet, she sat down, pulled off her shoes and stockings, left him and began to run. "You'll catch cold," he screamed, but the sand in his shoes weighed him down—he who had always been the agile one—and already the white spray creamed her feet.

He pulled her back, took a handkerchief to wipe off the wet and the sand. "Oh no," she said, "the sun will dry," seized the square and smoothed it flat, dropped on it a mound of sand, knotted the kerchief corners and tied it to a bag—"to look at with the strong glass" (for the first time in years explaining an action of hers) —and lay down with the little bag against her cheek, looking toward the shore that nurtured life as it first crawled toward consciousness the millions of years ago.

He took her one Sunday in the evil-smelling bus, past flat miles of blister houses, to the home of relatives. Oh what is this? she cried as the light began to smoke and the houses to dim and recede. Smog, he said, everyone knows but you. . . . Outside he kept his arms about her, but she walked with hands pushing the heavy air as if to open it, whispered: who has done this? sat down suddenly to vomit at the curb and for a long while refused to rise.

One's age as seen on the altered face of those known in youth. Is this they he has come to visit? This Max and Rose, smooth and pleasant, introducing them to polite children, disinterested grandchildren, "the whole family, once a month on Sundays. And why not? We have the room, the help, the food."

Talk of cars, of houses, of success: this son that, that daughter this. And *your* children? Hastily skimped over, the intermarriages, the obscure work—"my doctor son-in-law, Phil"—all he has to offer. She silent in a corner. (Car-sick like a baby, he explains.) Years since he has taken her to visit anyone but the children, and old apprehensions prickle: "no incidents," he silently begs, "no incidents". He itched to tell them. "A very sick woman," significantly, indicating her with his eyes, "a very sick woman." Their restricted faces did not react. "Have you thought maybe she'd do better at Palm Springs?" Rose asked. "Or at least a nicer section of the beach, nicer people, a pool." Not to have to say "money" he said instead: "would she have sand to look at through a magnifying glass?" and went on, detail after detail, the old habit betraying of parading the queerness of her for laughter.

After dinner—the others into the living-room in men- or women-clusters, or into the den to watch TV—the four of them alone. She sat close to him, and did not speak. Jokes, stories, people they had known, beginning of reminiscence, Russia fifty-sixty years ago. Strange words across the Duncan Phyfe table: *hunger; secret meetings; human rights; spies; betrayals; prison; escape*—interrupted by one of the grandchildren: "Commercial's on; any Coke left? Gee, you're missing a real hair-raiser." And then a granddaughter (Max proudly: "look at her, an American queen") drove them home on her way back to U.C.L.A. No incident—except that there had been no incidents.

The first few mornings she had taken with her the magnifying glass, but he would sit only on the benches, so she rested at the foot, where slatted bench shadows fell, and unless she turned her hearing aid down, other voices invaded.

Now on the days when the sun shone and she felt well enough, he took her on the tram to where the benches ranged in oblongs, some with tables for draughts or cards. Again the blanket on the sand in the striped shadows, but she no longer brought the magnifying glass. He played cards, and she lay in the sun and looked towards the waters; or they walked—two blocks down to the scaling hotel, two blocks back—past chili-hamburger stands, open-doored bars. Next to New and Perpetual Rummage Sale stores.

Once, out of the aimless walkers, slow and shuffling like themselves, someone ran unevenly towards them, embraced, kissed, wept: "dear friends, old friends." A friend of *hers*, not his: Mrs. Mays who had lived next door to them in Denver when the children were small.

Thirty years are compressed into a dozen sentences; and the present, not even in three. All is told: the children scattered; the husband dead; she lives in a room two blocks up from the sing hall—and points to the domed auditorium jutting before the pier. The leg? phlebitis; the heavy breathing? that, one does not ask. She, too, comes to the benches each day to sit. And tomorrow, tomorrow, are they going to the community sing? Of course he would have heard of it, everybody goes—the big doings they wait for all week. They have never been? She will come for them to dinner tomorrow and they will all go together.

So it is that she sits in the wind of the singing, among the thousand various faces of age.

She had turned off her hearing aid at once they came into the auditorium—as she would have wished to turn off sight.

One by one they streamed by and imprinted on her—and though the savage zest of their singing came voicelessly soft and distant, the faces still roared—the faces densened the air—chorded into.

children-chants, mother-croons, singing of the
chained;
love serenades, Beethoven storms, mad Lucia's
scream;
drunken joy-songs, keens for the dead, work-singing

while from floor to balcony to dome a bare-footed sore-covered little girl threaded the sound-thronged tumult, danced her ecstasy of grimace to flutes that scratched at a cross-roads village wedding

Yes, faces became sound, and the sound became faces; and faces and sound became weight—pushed, pressed

"Air"—her hand claws his.

"Whenever I enjoy myself. . . ." Then he saw the grey sweat on her face. "Here. Up. Help me, Mrs. Mays," and they support her out to where she can gulp the air in sob after sob.

"A doctor, we should get for her a doctor."

"Tch, it's nothing," says Ellen Mays, "I get it all the time. You've missed the tram; come to my place. Fix your hearing aid, honey . . . close . . . tea. My view. See, she *wants* to come. Steady now, that's how." Adding mysteriously: "Remember your advice, easy to keep your head above water, empty things float. Float."

The singing a fading march for them, tall woman with a swollen leg, weaving little man, and the swollen thinness they help between.

The stench in the hall: mildew? decay? "We sit and rest then climb. My gorgeous view. We help each other and here we are."

The stench along into the slab of room. A washstand for a sink, a box with oilcloth tacked around for a cupboard, a three-burner gas plate. Artificial flowers, colourless with dust. Everywhere pictures foaming: wedding, baby, party, vacation, graduation, family pictures. From the narrow couch under a slit of window, sure enough the view: lurching rooftops and a scallop of ocean heaving, preening, twitching under the moon.

"While the water heats. Excuse me . . . down the hall." Ellen Mays has gone.

"You'll live?" he asks mechanically, sat down to feel his fright; tried to pull her alongside.

She pushed him away. "For air," she said; stood clinging to the dresser. Then, in a terrible voice:

After a lifetime of room. Of many rooms.

Shhh.

You remember how she lived. Eight children. And now one room like a coffin

She pays rent!

Shrinking the life of her into one room like a coffin. Rooms and rooms like this. I lie on the quilt and hear them talk

Please, Mrs. Orator-without-breath.

Once you went for coffee I walked I saw A Balzac a Chekhov to write it.

Rummage . . . Alone . . . On scraps . . .

Better here old than in the old country!

On scraps Yet they sang like . . . like . . . Wondrous! *Humankind, one has to believe.* So strong. For what? To rot not grow?

Your poor lungs beg you. They sob between each word.

Singing. Unused the life in them. She in this poor room with her pictures. Max You The children Everywhere unused the life. . . And who has meaning? Century after century still all in us not to grow?

Coffins, rummage, plants: sick woman. Oh lay down. We will get for you the doctor.

"And when will it end. Oh, *the end.*" *That* nightmare thought, and this time she writhed, crumpled beside him, seized his hand (for a moment again the weight, the soft distant roaring of humanity) and on the strangled-for breath, begged: "Man . . . will destroy ourselves?"

And looking for answer—in the helpless pity and fear for her (for *her*) that distorted his face—she understood the last months, and knew that she was dying.

4

"Let us go home," she said after several days.

"You are in training for a cross-country run? That is why you do not even walk across the room? Here, like a prescription Phil said, till you are stronger from the operation. You want to break doctor's orders?"

She saw the fiction was necessary to him, was silent; then: "At home I will get better. If the doctor here says?"

"And winter? And the visits to Lennie and to

Clara? All right," for he saw the tears in her eyes, "I will write Phil, and talk to the doctor."

Days passed. He reported nothing. Jeannie came and took her out for air, past the boarded concessions, the hooded and tented amusement rides, to the end of the pier. They watched the spent waves feeding the new, the gulls in the clouded sky; even up where they sat, the wind-blown sand stung.

She did not ask to go down the crooked steps to the sea.

Back in her bed, while he was gone to the store, she said: "Jeannie, this doctor, he is not one I can ask questions. Ask him for me, can I go home?"

Jeannie looked at her, said quickly: "Of course, poor Granny. You want your own things around you, don't you? I'll call him tonight. . . . Look, I've something to show you," and from her purse unwrapped a large cookie, intricately shaped like a little girl. "Look at the curls—can you hear me well, Granny?—and the darling eyelashes. I just came from a house where they were baking them."

"The dimples," she marvelled, "there in the knees," holding it to the better light, turning, studying, "like art. Each singly they cut, or a mould?"

"Singly," said Jeannie, "and if it is a child only the mother can make them. Oh Granny, it's the likeness of a real little girl who died yesterday—Rosita. She was three years old. *Pan del Muerto*, the Bread of the Dead. It was the custom in the part of Mexico they came from."

Still she turned and inspected. "Look, the hollow

in the throat, the little cross necklace. . . . I think for the mother it is a good thing to be busy with such bread. You know the family?"

Jeannie nodded. "On my rounds. I nursed. . . . Oh Granny, it is like a party; they play songs she liked to dance to. The coffin is lined with pink velvet and she wears a white dress. There are candles. . . ."

"In the house?" Surprised, "They keep her in the house?"

"Yes," said Jeannie, "and it *is* against the health law. The father said it will be sad to bury her in this country; in Oaxaca they have a feast night with candles each year; everyone picnics on the graves of those they loved until dawn."

"Yes, Jeannie, the living must comfort themselves." And closed her eyes.

"You want to sleep, Granny?"

"Yes, tired from the pleasure of you. I may keep the Rosita? There stand it, on the dresser, where I can see; something of my own around me."

In the kitchenette, helping her grandfather unpack the groceries, Jeannie said in her light voice:

"I'm resigning my job, Grandaddy."

"Ah, the lucky young man. Which one is he?"

"Too late. You're spoken for." She made a pyramid of cans, unstacked, and built again.

"Something is wrong with the job?"

"With me. I can't be"—she searched for the word—"What they call professional enough. I let myself feel things. And tomorrow I have to report a family. . . ." The cans clicked again. "It's not that, either. I just don't know what I want to do, maybe go back to school, maybe go to art school. I thought if you went to San Francisco I'd come along and talk it over with Mommy and Daddy. But I don't see how you can go. She wants to go home. She asked me to ask the doctor."

The doctor told her himself. "Next week you may travel, when you are a little stronger." But next week there was the fever of an infection, and by the time that was over, she could not leave the bed—a rented hospital bed that stood beside the double bed he slept in alone now.

Outwardly the days repeated themselves. Every other afternoon and evening he went out to his new-found cronies, to talk and play cards. Twice a week, Mrs. Mays came. And the rest of the time, Jeannie was there.

By the sickbed stood Jeannie's FM radio. Often into the room the shapes of music came. She would lie curled on her side, her knees drawn up, intense in listening (Jeannie sketched her so, coiled, convoluted like an ear), then thresh her hand out and abruptly snap the radio mute—still to lie in her attitude of listening, concealing tears.

Once Jeannie brought in a young Marine to visit, a friend from high-school days she had found wandering near the empty pier. Because Jeannie asked him to, gravely, without self-consciouness, he sat himself cross-legged on the floor and performed for them a dance of his native Samoa.

Long after they left, a tiny thrumming sound could be heard where, in her bed, she strove to repeat the beckon, flight, surrender of his hands, the fluttering footbeats, and his low plaintive calls.

Hannah and Phil sent flowers. To deepen her pleasure, he placed one in her hair. "Like a girl," he said, and brought the hand mirror so she could see. She looked at the pulsing red flower, the yellow skull face; a desolate, excited laugh shuddered from her, and she pushed the mirror away—but let the flower burn.

The week Lennie and Helen came, the fever returned. With it the excited laugh, and incessant words. She, who in her life had spoken but seldom and then only when necessary (never having learned the easy, social uses of words), now in dying, spoke incessantly.

In a half-whisper: "Like Lisa she is, your Jeannie. Have I told you of Lisa, she who taught me to read? Of the highborn she was, but noble in herself. I was sixteen; they beat me; my father beat me so I would not go to her. It was forbidden, she was a Tolstoyan. At night, past dogs that howled, terrible dogs, my son, in the snows of winter to the road, I to ride in her carriage like a lady, to books. To her, life was holy, knowledge was holy, and she taught me to read. They hung her. Everything that happens one must try to understand why. She killed one who betrayed many. Because of betrayal, betrayed all she lived and believed. In one minute she killed, before my eyes (there is so much blood in a human being, my son), in prison with me. All that happens, one must try to understand.

"The name?" Her lips would work. "The name that was their pole star; the doors of the death houses fixed to open on it; I read of it my year of penal servitude. Thuban!" very excited, "Thuban, in ancient Egypt the pole star. Can you see, look out to see it, Jeannie, if it swings around *our* pole star that seems to *us* not to move.

"Yes, Jeannie, at your age my mother and grandmother had already buried children . . . yes, Jeannie, it is more than oceans between Olshana and you . . . yes, Jeannie, they danced, and for all the bodies they had they might as well be chickens, and indeed, they scratched and flapped their arms and hopped.

"And Andrei Yefimitch, who for twenty years had never known of it and never wanted to know, said as if he wanted to cry: but why my dear friend this malicious laughter?" Telling to herself half-memorized phrases from her few books. "Pain I answer with tears and cries, baseness with indignation, meanness with repulsion . . . for life may be hated or wearied of, but never despised."

Delirious: "Tell me, my neighbour, Mrs. Mays, the pictures never lived, but what of the flowers? Tell them who ask: no rabbis, no ministers, no priests, no speeches, no ceremonies: ah, false—let the living comfort themselves. Tell Sammy's boy, he who flies, tell him to go to Stuttgart and see where Davy has no grave. And what?" "And what? where millions have no graves save air."

In delirium or not, wanting the radio on; not seeming to listen, the words still jetting, wanting the music on. Once, silencing it abruptly as of old, she began to cry, unconcealed tears this time. "You have pain, Granny?" Jeannie asked.

"The music," she said, "still it is there and we do not hear; knocks, and our poor human ears too weak. What else, what else we do not hear?"

Once she knocked his hand aside as he gave her a pill, swept the bottles from her bedside table: "no pills, let me feel what I feel," and laughed as on his hands and knees he groped to pick them up.

Night-times her hand reached across the bed to hold his.

A constant retching began. Her breath was too faint for sustained speech now, but still the lips moved:

When no longer necessary   to injure others
Pick   pick pick   Blind chicken
As a human being   responsibility for

"David!" imperious, "Basin!" and she would vomit, rinse her mouth, the wasted throat working to swallow, and begin the chant again.

She will be better off in the hospital now, the doctor said.

He sent the telegrams to the children, was packing her suitcase, when her hoarse voice startled. She had roused, was pulling herself to sitting.

"Where now?" she asked. "Where now do you drag me?"

"You do not even have to have a baby to go this time," he soothed, looking for the brush to pack. "Remember, after Davy you told me—worthy to have a baby for the pleasure of the ten-day rest in the hospital?'

"Where now? Not home yet?" Her voice mourned. "Where *is* my home?"

He rose to ease her back. "The doctor, the hospital," he started to explain, but deftly, like a snake, she had slithered out of bed and stood swaying, propped behind the night table.

"Coward," she hissed, "runner."

"You stand," he said senselessly.

"To take me there and run. Afraid of a little vomit."

He reached her as she fell. She struggled against him, half slipped from his arms, pulled herself up again.

"Weakling," she taunted, "to leave me there and run. Betrayer. All your life you have run."

He sobbed, telling Jeannie. "A Marilyn Monroe to run for her virtue. Fifty-nine pounds she weighs, the doctor said, and she beats at me like a Dempsey. Betrayer, she cries, and I running like a dog when she calls; day and night, running to her, her vomit, the bedpan. . . ."

"She wants you, Grandaddy," said Jeannie. "Isn't that what they call love? I'll see if she sleeps, and if she does, poor worn-out darling, we'll have a party, you and I; I brought us rum babas."

They did not move her. By her bed now stood the tall hooked pillar that held the solutions—blood and dextrose—to feed her veins. Jeannie moved down the hall to take over the sickroom, her face so radiant, her grandfather asked her once: "you are in love?" (Shameful the joy, the pure overwhelming joy from being with her grandmother; the peace, the serenity that breathed.) "My darling escape," she answered incoherently, "my darling Granny"—as if that explained.

Now one by one the children came, those that were able. Hannah, Paul, Sammy. Too late to ask: and what did you learn with your living, Mother, and what do we need to know?

Clara, the eldest, clenched:

Pay me back, Mother, pay me back for all you took from me. Those others you crowded into your heart. The hands I needed to be for you, the heaviness, the responsibility.

Is this she? Noises the dying make, the crablike hands crawling over the covers. The ethereal singing.

She hears that music, that singing from childhood; forgotten sound—not heard since, since. . . . And the hardness breaks like a cry: Where did we lose each other, first mother, singing mother?

Annulled: the quarrels, the gibing, the harshness between; the fall into silence and the withdrawal.

I do not know you, Mother. Mother, I never knew you.

Lennie, suffering not alone for her who was dying, but for that in her which never lived (for that which in him might never live). From him too, unspoken words: *good-bye Mother who taught me to mother myself.*

Not Vivi, who must stay with her children; not Davy, but he is already here, having to die again with *her* this time, for the living take their dead with them when they die.

Light she grew, like a bird, and, like a bird, sound bubbled in her throat while the body fluttered in agony. Night and day, asleep or awake (though indeed there was no difference now) the songs and the phrases leaping.

And he, who had once dreaded a long dying (from fear of himself, from horror of the dwindling money) now desired her quick death profoundly, for *her* sake. He no longer went out, except when Jeannie forced him to; no longer laughed, except when in the bright kitchenette, Jeannie coaxed his laughter (and she, who seemed to hear nothing else, would laugh too, conspiratorial wisps of laughter).

Light, like a bird, the fluttering body, the little claw hands, the beaked shadow on her face; and the throat, bubbling, straining.

He tried not to listen, as he tried not to look on the face in which only the forehead remained familiar, but trapped with her the long nights in that little room, the sounds worked themselves into his consciousness with their punctuation of death swallows, whimpers, gurglings.

Even in reality (swallow) *life's lack of it*

The bell Summon what enables

78,000 in one minute (whisper of a scream) *78,000 human beings.*

We'll destroy ourselves?

"Aah, Mrs. Miserable," he said, as if she could hear, "all your life working, and now in bed you lie, servants to tend, you do not even need to call to be tended, and still you work. Such hard work it is to die? Such hard work?"

The body threshed, her hand clung in his. A melody, ghost-thin, hovered on her lips, and like a guilty ghost, the vision of her bent in listening to it, silencing the record instantly he was near. Now, heedless of his presence, she floated the melody on and on.

"Hid it from me," he complained, "how many times you listened to remember it so?" And tried to think when she had first played it, or first begun to silence her few records when he came near—but could reconstruct nothing. There was only this room with its tall hooked pillar and its swarm of sounds.

No man one   except through others
Strong   with the not yet   in the now
Dogma dead   war dead   one country

"It helps, Mrs. Philosopher, words from books? It helps?" And it seemed to him that for seventy years she had hidden a tape recorder, infinitely microscopic, within her, that it had coiled infinite mile on mile, trapping every song, every melody, every word read, heard and spoken—and that maliciously she was playing back only what said nothing of him, of the children, of their intimate life together.

"Left us indeed, Mrs. Babbler," he reproached, "you who called others babbler and cunningly saved your words. A lifetime you tended and loved, and now not a word of us, for us. Left us indeed? Left me."

And he took out his solitaire deck, shuffled the cards loudly, slapped them down.

Lift high banner of reason justice freedom light (tatter of an orator's voice)

Humankind life worthy heroic capacities

Seeks (blur of shudder) *belong human being*

"Words, words," he accused, "and what human beings did *you* seek around you, Mrs. Live Alone, and what mankind think worthy?"

Though even as he spoke, he remembered she had not always been isolated, had not always wanted to be alone (as he knew there had been a voice before this gossamer one; before the hoarse voice that broke from silence to lash, make incidents, shame him—a girl's voice of eloquence that spoke their holiest dreams). But again he could reconstruct, image, nothing of what had been before, or when, or how, it had changed.

Ace, queen, jack. The pillar shadow fell, so, in two tracks; in the mirror depths glistened a moonlike blob, the empty solution bottle. And it worked in him: *of reason and justice and freedom. Dogma dead:* he remembered the full quotation, laughed bitterly. "Hah, good you do not know what you say; good Victor Hugo died and did not see it, his twentieth century."

Deuce, ten, five. Dauntlessly she began a song of their youth of belief:

These things shall be, a loftier race
than e'er the world hath known shall rise

with flame of freedom in their souls
and light of knowledge in their eyes

King, four jack. "In the twentieth century, hah!"

They shall be gentle, brave and strong
to spill no drop of blood, but dare
all . . .
on earth and fire and sea and air

"To spill no drop of blood, hah! So, cadaver, and you too, cadaver Hugo, 'in the twentieth century ignorance will be dead, dogma will be dead, war will be dead, and for all mankind one country—of fulfilment.' Hah!"

And every life (long strangling cough) *shall*
be a song

The cards fell from his fingers. Without warning, the bereavement and betrayal he had sheltered—compounded through the years—hidden even from himself—revealed itself,
uncoiled,
released,
sprung
and with it the monstrous shapes of what had actually happened in the century.

A ravening hunger or thirst seized him. He groped into the kitchenette, switched on all three lights, piled a tray—"you have finished your night snack, Mrs. Cadaver, now I will have mine." And he was shocked at the tears that splashed on the tray.

"Salt tears. For free. I forgot to shake on salt?"

Whispered: "Lost, how much I lost."

Escaped to the grandchildren whose childhoods were childish, who had never hungered, who lived unravaged by disease in warm houses of many rooms, had all the school for which they cared, could walk on any street, stood a head taller than their grandparents, towered above—beautiful skins, straight backs, clear straightforward eyes. "Yes, you in Olshana," he said to the town of sixty years ago, "they would be nobility to you."

And was this not the dream then, come true in ways undreamed? he asked.

And are there no other children in the world? he answered, as if in her harsh voice.

And the flame of freedom, the light of knowledge?
And to spill no drop of blood?

And he thought that at six Jeannie would get up and it would be his turn to go to her room and sleep, that he could press the buzzer and she would come now; that in the afternoon Ellen Mays was coming, and this time they would play cards and he could marvel at how rouge can stand half an inch on the cheek; that in the evening the doctor would come, and he could beg him to be merciful, to stop the feeding solutions, to let her die.

To let her die, and with her their youth of belief out of which her bright, betrayed words foamed; stained words, that on her working lips came stainless.

Hours yet before Jeannie's turn. He could press the

buzzer and wake her to come now; he could take a pill, and with it sleep; he could pour more brandy into his milk glass, though what he had poured was not yet touched.

Instead he went back, checked her pulse, gently tended with his knotty fingers as Jeannie had taught.

She was whimpering; her hand crawled across the covers for his. Compassionately he enfolded it, and with his free hand gathered up the cards again. Still was there thirst or hunger ravening in him.

That world of their youth—dark, ignorant, terrible with hate and disease—how was it that living in it, in the midst of corruption, filth, treachery, degradation, they had not mistrusted man nor themselves; had believed so beautifully, so . . . falsely?

"Aaah, children," he said out loud, "how we believed, how we belonged." And he yearned to package for each of the children, the grandchildren, for everyone, *that joyous certainty, that sense of mattering, of moving and being moved, of being one and indivisible with the great of the past, with all that freed, ennobled.* Package it, stand on corners, in front of stadiums and on crowded beaches knock on doors, give it as a fabled gift.

"And why not in cereal boxes, in soap packages?" he mocked himself. "Aah. You have taken my senses, cadaver."

Words foamed, died unsounded. Her body writhed; she made kissing motions with her mouth. (Her lips moving as she read, poring over the Book of the Martyrs, the magnifying glass superimposed over the heavy eyeglasses.) *Still she believed?* "Eva!" he whispered. "Still you believed? You lived by it? These Things Shall Be?"

"One pound soup meat," she answered distinctly, "one soup bone."

"My ears heard you. Ellen Mays was witness: 'Man . . . one has to believe.' " Imploringly: "Eva!"

"Bread, day-old." She was mumbling. "Please, in a wooden box . . . for kindling. The thread, hah, the thread breaks. Cheap thread"—and a gurgling, enormously loud, began in her throat.

"I ask for stone; she gives me bread—day-old." He pulled his hand away, shouted: "Who wanted questions? Everything you have to wake?" Then dully, "Ah, let me help you turn, poor creature."

Words jumbled, cleared. In a voice of crowded terror:

"Paul, Sammy, don't fight.

"Hannah, have I ten hands?

"How can I give it, Clara, how can I give it if I don't have?"

"You lie," he said sturdily, "there was joy too." Bitterly: "Ah how cheap you speak of us at the last."

As if to rebuke him, as if her voice had no relationship with her flailing body, she sang clearly, beautifully, a school song the children had taught her when they were little; begged:

"Not look my hair where they cut. . . ."

(The crown of braids shorn.) And instantly he left the mute old woman poring over the Book of the Martyrs; went past the mother treadling at the sewing machine, singing with the children; past the girl in her wrinkled prison dress, hiding her hair with scarred hands, lifting to him her awkward, shamed, imploring eyes of love; and took her in his arms, dear, personal, fleshed, in all the heavy passion he had loved to rouse from her.

"Eva!"

Her little claw hand beat the covers. How much, how much can a man stand? He took up the cards, put them down, circled the beds, walked to the dresser, opened, shut drawers, brushed his hair, moved his hand bit by bit over the mirror to see what of the reflection he could blot out with each move, and felt that at any moment he would die of what was unendurable. Went to press the buzzer to wake Jeannie, looked down, saw on Jeannie's sketch pad the hospital bed, with *her*; the double bed alongside, with him; the tall pillar feeding into her veins, and their hands, his and hers, clasped, feeding each other. And as if he had been instructed he went to his bed, lay down, holding the sketch (as if it could shield against the monstrous shapes of loss, of betrayal, of death)—and with his free hand took hers back into his.

So Jeannie found them in the morning.

That last day the agony was perpetual. Time after time it lifted her almost off the bed, so they had to fight to hold her down. He could not endure and left the room; wept as if there never would be tears enough.

Jeannie came to comfort him. In her light voice she said: Grandaddy, Grandaddy don't cry. She is not there, she promised me. On the last day, she said she would go back to when she first heard music, a little girl on the road of the village where she was born. She promised me. It is a wedding and they dance, while the flutes so joyous and vibrant tremble in the air. Leave her there, Grandaddy, it is all right. She promised me. Come back, come back and help her poor body to die.

For my mother and two others of that generation
Seevya and Genya
Infinite, dauntless, incorruptible

Death deepens the wonder

Yonnondio
From the Thirties

For Jack

(*Lament for the Aborigines*)
A song, a poem of itself—the word itself a dirge

Race of the woods, the landscapes free, and the falls!
No picture, poem, statement, passing them to the
  future:
Yonnondio! Yonnondio!—unlimn'd they disappear;
To-day gives place, and fades—the cities, farms,
  factories fade;
A muffled sonorous sound, a wailing word is borne
  through the air for a moment,
The blank and gone and still, and utterly lost.

from Walt Whitman's "Yonnondio"

The time at the opening of this
book is the early 1920's;

the place: a Wyoming mining town.

A Note About This Book

This book, conceived primarily as a novel of the 1930's, was begun in 1932 in Faribault, Minnesota, when the author was nineteen, and worked on intermittently into 1936 or perhaps 1937 in Omaha, Stockton, Venice (Calif.), Los Angeles and San Francisco. Unfinished, it yet bespeaks the consciousness and roots of that decade, if not its events.

Thought long since lost or destroyed, some of its pages were found intermixed with other old papers last winter, during the process of searching for another manuscript. A later, more thorough, search turned up additional makings: odd tattered pages, lines in yellowed notebooks, scraps. Other parts, evidently once in existence, seem irrevocably lost.

The first four chapters, in final or near-final form when fitted together, presented only minor problems. The succeeding pages were increasingly difficult to reclaim. There were usually two to fourteen versions to work from: 38 to 41 year old penciled-over scrawls and fragments to decipher and piece together. Judgment had to be exercised as to which version, revision or draft to choose or combine; decisions made whether to include or omit certain first drafts and notes; and guessing had to be done as to where several scenes belonged. In this sense—the choices and omissions, the combinings and reconstruction—the book ceased to be solely the work of that long ago young writer and, in arduous partnership, became this older one's as well. But it is all the old manuscripts—no rewriting, no new writing.

TILLIE OLSEN

San Francisco, February 1973

INTRODUCTION

Tillie Olsen has said that to be a writer of her class and sex is to be both "fortunate" and "a survivor". *Yonnondio: From the Thirties* calls back the unrecorded suffering of the midwestern working class of the twenties and thirties. It is a vital response to its suggestive title, from Walt Whitman's poem: the "muffled sonorous sound" that laments the passing of the aborigines, a "dirge" for the lost history of all "unlimned" peoples. *Yonnondio* is the "picture, poem, statement" that Whitman sought; it answers, too, his 1871 comment that "Literature has never recognized the common people" or given a truthful portrait of "typical" independent American working women. Since Whitman wrote there has grown up in America a fragmentary literature of common people. Much of it, written and published in the Depression, deserves our attention but is rarely read. *Yonnondio*, although written in the Depression when the Nebraska-born author was in her late teens and early twenties, was laid aside, then lost for almost forty years. Its publication in 1974 was thus a double retrieval of lost lives.

In the novel, the world is largely seen through the alternating, counterpointed awareness of Anna Holbrook and her child Mazie. The book itself is a project of two consciousnesses, both Tillie Olsen's. When the text was discovered in manuscript in the early seventies only the first four chapters were in "final or near final form". Her reconstruction of the remaining drafts and fragments involved a delicate and painstaking task in which no word was altered, but the older writer, "the woman of the seventies" in "arduous partnership" with " the girl of the thirties" selected and ordered. *Yonnondio* comes to us "unfinished" in the sense that the young author meant to write more, but it is not therefore rough or incomplete. On the contrary, as it stands it is one of the great short novels in English. The triumphant result of this joint effort might be seen as a small reparation from history for the faith which the older writer always kept with her younger self.

Wide public recognition came to Tillie Olsen with the publication in 1962 of *Tell Me a Riddle*, her collected short fiction written in the preceding decade. It came late; she was fifty. With the platform made available to her she has campaigned for an audience for other forgotten or muffled women writers, forerunners, contemporaries, rising talents. She inaugurated an incisive analysis of the social forces that keep writers, especially women writers "silent", limiting their production, cutting off or cutting up their writing lives. In two major talks, "Silences" (1962) and "Women Who Are Writers in Our Century" (1971), later published as essays and collected in *Silences* (1978) she anatomised the circumstances which accounted for so few published writers of her sex and class, dispelling as she wrote the myth that writing is a wholly mysterious art for which men have a special unnurtured gift. To her bulging dossier, which includes the foreshortened careers of many admired male authors, she appended her own history of silence, for what " the individual experience may add":

> In the twenty years I bore and reared my children, usually had to work on a paid job as well, the simplest circumstances for creation did not exist. Nevertheless writing, the hope of it, was 'the air I breathed, so long as I shall breathe at all.' In that hope, there was conscious storing, snatched reading, beginnings of writing, and always 'the secret rootlets of reconnaissance'.
>
> . . .
>
> A full extended family life; the world of my job (transcriber in a diary-equipment company); and the writing, which I was somehow able to carry around within me through work, through home. Time on the bus, even when I had to stand, was

> enough; the stolen moments at work, enough; the deep night hours for as long as I could stay awake, after the kids were in bed, after the household tasks were done, sometimes during . . .

After this period, the "triple life" became too costly, the "craziness of endurance" lost. An eight month's writing grant allowed her to give up her job; returning to it she shielded the writing for a little, but it was a time of "festering and congestion", when she was "always roused by the writing, always denied". When fuller freedom came she had "to learn response".

Her personal account in *Silences* particularised women's oppression and highlighted the extra burdens stemming from the sexual division of labour that keep women writers from their art. It was part of a vanguard feminist analysis, for which, in 1962 there was almost no current context. Like *Yonnondio* itself, it arose out of the left-wing political consciousness of the nineteen thirties, forgotten or despised, that contained a strong feminist element. The subtitle *From the Thirties* for a novel that begins, and in the form it has reached us, ends in the twenties, marks out the political base and perspective from which it was written. From the thirties onward Tillie Olsen was a political activist. The working conditions she describes were well-known to her. The packinghouse scenes were drawn from first hand knowledge of the Kansas City industry where she was jailed for organising workers. *Yonnondio* was begun shortly afterwards, during a period of illness, and worked on intermittently thereafter. During this time she was writing political journalism, involved in the 1934 Longshoreman's strike, union activity, opposing the rise of fascism and other threats to human rights and world peace of that decade, the Spanish Civil War. The first chapter of the Yonnondio manuscript, titled "The Iron Throat", appeared in the second issue of the radical journal the *Partisan Review* in 1934 and was praised as "unmistakably the work of early genius" but children, home, jobs and politics were devouring the young author's time and energies.

The retrieval and publication of *Yonnondio* reminds us of the importance to feminism of its own history, and the ease with which that history can be deracinated, especially when, as here, it is both by and of the poor. In the novel, Old Man Caldwell, the educated farmer with socialist sympathies tells the child Mazie "Whatever happens, remember, everything, the nourishment, the roots you need, are where you are now." Caldwell puts into question the political and social value of the education Anna wants for her children, telling her his "education began after I got out of college". He recognises in Anna the survival of intelligence and feeling, in Mazie the imagination and tenacious curiosity which may remember in order to change. Transmission is a chancy business. Jim sells the books that Caldwell has bequeathed to Mazie for "half a dollar".

Tillie Olsen has taught at, but never attended college. Today a small army of talented, determined university trained feminist historians and social scientists work to expose and analyse the twin oppressions of class and gender – for which *Yonnondio* could serve as a text. With wonderful economy it sets out, even in its first few pages, the material and ideological situation under which Anna and Jim Holbrook labour, yoked and divided and the children are formed into female or male. We overhear with six-year-old Mazie, the conditions and contradictions into which she has been born.

We may begin to understand Tillie Olsen's reverence for literature as an "incomparable medium" when we realise how much subtle analysis she can pack into two moving pages of expository narrative. Mazie wakes in a Wyoming town in the early twenties to the mining whistle that can mean death to "somebody's poppa or brother". She listens as her parents discuss their immigrant neighbours, father dead in the mine, son rising fourteen about to go down, bitter mother, the dream of America blasted. Immigrant and native perspectives clash; more profoundly men and women's visions conflict. Anna has absorbed Marie's grief that the children will go uneducated, is thoughtful about Marie's wish that the girls enter convents rather than live in poverty, to rear more kids "to get their heads blowed off in the mine". She passes on with tacit agreement Marie's passionate utterance that the coal should be "blood-coloured". Jim resists the "funny ideas" of foreigners and wonders "what earthly use can a woman have" except childbearing. When pushed to consider the dangers of the job he tells Anna "Quit your woman's blabbin. . . " The narrative shifts into Anna's mind where thoughts creep "like worms" over mine disasters, her four children's fragile future, entwined with a dull sad insight into Mazie's precocity: "Its living like this does it. . . . Makes 'em old before their time." It is a comment on herself as well.

The opening episode indicates a psychic as well as material sexual division of labour. Forms of consciousness are gendered by the division of tasks, that separation passed on from parents to children in spite of themselves. The men "never let on" if they are afraid of the mine; women let the fear of it run free in their thoughts and words. Their "woman's blabbin" is an acute assessment of the conditions of the men's labour which the men cannot bear, literally, to think of. Marie and Anna have a bloody understanding, of which Mazie acquires a frightening fragment, that women are there to reproduce a labour force that capital will use and kill. In her later story, "I Stand Here Ironing", (from *Tell Me a Riddle*) the mother-speaker, knowing her teenage child to be damaged by the depression and the war, asks only that she have "enough to live by" and know her human capacity to resist being merely victim. The younger author has Anna say to the sympathetic Caldwell " 'Better. . . to be a cripple and alive than dead, not able to feel anything.' " The bass line of the novel is the harsh rhythm of the Holbrooks' unsuccessful struggle against successive, but only quantitively different forms of economic exploitation; the melody is Anna's emergence alive, if crippled, Mazie's undiminished quest for answers. The characters of the mother and child are so densely imagined and rendered, as is their world, that there is a danger that we, the readers, pleasure ourselves with a vicarious experience of their pain. But an authorial voice interrupts the fiction, disturbs this identification. Sometimes it is the voice of history and fate to remind Jim's workmates that they are dying or doomed, once it is strategically placed to prevent us from taking up Caldwell's larger vision as the controlling philosophy of the narrative. Most important, the author intervenes to warn the reader against the conservative tendency and effect that art can have. When the mine explodes, before the scene is fully described:

> And could you not make a cameo of this and pin it onto your aesthetic hearts? So sharp it is, so clear, so classic. The shattered dusk, the mountain of calm, the tipple; clean lines, bare beauty – and carved against them dwarfed by the vastness of night and the towering tipple, these black figures with bowed heads, waiting, waiting.
>
> Surely it is classical enough for you – the Greek marble of the women, the simple, flowing lines of sorrow, carved so rigid and eternal.

A thrust, this, "from the thirties" against an art that made abstract pseudo-classical still-lives out of ongoing injustice and misery. The author makes clear that her language has not been mobilised for the aesthetic gratification of readers or critics – if the readers "feel" with Mazie and Anna it is so that they may, like them "rebel against what will not let life be". The polemic informs, deepens, shapes the fiction, but must not alienate it into another commodity called art, which is elevated and depoliticised.

The women imagined in the author's satirical "cameo" of grief are eternal, frozen figures, symbols, watchers, of natural catastrophe. *Yonnondio* refuses this aesthetic representation of women, instead it strongly affirms that women have much more than an "earthly use", sexual, reproductive, nurturant. Neither mothering nor domestic tasks wholly define them, nor are the women identified with benign or malignant nature, with security or organic forces, as they so frequently are in men's fiction and poetry, even where the political impulse is "radical". Tillie Olsen foregrounds mothers and daughters, balancing perhaps, the emphasis on mothers and sons in male proletarian writing. The daughters carry the future, the mothers bear witness to past and present. Experience is exposed and spoken by the women in *Yonnondio*: Marie, Anna, Mazie, Else, Ella. In the penultimate scene in the packinghouse which employs both sexes, it is Ella "who has a need to put things into words" who chants their suffering in kitchen imagery " 'steamed, boiled, broiled, fried, cooked' ", and finally "scalded". In the opening pages Mazie lists to herself the words she knows, tells her brother stories. The novel ends with baby Bess banging out her emerging identity with a jam jar lid.

Significantly, sexuality as a positive force, a woman's right, is never emphasised in Tillie Olsen's fiction, as it is in so much literature by women before and after. In *Yonnondio* sex is the madman's possible threat to Mazie, Jim's brutal and thoughtless rape of Anna when she is pregnant, the fantasies engendered by the media. There is kindness and affection as well as anger and cruelty between Jim and Anna, and an unstated mutual struggle to maintain the family. But the absence of familiar discussions of love and passion in the text is deliberate, not the result of puritanism, rather a desire for us to see women's lives and needs outside, beyond, sexual desire.

Women are oppressed in these pages, but not silenced. Anna's madness, brought on by overwork, miscarriage and unendurable stress, induces in her a state where the children are *not*, a sublime sense out of which comes, at the end, a brief moment of expressed, nonverbal tenderness to Mazie.

> She began stroking Mazie's hair in a kind of languor, a swoon. Gently and absently she stroked. . . .. A fragile old remembered comfort streamed from the stroking fingers into Mazie, gathered to some shy bliss that shone despairingly over suppurating hurt and want and fear and shamings, the Harm of years. . . . The fingers stroked, spun a web, cocooned Mazie into happiness and intactness and selfness. Soft wove the bliss round hurt and fear and want and shame – the old worn fragile bliss, a new frail selfness bliss, healing, transforming. . . . The air and self shone boundless. Absently her mother stroked; stroked unfolding, wingedness, boundlessness.

The novel insists on the survival of a creative consciousness for women in the very worst material circumstance. It also explores what the author felt, as late as 1971, to be "an almost taboo area; the last refuge of sexism. . . the least understood, least and last explored, tormentingly complex *core* of woman's oppression (and I believe, transport as woman) – motherhood." The heart of *Yonnondio* turns, twists on this contradictory "area" so movingly opened out for us by its author, young and old. Its existence is responsible for the book's creation and recreation, part of the circumstance of silence that delayed its delivery to us.

Cora Kaplan, 1980

ONE

The whistles always woke Mazie. They pierced into her sleep like some guttural-voiced metal beast, tearing at her; breathing a terror. During the day if the whistle blew, she knew it meant death—somebody's poppa or brother, perhaps her own—in that fearsome place below the ground, the mine.

"God damn that blowhorn," she heard her father mutter. Creak of him getting out of bed. The door closed, with yellow light from the kerosene lamp making a long crack on the floor. Clatter of dishes. Her mother's tired, grimy voice.

"What'll ya have? Coffee and eggs? There aint no bacon."

"Dont bother with anything. Havent time. I gotta stop by Kvaternicks and get the kid. He's starting work today."

"What're they going to give him?"

"Little of everything at first, I guess, trap, throw switches. Maybe timberin."

"Well, he'll be starting one punch ahead of the old man. Chris began as a breaker boy." (Behind both stolid faces the claw of a buried thought—and maybe finish like him, buried under slaty roof that the company hadn't bothered to timber.)

"He's thirteen, aint he?" asked Anna.

"I guess. Nearer to fourteen."

"Marie was tellin me, it would break Chris's heart if he only knew. He wanted the kid to be different, get an edjication."

"Yeah? Them foreigners do have funny ideas."

"Oh, I dunno. Then she says that she wants the girls to become nuns so they won't have to worry where the next meal's comin from, or have to have kids."

"Well, what other earthly use can a woman have, I'd like to know?"

"She says she doesnt want 'em raisin a lot of brats to get their heads blowed off in the mine. I guess she takes Chris's . . . passing away pretty hard. It's kinda affected her mind. She keeps talkin about the old country, the fields, and what they thought it would be like here—all buried in da bowels of earth, she finishes."

"Say, what does she think she is, a poet?"

"And she talks about the coal. Says it oughta be red, and let people see how they get it with blood."

"Quit your woman's blabbin," said Jim Holbrook, irritated suddenly. "I'm goin now."

Morning sounds. Scrunch of boots. The tinkle of his pail, swinging. Shouted greetings to fellow workers across the street. Her mother turning down the yellow light and creaking into bed. All the sounds of the morning weaving over the memory of the whistle like flowers growing lovely over a hideous corpse. Mazie slept again.

Anna Holbrook lay in the posture of sleep. Thoughts, like worms, crept within her. Of Marie Kvaternick, of Chris's dreams for the boys, of the paralyzing moment when the iron throat of the whistle shrieked forth its announcement of death, and women poured from every house to run for the tipple. Of her kids—Mazie, Will, Ben, the baby. Mazie for all her six and a half years was like a woman sometimes. It's living like this does it, she thought; makes 'em old before their time. Thoughts of the last accident writhed in her blood—there were whispered rumors that the new fire boss, the super's nephew, never made the trips to see if there was gas. Didn't the men care? They never let on. The whistle. In her a deep man's voice suddenly arose, moaning over and over, "God, God, God."

The sun sent its grimy light through the window of the three-room wooden shack, twitching over Mazie's face, filtering across to where Anna Holbrook bent over the washtub. Mazie awoke suddenly; the baby was crying. She stumbled over to the wooden box that held him, warming the infant to her body. Then she dressed, changed the baby's diaper with one of the old flour sacks her mother used for the purpose and went into the kitchen.

"Ma, what's there to eat?"

"Coffee. It's on the stove. Wake Will and Ben and dont bother me. I got washin to do."

Later. "Ma?"

"Yes."

"What's an edication?"

"An edjication?" Mrs. Holbrook arose from amidst the shifting vapors of the washtub and, with the suds dripping from her red hands, walked over and stood impressively over Mazie. "An edjication is what you kids are going to get. It means your hands stay white and you read books and work in an office. Now, get the kids and scat. But dont go too far, or I'll knock your block off."

Mazie lay under the hot Wyoming sun, between the outhouse and the garbage dump. There was no other place for Mazie to lie, for the one patch of green in the yard was between these two spots. From the ground arose a nauseating smell. Food had been rotting in the garbage piles for years. Mazie pushed her mind hard against things half known, not known. "I am Mazie Holbrook," she said softly. "I am a-knowen things. I can diaper a baby. I can tell ghost stories. I know words and words. Tipple. Edjication. Bug dust. Supertendent. My poppa can lick any man in this here town. Sometimes the whistle blows and everyone starts a-runnen. Things come a-blowen my hair and it is soft, like the baby laughin." A phrase trembled into her mind, "Bowels of earth." She shuddered. It was mysterious and terrible to her. "Bowels of earth. It means the mine. Bowels is the stummy. Earth is a stummy and mebbe she eats the men that come down. Men and daddy goin' in like the day and comin out black. Earth black and pop's face and hands black, and he spits from his mouth black. Night comes and it is black. Coal is black—it makes a fire. The sun is makin a fire on me, but it is not black. Some color I am not knowen it is," she said wistfully, "but I'll have that learnin' someday. Poppa says the ghosts down there start a fire. That's what blowed Sheen McEvoy's face off so it's red. It made him crazy. Night be comen and everything becomes like under the ground. I think I could find coal then. And a lamp like poppa's comes out, but in the sky.

Momma looks all day as if she thinks she's goin to be hearin something. The whistle blows. Poppa says it is the ghosts laughin 'cause they have hit a man in the stummy, or on the head. Chris, that happenened too. Chris, who sang those funny songs. He was a furriner. Bowels of earth they put him in. Callin it dead. Mebbe it's for coal, more coal. That's one thing I'm not a-knowen. Day comes and night comes and the whistle blows and payday comes. Like the flats runnin on the tipple they come—one right a-followen the other. Mebbe I am black inside too. . . . The bowels of earth. . . . The things I know but am not knowen. . . . Sun on me and bowels of earth under . . ."

Andy Kvaternick stumbles through the night. The late September wind fills the night with lost and crying voices and drowns all but the largest stars. Chop, chop goes the black sea of his mind. How wild and stormy inside, how the shipwrecked thoughts plunge and whirl. Andy lifts his face to the stars and breathes frantic, like an almost drowned man.

But it is useless, Andy. The coal dust lies too far inside; it will lie there forever, like a hand squeezing your heart, choking at your throat. The bowels of earth have claimed you.

Breathe and breathe. How fresh the night. But the air you will know will only be sour with sweat, and this strong wind on your body turn to the clammy hands of sweat tickling under your underwear.

Breathe and breathe, Andy, turn your eyes to the stars. Their beauty, never known before, pricks like tears. You belong to a starless night now, unimaginably black, without light, like death. Perhaps the sweat glistening on the roof rock seen for an instant will seem like stars.

And no more can you stand erect. You lose that heritage of man, too. You are brought now to fit earth's intestines, stoop like a hunchback underneath, crawl like a child, do your man's work lying on your side, stretched and tense as a corpse. The rats shall be your birds, and the rocks plopping in the water your music. And death shall be your wife, who woos you in the brief moments when coal leaps from a bursting side, when a cross-piece falls and barely misses your head, when you barely catch the ladder to bring you up out of the hole you are dynamiting.

Breathe and lift your face to the night, Andy Kvaternick. Trying so vainly in some inarticulate way to purge your bosom of the coal dust. Your father had dreams. You too, like all boys, had dreams—vague dreams, of freedom and light and cheering throngs and happiness. The earth will take those too. You will leave them in, to replace the coal, to bear up the roof instead of the pillar the super ordered you to rob. Earth sucks you in, to spew out the coal, to make a few fat bellies fatter. Earth takes your dreams that a few may languidly lie on couches and trill "How exquisite" to paid dreamers.

Someday the bowels will grow monstrous and swollen with these old tired dreams, swell and break, and strong fists batter the fat bellies, and skeletons of starved children batter them, and perhaps you will be slugged by a thug hired by the fat bellies, Andy Kvaternick. Or death will take you to bed at last, or you will strangle with that old crony of miners, the asthma.

But walk in the night now, Andy Kvaternick, lift your face to the night, and desperately, like an almost drowned man, breathe and breathe. "Andy," they are calling to you, in their lusty voices, your fellow workers—it is an old story to them now. "Have one on us." The stuff burns down your throat. The thoughts lie shipwrecked and very still far underneath the black sea of your mind; you are gay and brave, knowing that you can never breathe the dust out. You have taken your man's burden, and you have the miner's only friend the earth gives, strong drink, Andy Kvaternick.

For several weeks Jim Holbrook had been in an evil mood. The whole household walked in terror. He had nothing but heavy blows for the children, and he struck Anna too often to remember. Every payday he clumped home, washed, went to town, and returned hours later, dead drunk. Once Anna had questioned him timidly concerning his work; he struck her on the mouth with a bellow of "Shut your damn trap."

Anna too became bitter and brutal. If one of the children was in her way, if they did not obey her instantly, she would hit at them in a blind rage, as if it were some devil she was exorcising. Afterward, in the midst of her work, regret would cramp her heart at the memory of the tear-stained little faces. " 'Twasn't them I was beatin up on. Somethin just seems to get into me when I have somethin to hit."

Friday came again. Jim returned with his pay, part money, most company script. Little Will, in high spirits, ran to meet him, not noticing his father's sullen face. Tugging on his pant's leg, Willie begged for a ghost story of the mine. He got a clout on the head that sent him sprawling. "Keep your damn brats from under my feet," Jim threatened in a violent rage, while Anna only stared at him, almost paralyzed, "and stop looking at me like a stuck pig."

The light from the dusk came in, cold, malignant. Anna sat in the half dark of the window, her head bent over her sewing in the attitude of a woman weeping. Willie huddled against her skirt, whimpering. Outside the wind gibbered and moaned. The room was suddenly chill. Some horror, some sense of evil seemed on everything.

It came to Mazie like dark juices of undefined pain, pouring into her, filling the heart in her breast till it felt big, like the world. Fear came that her heart would push itself out, roll out like a ball. She clutched the baby closer to her, tight, tight, to hold the swollen thing inside. Her dad stood in the washtub, nude, splashing water on his big chunky body. The menacing light was on him, too. Fear for him came to Mazie, yet some alien sweetness mixed with it, watching him there.

"I would be a-cryen," she whispered to herself, "but all the tears is stuck inside me. All the world is a-cryen, and I don't know for why. And the ghosts may get daddy. Now he's goin' away, but he'll come back with somethin sweet but sicklike hangin on his breath, and hit momma and start the baby a-bawlen. If it was all a dream, if I could only just wake up and daddy'd be smilin, and momma laughin, and us playin. All the world a-cryen and I don't know for why. . . . Maybe daddy'll know—daddy knowen everything." The huge question rose in her, impossible to express, too huge to understand. She ached with it. "I'll ask Daddy." To ask him—to force him into some recognition of her existence, her desire, her emotions.

As Jim Holbrook strode down the dirt street, he heard a fine patter-patter and a thin "Pop." He wheeled. It was Mazie. "You little brat," he said, the anger he had felt still smoldering in him. "What're you runnin away from home for? Get back or I'll skin you alive."

She came toward him, half cringing. "Pop, lemme go with you. Pop, I wanna know what . . . what makes people a-cryen. Why don't you tell us ghost stories no more, Pop?" The first words had tumbled out, but now a silence came. "Don't send me home, Pop."

The rough retort Jim Holbrook had meant to make vanished before the undersized figure of Mazie, outlined so clearly against the cold sunset. In some vague way, the questions hurt him. What call's a kid got, he thought, asking questions like that? Though the cramp in his back from working, lying on his side all day, shot through him like hot needles, he stopped and took her hand.

"Don't be worryin your head with such things, Big-eyes—it'll bust. Wait'll you grow up."

"Pop, you said there was ghosts in the mine, black, not white, so's you couldn't see 'em. And they chased a feller, and then when they got him they laughed, but people think it's just the whistle. Pop, they wouldn't chase you, would they?" The fear was out at last.

"Why," chuckled Jim, "I'd like to see 'em try it. I'd just throw them over my shoulder, like this." He lifted her, swung her over his shoulder, set her down. "My right shoulder, or it wouldn't work. And then I'd pin 'em down with the crossbar so they'd have as much chance as a turkey at Thanksgiving. Now, how'd you like to ride to town on poppa's shoul-diehorse and buggy, and get served with a sucker?"

Mazie smiled, but her heart was still sad. "Pop, does the boss man honest have a white shiny tub bigger than you and he turns somethin and the water comes out? Or is it a story? And does he honest have a toilet right inside the house? And silks on the floor?" She held her breath.

"Sure, Big-eyes. And they eat on white tablecloths, a new one, every night."

"How come he aint livin like we do? How come we aint livin like him, Pop?"

Why indeed? For a moment Jim was puzzled. "'Cause he's a coal operator, that's why."

"Oh"—another wall of things not understood gone up. Something made the difference. A big word. Like what happened to Miss Tikas when she was cut up. But how could he cut up a mine? His knife would have to be awful big.

"But you could lick him, Pop, couldn't you? Couldn't you lick anybody?"

"Sure." And to prove it he told her an elaborate story of three dogs he fought, each big as a horse, finishing triumphantly, "Now, do you think anybody could lick your daddy?"

"Pop, I can make the bacon when I stand up on the box, and I can wash the baby, honest. Pop, momma says I'm gonna get an edjication, and my hands white. Is that a story, Pop?"

Fillin the kid's head with fool ideas, he thought wrathfully. But she could become a teacher. Aloud—"Sure you are. You'll go to college and read books and marry a—" his stomach revolted at the thought of a mine boss—"a doctor. And," he finished, "eat on white tablecloths."

She trotted along. Somehow the question she had meant to have answered could not be clamped into words. They reached the one street. Her dad went into the company store to buy her a sucker. Afterward when he went into the saloon, she slipped out to the culm bank that rose like an enormous black mountain at the edge of the street. One side was on fire and weird; gorgeous colors flamed from it. The colors swirled against the night, reds and blues, oranges and yellows. "Like babies' tongues reachin out to you. Like what happens to the back of your eyes when you close 'em after seein the sun, only that hurts. Like all the world come a-colored," she whispered softly to herself. "Mazie Holbrook is a-watchin you," she whispered, "purty tongues." And gently, gently, the hard swollen lump of tears melted into a swell of wonder and awe.

It was cold and damp. Mazie shivered a little, but the shiver was pleasant. The wind came from the north, flinging fine bits of the coal dust from the culm against her face. They stung. Somehow it reminded her of the rough hand of her father when he caressed her, hurting her, but not knowing it, hurting with a pleasant hurt. "I am a-watching you, purty tongues."

Sheen McEvoy, lurching out of the saloon, saw a fluttering patch of white against the black culm. "Ghosts," he whispered to himself. His throat became dry. A lost ghost, sent out of the mine, and *white.* "God." The wind shivered against him. Against the culm he saw letters of fire dancing a devil's dance. For a paralyzing instant they danced together, writing a mine blowup. They seared Sheen McEvoy's eyes almost with the terrifying pain of the gas explosion that had blown his face off and taken his mind. The culm made a long finger of shadow toward him—the stars pointed, pointed. "No, no," he moaned, "don't make me have to save 'em."

In Sheen McEvoy's mind insanity dwelled, like a caged wind. Sometimes it was a hurricane, whistling crazily, tearing, making whirlpools of thought, driving his body to distorted movements. Sometimes an old forlorn wind, with the tired voice of dead people, barely touching him, creeping along the sensitive surface. Sometimes the wind spoke or laughed in him. Then awful prophecies came to his tongue. To him, the mine was alive—a thousand-armed creature, with ghosts hanging from the crossbeams, ghosts living in the coal swearing revenge when their homes were broken into. Once fire had risen from earth to sky, clutched at his face, borne it away. Looking in the mirror at himself, he thought now some ghost in the coal was wearing it, laughing.

The wind began its whining. He ran unsteadily for the white flutterflutter. Dazed, he saw it was a small child, with unholy eyes, green. A voice spoke in him, "A little child, pure of heart." *That* was it. The mine was hungry for a child; she was reaching her thousand arms for it. "She only takes men 'cause she aint got kids. All women want kids." Thoughts whirled in colors—licking to flame; exultation leaped up in him.

Sheen McEvoy will fill you, ol' lady. His laugh, horrible as the cracked thin laughter of old breastless women watching youth, sent the night unsteady. Mazie looked up. Sheen McEvoy was standing above her, laughing. Her heart congealed. The red mass of jelly that was his face was writhing, like a heart torn suddenly out of the breast, and he laughed and laughed. Mazie wanted to run; her mind fainted on the thought of her father, strong and tall, so far away. She turned to go.

He held her. His body was hot and putrid. Stinking. "You're the mine's baby now," he said, holding her tight. "The mine'll hold ya like that, pretty baby." Screams tore at Mazie's throat, caged there. Sweat poured over her. She closed her eyes. He strode toward the shaft. He kissed her with his shapeless face. In Mazie her heart fainted, and fainted, but her head stayed clear. "Make it a dream, Momma, Poppa, come here, make it a dream." But no words would come.

Instead another voice, thundering. "What are you doing with that kid, McEvoy?" No words would come. But he—his breath stinking, the jelly opening in the middle. "Stand out of my way. The mine is calling for her baby. Men'll die—but they'll live if she gets the baby. Stand back."

The night watchman's mouth came open. "Put her down."

Sheen McEvoy strode on, oblivious. Angels were singing in his head, men were singing—glad praise, saved men. Her body was soft and warm. "Lift my arms and throw her down the shaft and the mine'll forget about men."

"Put her down."

"Give her a sweet baby, and she'll want no more." Angels singing, men, strong-bodied men, marching and singing, saved. Her body, soft, trembled against him. Ecstasy sang. Now the shaft, hungry mouth.

"I am giving you your baby." He lifted his arms. Mazie saw down, but there was no bottom. Her scream sounded now, answered by his laughter: shrill, cracked, horrible.

Darkness came like lightning. His arms loosened. Mazie rolled, barely missing the shaft. Rising, she crawled, toward what she did not know. The tipple rose like a tree, without leaves, above her. Words came, drunken. Fear. "Poppa." Behind a figure rose, menacing; swung. A miner's pickax. Blindness on two men, fighting. The ax swings, misses. A gun spurts, one, two, three; lovely fire colored like on the culm, colored like the thoughts in McEvoy's head. One instant angels singing, men marching and singing, saved men; the mine yawning, hungry; soft body trembling to him. Blackness now. Black as the day in the mine. Over and over a body lurches, dips into a shaft, thuds thuds against the sides. The clouds, throwing their shadow, give for an instant a smile, inscrutable, to the mouth of the mine.

Into the saloon, like some apparition, came the nightman, bloody of face and clothes, carrying a child. The men looking up from their drink, laughter and oaths cut off, stared astounded. Breathing heavily, he walked to the center of the room and asked fiercely, "Whose kid is this?"

The whiskey making giddiness of his veins, Holbrook turned. The oath, so like a laugh, died on his lips. The kid was Mazie. "It's my kid," he answered gruffly. "What the hell are *you* doin with her?"

"You oughta thank your damn guts I am doin something with her. Why didn't you watch her, if she's your kid?"

The whiskey made a lovely golden fog in his head. Not understanding, he lurched to the nightman, taking the kid away. "What you been doin?" he asked sharply. "What did you run away for?" Her eyes opened for an instant. Questioning and impersonal like a wounded animal's, they stared at him. Uncomprehending, meaning to roar some oath, he looked toward the nightman. The tense, accusing face came like a wind, blowing the fog with cold sharp wings. "What happened?" he asked tersely, still shaking Mazie.

"Stop shaking the kid, she can't answer you, she's sick. And who wouldn't be? That bastard McEvoy went on another loony spree. Picked her up somewhere and gets the idea the mine wants a baby, as if it don't get enough grownups. Comes to the shaft laughing and singing about the men he's going to 'deliver.' When I looked for the kid she was crawlin like some blind animal. Scared to death."

"The sonofabitch," roared Holbrook, "I'll kill him. Where is he?"

"Keel him, leench him," one man muttered angrily.

"The mine done the job for you. He fell down the shaft he was aimin to throw her down."

Holbrook felt as if he were drowning. He felt weak, like a child. My baby, this happened too, he thought. He shook her again, but gently. The stirring of her body against him was insufferably sweet anguish.

"Geev her a sweeg dees," one of the Greeks offered roughly. "That waken her up."

"No, Nick, I'm taking her home. Anna'll fix her up. Got a coat, anybody?"

Tenderly he wrapped her in one, letting no one else touch her. Walking home, he still felt as if he were drowning. Once when she opened her eyes and in a dream-voice murmured, "Poppa, you came," tears stung his eyes.

"My baby, this had to happen too." A monstrous

thought gripped him. Frightened, he shook her roughly. "What did he do to you, Mazie, Big-eyes, what did he do to you?" He ran for the yellow light that made a neat block on the road.

Anna was still by the window sewing, in the attitude of a woman weeping. But her eyes were tearless —they shone at him like hard bright steel. "You're home early. Get homesick?"

Remorse added to terror and shame. "Anna," he said, so broken, so tender, her heart leaped.

"Jim?"

"The kid. She. Maybe . . ." He could not speak.

"Mazie?" cried Anna, shrill. "What happened? What've you done to her?" She snatched the child, spoke to her, took her to the light. There was a small bruise on her forehead, scratches on her face.

"You beat up on her, you dirty bastard."

"No, listen, Anna." He told her the story, tremblingly told his fear. He was like a child. Terrified, he heard Anna's hysterical laughter—then her calm.

"She hasn't been touched. She'd have been all bloody if he had. But God only knows how hurt she is. Put on hot water, you, and bring some whiskey into the bedroom." She carried Mazie onto their cot and tumbled hot whiskey and tea down her throat.

Jim sat and held the lamp. His wavering shadow looked at him from the wall. Feeling Mazie's burning head, her body moist with sweat, he asked, "Shouldn't I get a doctor?"

"Forget where you are? You know there's only the company doc—and a vets better'n him. She'll be all right. Looks like she might've hurt her head fallin, or maybe she's just scared. Poor baby, poor baby, I'll give her more hot whiskey."

The wind, starting up outside, shook against the house, and Mazie in the quiet of the bedroom began crying, tossing, calling out fragments of sentences, incoherent words. Will, waking, saw how his father sat so still and terrible. Still in his sleep, he began to whimper—"Dont hit me, Poppa, dont. I didn't mean nothing." Unsteadily Jim stood up. The waters seemed closing over his head again: a grimy face turned up to him, pleading, "A story, Pop," and a hand that had crashed down over it. Almost timidly he rubbed that hand against the soft head. "You're dreaming, Will boy," he whispered. "Sleep agin. Try to sleep."

He turned down the light. The new-made, concealing darkness came welcome to them both. "Listen." He gripped her shoulders. "We're clearin out in spring, you hear? We'll save every cent. We'll go to Dakota. Spring's the time to begin a new life, aint it? I'll farm. That's a good job—I could do it, tried my hand at everything else. Or maybe we'll go to Omaha—get on at the slaughterhouse. No—it'll be farmin, workin with ground, not rock. Ground smells sweet. And it's good for the kids, right, Anna? We'll make it a new life in the spring?"

In her delirium Mazie laughed—terrible laughter, mocking, derisive, not her own. Anna and Jim, hearing it mix with their words, shuddered.

TWO

A new life in the spring. But now fatback and cornmeal to eat. Newspapers stuffed in the shoes so that new ones need not be bought, and the washing done without soap. Somehow to skimp off of everything that had long ago been skimped on, somehow to find more necessities the body can do easiest without. The old quilt will make coats for Mazie and Ben; Will can wear Mazie's old one. This poverty's arithmetic for Anna, and for Jim—hunger for the gayness whiskey gives the world, battling fear that before spring the mine will engulf him.

A new life . . . in the spring. Once Anna tried to tell the children. Illumining her drab words with her glowing face, Anna told them of living among trees, having Daddy work where they all could see him, of a good school—not a Catholic one—and milk from cows. Will, watching her face with burning eyes, said, "That a fairy story,

Mom?" but Mazie hardly seemed to listen; crept out of the house, restless, before Anna was through.

The children were changed. Even their "Aint there nothing else to eat, Mom?" was apathetic. The peace at home, their father so awkwardly gentle, sitting home nights now, frightened them. Always they were expecting something else. Mazie sat still the evenings staring into the stove, and when Jim tried to woo her to smiles, she gave him such objective ones, they froze him.

In the coal town too there lived a subtle fear. The new fire boss was the super's nephew, too scared, too lazy, it was said, to go stumbling through the foggy workings alone, testing to find out if gas had collected. In everyone's heart coiled the fear of a blowup. Nights the saloon jetted with fiery laughter, reckless song, hard evil fights. On the women's faces lived the look of listening. And the autumn days, shaken with rain and restless wind, brought always the sound of fear, undefinable, into the air.

One November day the sky was packed so thick with clouds, heavy, gray, Marie Kvaternick said it had the look of an eyelid shut in death. Leaves dashed against the houses, giving a dry nervous undertone to everything, and the maniac wind shrieked and shrieked.

Anna's face that day had the look of a mask, racked listening hidden underneath. It drove the children restless. Even the baby, sensing the tension, whimpered. "Shut that kid up," Anna demanded of Mazie. "I dont care how." Mazie gathered him up, with a bread crust for him to suck on, and a diaper, and slipped out. Will came alongside.

Above colors were gathering in the sky. Sunset colors, though it was early afternoon. Mazie remembered the colors in the culm and shuddered. There was a grove away from the town—a long way—but they went there. Will played with his stocking ball, and she lay down in the rustling autumn leaves, one hand over her eyes, shielding them from what she did not know. The baby lay warm in her other arm, there where it ached from carrying him.

High up the wind was whirring, but here there was only a gentle shadow of it. "All that be here is the end of its skirt," Mazie whispered. And in the darkness of her arm, the tightness that had been around her heart slackened, eased, was no more.

Will came over. Lay down, his head snuggled on her stomach. "Five years. I'm five years old. What be it to be five years?"

"Five years you've lived, Will."

"Five years. I'm wearin your old coat, a girl's coat. For why?"

"For that's all there is. Shush now, let baby sleep. Shush, and hear the wind cryin."

"The wind? What's wind?"

"It's people cryin and talkin."

"People?"

"Yes, people in the sky."

"Sky? What be sky?"

"Shush. That's something I'm not knowin."

"Sky be a winder?"

"A window."

"You can't see through it, 'cause its dirty?"

"No, your breath's blowin up on it, everybody's breath—open your eyes and you see it go up, and it makes it cloudy."

"Breath? Not rags. Looks like rags stuck in the window, a-flappin."

"Shush, Will, not rags. Listen to the leaves. Sounds like people walkin quiet, quick—walkin past on tiptoe."

"Fatback tastes in my mouf."

"Eyes closed and you hear better."

"Fatback sour in my mouth. Wish I had a apple."

"Poppa comes home and stays." Something stirred in her breast faint like the leaves about her. Dont think of poppa. Hear the leaves.

"Ask momma for a apple. She says no."

"He never hits no more. Looks at me like he got

something good, but he never gives it to me, only looks."

"Johnny tole me what you eat grows in your belly. I gonna grow fatback."

"And momma . . . bein mad, then bein sorry . . . momma always lookin as if she expects to hear somethin . . ."

"Grow fatback and be dead. Mazie, what's dead?"

"Momma listenin, always listenin." The tightness had come alive again; it strangled around her heart. She leaped to her feet with a cry, waking the baby. Some terror crept upon her.

"Mazie, whatsa matter?"

She pointed. Above the sky were ears. In all their different shapes they coiled, blurred ears, listening. And looking down, she saw that the wind was pitting the grasses and leaves, making little whirlpools, kitten-shaped ears, listening, listening. The face of her mother, the face of Mis' Connors, the face of Mis' Tikas came like a mist before her eyes—listening, everywhere, everywhere.

"Willie, lets go home, Willie. I'll race you, baby and all. Lets go. Put your hands in your ears and you dont hear nothin, lets go, run."

The wind was icy on her running body; the baby dragged. But everywhere the sky and earth were listening. And the whistle—yes, it was the whistle that was shrieking—not the finger in her ear, not the wind. At the tipple there would be . . . thinking of the tipple, her heart plunged, she wanted to fall, to stuff the leaves into her ears. "Willie, lets run, Willie." He moaned, "Momma be runnin, everyone runnin and screamin, Mazie."

"Lets run away, Will." A thought hung with bull-dog teeth to her mind—"It'll be daddy this time."

"Lets run away," but their feet were flying—flying to the tipple.

The women were there already. Tearless faces, watching. But no one brought up limp and sagging. Instead, frightened men, and the rest sealed in an open grave. A big explosion. It might take days to dig them up. Anna with bloodless lips formed "a new life," but Will and Mazie were pulling at her skirt, her baby was moving in her arms, and Marie Kvaternick hurting her shoulder. "You see, Anna. They be up. These big ones—they save; nothing happen. Only little accidents they die. But if Andy stay—" she pushed out fierce—"if Andy stay, better for Andy. Wots matter, Anna? You see, Jim'll be back, they be up. Only . . . Chris . . ."

> And could you not make a cameo of this and pin it onto your aesthetic hearts? So sharp it is, so clear, so classic. The shattered dusk, the moun-

tain of culm, the tipple; clean lines, bare beauty —and carved against them, dwarfed by the vastness of night and the towering tipple, these black figures with bowed heads, waiting, waiting.

Surely it is classical enough for you—the Greek marble of the women, the simple, flowing lines of sorrow, carved so rigid and eternal. Surely it is original enough—these grotesques, this thing with the foot missing, this gargoyle with half the face gone and the arm. In the War to Live, the artist, Coal, sculptured them. It was his Master hand that wrought the intricate mosaic on this face—splintered coal inlaid with patches of skin and threads of rock . . . You will have the cameo? Call it Rascoe, Wyoming, any of a thousand towns in America, the night of a mine blowup. And inside carve the statement the company already is issuing. "Unavoidable catastrophe . . . (O shrink, super's nephew, fire boss that let the gas collect) . . . rushing equipment . . . bending every effort . . . sparing no expense . . . to save—or recover the bodies . . ."

(Dear Company. Your men are imprisoned in a tomb of hunger, of death wages. Your men are strangling for breath—the walls of your company town have clamped out the air of freedom. Please issue a statement. Quick, or they start to batter through with the fists of strike, with the pickax of revolution.)

A cameo of this, then. Blood clot of the dying sunset and the hush. No sobs, no word spoken. Sorrow is tongueless. Apprehension tore it out long ago. No sound, only the whimpering of children, blending so beautifully with the far cry of blown birds. And in the smothered light, carved hard, distinct, against the tipple, they all wait. The wind, pitying, flings coal dust into their eyes, so almost they could imagine releasing tears are stinging.

"He'll be back." Brought up quiet and shaken five days later. Gaunt and bearded so that Ben wailed when he saw him. "In March, Anna," he said, "March, if I have to pick the sun outa the sky for a gold piece."

Whispering—"Just give me one third for the scrip. Just one third cash. You know it's worth more than that. I'll buy the stuff for you, so they'll think it's me, and you pay me one third cash."

Pushing the words out from where they stand so humbly in her throat. "I thought maybe around the holidays there might be extra work. Scrubbin or washin. I know you got a cook. I'm not askin much, just fifty cents the day."

Fear. You got no business doin it, Jim, workin under loose roof like that.

But March—a new life . . . And they dont pay for pullin it down and clearin. And I cant do nothin unless I'm gettin paid for it.

"Ma. They growin chicory instead of coffee? Aint we ever gonna have coffee again?" "Ma, my teef hurts."

"Ma, I can push my finger in Mazie's skin and it goes in, way deep."

"Ma, this all to eat, Ma?"

"In spring, in March, we're goin, baby. Hushabye now. Hushabye. Momma'll sing you to sleep."

March. Raw with blistering winds and snow. I see even the weather's against us. No use, we can't leave. But April. April first for sure.

All winter his reckless work under loose roof, because pulling down and clearing meant unpaid labor. All winter the children puffing out with starch. All winter her hands cracking with the extra work.

But the decrepit wagon waits outside, and Jim pounds on an extra rude seat, a rough removable canopy. There is an ancient truck horse bargained for and promised. And sometimes clearing the coal, walking to work in the morning darkness, scrubbing his face, Jim stops suddenly, and thickly, out of his throat, utters, "April." And Anna's hand goes often over her heart, remembering new life words of hope spoken through the weave of a child's delirious derisive laughter.

April at last. Delicate with shy greens and little winds blowing. A few of the women come to bid goodbye. And when Anna closes the door for the last time, quick, hard, dropping her hand from the latch, they watch as if it were a ceremony. Wistfulness is in their eyes, no envy. "Goodbye. Goodbye," they chorus. But the Holbrooks do not look back, only Mazie once, but there is nothing left, only a shadow of culm, rearing against the sky. Over it small white clouds forming and dissolving—almost fairy hands, waving goodbye, goodbye.

THREE

Three days they jolted through Wyoming and west Nebraska. The black cuts of the buttes against the sky, the colors in them like striped fire, the great quiet desolation of the mesa they passed, filled Mazie with some strange unhappiness, more like happiness than anything she had ever known. Anna felt like a bride; riding along, she sang and sang. Sometimes Jim whistled or sang with her in a depthless bass voice. And the wagon made gay silvery sounds accompanying them, and the sun laid warm hands on their backs.

The fourth day they came to South Dakota—breaths caught in sharp wonder at the green stretching for miles, at the small streamlets like open silver veins on the ground, and here and there dots of cattle grazing, heads down. The air was pure and soft like a baby's skin. "Breathe," Anna said, "breathe it in, kids." "Listen, Momma, there's birds." Birds, floating round shining bubbles of song on the air, jackrabbits rising suddenly from one end of the road to flee to the other.

And that day there was laughter. Nellie, refusing to trot, stopping stubbornly, haunches apart, head lifted up. In vain Jim beat her. When he clambered down to lead her; she galumphed away at a tremendous (for her) speed. Though Anna, frantic, tried to reach to dragging reins, the children screamed and laughed. Crazy, the wagon tipped, this side, that side. "Seesaw, Marjorie Daw," Will began. And Nellie, with immense dignity, stopped.

Five minutes later Jim came puffing up. A farmer stopped his plowing to lean over the fence. "Ya oughta get a mule, I reckon. They're not so stubborn."

"She *is* a mule in disguise." Jim climbed up again. But again she wouldn't budge. Leisurely she cropped the grass at her side.

"How about the old grass-on-the-end-of-a-stick gag?" the farmer asked. "That'll start her trottin."

It did. Jim, with one foot on the step, felt the wagon jerk forward and barely swung himself up in time. Nellie didn't wait to go for the food that hung tantalizingly beyond her nose. For two hours she ran, Jim precariously directing her with the reins over corners. Mazie stood up, her hands on the wagon seat, screaming with delight. The wind came over her body with a great rush of freedom; freedom and joy tingled to her hair roots. Anna swayed back and forth, clutching her hat and the baby, laughing too. Ridiculous Nellie with her huge buttocks moving in frenzied rhythm, the wagon bumping along after, and the wheels making their singy laughter. Laughter came from the skies, blowing something that was more than coal dust out of their hearts.

The sky tinged leaden. Enormous shadows began to shift over the face of the prairie, and above the whole sky came gray, with dull silver undersides to the clouds. Cold, the wind whirled from the north. Nellie set her head stubbornly against it, plodding along. Jim stopped to stretch the canopy over them, telling the children to scurry into their coats.

The wind began running a long hand under the dust, stirring it into a dervish dance. A steady moaning came from the grasses. Mazie leaned forward to catch the feel of the wind on her face—something seemed clawing in her to be out running with it. Anna for some reason was laughing.

A cold tongue licked their cheeks—snow. Jim shouted back, "Cover up with them blankets and throw another up here, Mazie. You better go back with the kids, Anna," and Mazie crept forward. The sky was invisible now. When she lifted her face, the snow stung like nails. Mistily she could see her father

—on his face a look of being intoxicated, his heavy brown hair blowing back, his blue eyes glittering. The snow fell thicker. The wind whirled it like a dancing skirt. Even following the road was difficult. The fences alone helped. And nowhere was there a farmhouse. Mazie did not care—it was enough to stumble on like this forever through a white whirling world. The wagon sank. Nellie pulled bravely but in vain. Jim got out. The back wheels were sunk deep in what had been a spring pool of water, under the snow.

"What's the matter?" Anna's shout came faintly.

"We're stuck," he yelled back—the futility of voices yelling loud but coming out like babies' piping voices obsessed him. With head down Jim pulled against the wind to win to the front of the wagon again. Snow was blowing in from the open front. "It'll be a minute."

Mazie awkwardly fought her way after her dad, watched him lay down in the snow, put his shoulder under the wheel. His body tautened, the wheel jerked. Again he straightened out tense, and the wheel lifted. Jim held the weight of the wagon on him, not knowing what to do next. Slowly he wriggled his body to the right, then crept from under. Mazie could hear his hoarse breathing pulsating with the wind. He was fumbling along the roadside, edging a rock on the ground under the other wheel. "Roll it under when I lift it up again," he commanded. Again, with terrible strength he lifted the wheel. To Mazie, her fingers frozen, rolling the rock seemed to take forever. Trembling, she got it under.

In an hour they found a small town, crouched in a hollow. In a one-story "hotel" run by an obese Swede and his lanky wife, they got shelter. She caressed the children, made a crackling fire, rubbed their hands, put on hot water for footbaths, exchanged recipes with Anna, talked of the marvelous farming country around Zell, where they were going.

Mazie, shivering before the fire, her eyes closed, remembered the feel of the wind and the culm left behind.

The morning was a dim smear of light. Jim, looking at the white country, shook his head. No travelin today. The sun made a wan smile of the afternoon, and all night the melting snow dripped, dripped. Morning came, and the road was clear but muddy. Ben cried at leaving the gaunt lady.

Two days later, the weather shining again, they came to a rise. Looking down, they could see for miles. Far east rolled the hills, the near ones flat brown, washed over with delicate green, the far ones repeating themselves over and over till they faded into blue hazes and dull mists—indistinct blurs of lines against the spring sky.

Below lay the farms, uneven patches of brown and plowed black and transparent green, and far stretched the river, dull yellow in the sun, glinting crystal, where the wind stirred it. Tiny as a toy, a man was plowing a thin thread of black in the brown square of field immediately below them.

Everyone's eyes were shining with wonder and promise. "We'll be living somewhere beyond that," Jim said, with a gesture of joy and freedom illimitable (goodbye, mole's life, goodbye, you're far behind me now); Willie babbled childishly of the man, grown so tiny, and the baby stretched his arms and crowed. One joy lay in their hearts like a warmth—hope. "A new life," Anna said, "in the spring."

With dusk a softness crept over the land. They were down in the lowlands now. Low curves cut into the sky. The earth glowed with reflected color, like light under green water, and Anna and Jim began singing, "Down in the valley, valley so low, hang your head over, feel the wind blow."

Willie slumbered against Mazie's shoulder. Ben drowsily had his head in her lap, staring into the depthless transparent green above. Even the gay tinkle of the wheel came subdued and the clop of Nellie's hoofs incredibly hushed and beautiful. "Roses love nightwinds, violets love dew, angels in heaven, know I love you." Their voices were slow curving rhythms, slow curving sounds. Voices, rising and twining, beauty curving on rainbows of quiet sound, filled their hearts heavy, welled happy tears to Mazie's eyes.

Anna singing, "In the gloaming, oh my darling, when the lights are dim and low," with bright eyes folded and unfolded memories of past years—plans for the years to come. School for the kids, Jim working near her, on the earth, lovely things to keep, brass lamps, bright tablecloths, vines over the doors, and roses twining. A memory, unasked, plunged into her mind—her grandmother bending in such a twilight over lit candles chanting in an unknown tongue, white bread on the table over a shining white tablecloth and red wine—she broke into the song to tell Jim of it . . .

They reached the farm at midnight. Anna had awakened Mazie so she could see. There were flatter fields, low houses, some with towers her father softly pointed out as silos. Sometimes Jim got out and fumbled with a match before a mailbox or signpost. At last there came a low rambling place, with three trees dwarfing it and barn larger than the house looming in the back. Above the stars glistened—and two twin stars hung over the roof. "The place," Jim said.

Mazie, sleepy, lay down immediately on the mattress stretched for her and, with Will and Ben breathing quietly beside her, fell asleep at once. Jim spent another hour getting the barn open, moving the one bed they had taken with them in and setting it up, while Anna, nursing the baby held in the crook of one arm, unpacked what would be needed for the morning. Then they too slept. And into their sleep wove a dream of beauty curving on rainbows of quiet sound over a land that stretched into mist, in which one figure, tiny as a toy, plowed a black thread in a square of brown.

FOUR

The farm. Oh Jim's great voice rolling over the land. Oh Anna, moving rigidly from house to barn so that the happiness with which she brims will not jar and spill over. Oh Mazie, hurting herself with beauty. Oh Will, feeling the eggs and radishes gurgle down his throat, tugging the woolly neck of the dog with reckless joy. Oh Ben, feeling smiles around and security.

Well, what of Benson? stoop-shouldered neighbor and his "I tell you, you cant make a go of it. Tenant farmin is the only thing worse than farmin your own. That way you at least got a chance a good year, but tenant farmin, bad or good year, the bank swallows everything up, and keeps you owin 'em. You'll see."

But land is here. Days falling freely into large rhythms of weather. Feet sinking into plowed earth, the plow making a bright furrow. Corn coming swiftly up. Tender green stalks with thin outer shoots, like grass. Oh Momma come look! Oh Daddy come look! Oh Mazie come look! Drama of things growing. You're browning, children. The world is an oven, and you're browning in it. How good the weariness—in the tiredness, the body may dream. How good the table, with the steam arising from the boiled potatoes and vegetables and the full-bellied pitcher of milk.

Around the house, the earth is hoed up for truck. Mazie and Will do the weeding, help feed the chickens, bring the cow from pasture, wring out the clothes. But strangely there is time. Sometimes Mazie pads with bare feet across the waving corn to the road—to watch the carriages and wagons bump by. When there are gay little girls sitting high and proud in the buggies, ribbons in their hair blowing a long streamer in the wind, shame and envy shudder over her, and she draws herself together to make herself nothing, to lose herself in the faded gray dress on her body. Then the sun and wind rippling over her skin, and the gold corn moving against the sky lull her into beauty again with the slenderest arms of rhythm.

Sometimes the neighbors come. Benson, he of the stoop shoulders, as if for all his six feet he were trying to get closer to the earth. Two furrows live on his brow and a curious compassion in his eyes. A compassion that is weariness and despair. He will start to talk of a new way of planting, of the good weather, and then cease suddenly, the compassion gray where the living was before. Missis Ellis, round and laughing, sure of touch, knowing the helplessness of newborn animals, how to bring animals and women out of labor, her voice the timbre of earth. She laughs, but a kernel of worry hides under the laughter. Her father is old Caldwell, pioneer, who had come west from college and wealth and chosen to live and build out of the wilderness.

Jim's big barn was the accustomed place for the midsummer dance in mid-July. Two days before, neighbor women came to prepare the floor, bring food, help with the cooking. Anna sewed over her good dress, bought bright ribbons recklessly for Mazie and herself, washed and starched the children's clothes.

The laughter of summer was on the earth. Trees, rich and voluptuous, flowered by the roadside, brimming fields of corn waved in the sun, roses were in bloom, and the days were bright with the colored balls of song, birds tossed back and forth.

The night of the dance was luminous with moonlight. Winds rushed over the fields, faded to small breezes, subsided into stillness, gathered again. Trees dipped and curtsied, the corn rippling like a girl's skirt. Very low, very misty, very tender, the stars shone, and over all flowered the smell of growing things, of fecund earth, overpowering.

Mazie, with the green ribbon glowing on her head,

felt like spring. To her, Anna, with her black eyes laughing, her black hair smooth and shiny to purple, was the handsomest woman there. But everyone had a look of beauty about them.

Withered and small, the fiddler seemed too frail for any sturdy music, but at his side the guitar and harmonica player rose strong and capable. The caller stood in the middle. The circle eights formed. Then the music rocked in the air. Some of the dancers were young girls and boys, quick of step, their laughter rising like a froth, quick colors, step on step, bubble on bubble. Most were middle-aged men, women, still young, if not in body. They gave themselves easily to the dance, backs curved, skirts flying round and round. Round and round in the intricate steps, and, at the end of each circle eight, the men gave out a long cry that beat up the blood. Summer was in their hearts, high summer brimming like a tide.

Swiftly the summer days blended into one another. Heat throbbed like a great anvil, and hot glassy air shimmered over the dusty-smelling corn. Or a burst of rain would come, in a great glistening mesh. Nights were vast and fragrant with wind and stars and the wavering sound of far frogs. Weariness, like armor, over their bodies, Jim and Anna would sit in the blue night; Anna, her head against the top step of the porch, caressing the flowers in her lap as if they were about to vanish; Jim, puffing a pipe, trying to empty his mind, keep it motionless on the *now,* not on the past or what might come. The breath of the moon, mist and silver, lay on the fields; the flowers clustered in bright shadows in the darkness. After a long while Anna would laugh, a strange mirthless laugh, and rise to go into the house. Then Jim, too, would follow, knocking the ashes out of his pipe onto the vine, giving a last broad look over the night and the earth. Sometimes seeing them sit so in the night, a sharp unhappiness would pierce the golden haze in Mazie's heart; but the blur of days descending so swiftly would wash it out again.

Once, hungry, degraded, after a beating from Anna for some mischief, Mazie lay by the roadside, bedded in the clover, belly down, feeling the earth push back against her, feeling the patterns of clover smell twine into her nostrils till she was drugged with the scent. The soft plodding of a buggy gathered into her consciousness.

She turned on her back. Above the stars clustered, low, bright, still-winged. As if she had never seen them before. Her breath caught. The buggy was stopping, and an old man got out. Old Man Caldwell.

"Lost?" he breathed softly in the soft night.

"No, just watchin the stars. I live in that house over there—Holbrook's house. My name's Mazie Holbrook."

He came over and lay down beside her, so quiet in the dimness he did not seem to be there. He was looking up too, making it a trusting dark.

"Stars," she began. "What are they now? Splinters offn the moon, I've heard it said. But more likely they're lamps in houses up there, or flowers growin in the night. I'd like to smell the smell that would be comin offn those flowers."

He raised up on his elbow, staring at her. Then said, "Stars are suns. Like our sun. But so far away—so many miles no one can imagine—they look tiny."

"You know them things? Then what is the sun, a fire?"

"Miles of fire, many times bigger than the earth. But more than fire."

"Yes, a fire. Now I know I can see that the stars are fire, for they are dancin now like a fire movin."

He laughed. Then told her why the stars seemed dancing, how old stars were, how they lived and died, and of a people living long ago, the Greeks, who had named these stars and had found in their shapes images of what was on earth below. As his words misted into the night and disappeared, she scarcely listened—only the aura over them, of timelessness, of vastness, of eternal things that had been before her and would be after her, remained and entered into her with a great hurt and wanting.

Hot midsummer nights when the bedroom of sweating, tossing bodies was too much for her, she would slip out into the fields and the sad hurt would gather into her again, seeing an old old people lying in just such a field, tracing out names and images in the heavens where splashes of enormous fire whirled, eternal and timeless, and tangled comets hissed.

One day, coming in because the hot dust pricked her feet so, she saw him again, sitting with Ben on his lap, watching Anna put up tomato preserve. He was saying, "Vultures running it now. It doesn't make any difference whether it's Republican or Democrat; the same hand pulls the strings." She was going to ask him what he meant, but Anna answered into the kettle of steaming tomatoes, "The bellwether leads the flock all right, but who is it sees they go how he wants? The one that trains the bellwether."

"Exactly . . . when I came out, a man had some chance. The only thing against him was nature, locusts and drought and late frost. You took your chance. That was all you had to fight. But now that hardly matters. There's mortgage, taxes, the newest kind of machinery to buy so you do as good as the other fellow, and the worry—will it get a price this year."

Anna stopped stirring, straightened up, steam or sweat beaded on her intense face. "In college, did you learn why all that is?"

"In college . . ." He choked off his words and his face went frozen. "My education began after I got out of college." Then seeing Mazie, "Hello, my stargazing companion . . . Mrs. Holbrook, children have marvelous minds. I hate to see what life does to 'em."

Fall came. A dribble of gaudy leaves over the roads. Sheets of taffeta-gold corn brimming the fields. Days alive with the throb of the threshing machine and the low moo of cows calling across the meadows. Under the full moon, the kids sang and played hide-go-seek in the hay, or listened to hear the apple trees plop their fruit upon the ground.

School began. Mazie and Will went for the first time. The playground squirming with kids was wonderful, but the teacher that waddled and held her head like a duck and her wheezing horror—"Eight years old and can't read yet, you'll have to go in the first grade with your brother Will"—was shame. Yet the lessons came easy—the crooked white worms of words on the second-grade blackboard magically transforming into words known and said, although they were still stumbling over the first-grade alphabet. Finding the two could suddenly read, the teacher put them both up one grade, but the primer already breathlessly raced through with only silly sentences as a reward, they spent most of their time secretly listening to the upper grades recite geography and history—far countries, strange peoples.

Anna's face would glow. "What did you learn today?" And Mazie would try to tell her. "See, Jim," she would say, handing Mazie or Will a catalogue, hearing them stumble through the words. "See? They're reading. They'll be something, these kids."

For the first time, Mazie was acutely conscious of her scuffed shoes, rag-bag clothes, quilt coat. Stripping corn, she kept the soft silk; buried in the hay, she would dream of somehow weaving it into garments incredible. But the tassels withered, grew brown and smelly, and she had to throw them away. Sometimes, when the sadness in her heart became intolerable, she gathered Will and Ben and baby Jim about her and recited for them a poem learned from Old Man Caldwell. Not in his chaffing tones, but in a deep mysterious voice:

> O Were I a Lum Ti Tum Tum
> In the land of the alivoo fig
> I'd play on the strum ti tum tum
> To the tune of the thinguma jig.

Here, her voice would ripen into tragedy:

And if in the Lum Ti Tums battle I fall
A thingamys all that I crave
Oh bury me deep in the whatcha may call
And plant thingumbobs over my grave.

Reciting it, the sadness would ebb; the autumn world became blue and gold again.

One autumn dusk, with the calling of birds making her restless and a great gilt sunset clotting over the prairie, Mazie left the smoky kitchen and ran down the road. There was something to escape from. The autumn air, sweet with mellow death. But more, something in the kitchen; her father with anger riding on his brow, the shadow curtaining her mother's eyes. Momma'll hit me for runnin way thout doin the dishes, she thought, but a hunger and fear pushed her forward.

There was a great star glowing in the heart of the sunset, like a still candle in a vast unmoving flame. She could feel its glow on her face. As it sank, she began to run across the fields, to follow it; the corn stubble cut into her bare feet, but she knew only the sky dimming, the great star pulling down over the horizon, into the night, and something vanishing with it. Then it was gone, only darkness left, standing very tall and black about her.

With a bite of agony, she felt the slashes in her feet. Whimpering softly, a great void swelling in her, she started to find the road. Up ahead a big quiet hulk loomed, with a sultry light in one window. Caldwell's house, she thought; that must be Caldwell's house.

Bess Ellis answered the door. "Why, Mazie! What's brought you all the way up here?"

"I . . ." Her feet made a silent screaming. "I come to borry a book or a catalogue for to read."

Bess opened her mouth to say something, then closed it again. "Well, come in. Dad's pretty sick, I guess you know; but he'll be glad to see you."

Mazie walked into the light; stared incredulous. There was a gleaming sink and a great white cabinet. Upon the table, on a white tablecloth, glowed a bowl of vegetables bursting with snow cabbage and crimson tomatoes and hard round radishes. In the other room she could see a white plaster head and a wall of books.

Blood dribbled from her feet onto the kitchen linoleum; guiltily she forbade herself to notice. Bess was calling from the other room, "Come on into Dad's room—he wants to see you." He lay in the bed, curiously withered. Unmoving, only his eyes alive. Mazie took a step backward.

His fragile voice shattered about her. "Come by the bed, child." His hand, only a shadow of weight, embraced her shoulder. "I'm glad you came, Mazie. I think about you. How is your mother?"

She did not know what to say. A fear hovered. Outside the window there was still a faint light low in the west, like vanishing wings of birds. She fastened her eyes there. He kept on talking.

"Tell her to come see me, your mother. You remember what you thought the stars were, Mazie, before I told you?"

She nodded.

"Splinters of the moon, you said. Or maybe flowers in the night. Keep that wondering, Mazie, but try to know. Build on the knowing with the wondering. Mazie . . ."

She had to turn her eyes to him. His head was moving from side to side as if something were caught choking in his throat.

"Mazie. Live, don't exist. Learn from your mother, who has had everything to grind out life and yet has kept life. Alive, felt what's real, known what's real. People can live their whole life not knowing."

The words were incomprehensible. They parched the fear, but thirstily she still watched his eyes.

"You don't know how few . . . 'Better,' your mother says, 'to be a cripple and alive than dead, not able to feel anything.' No, there is more—to rebel against what will not let life be. Your mother thought to move from the mine to the farm would be enough, but . . ."

The hand was suddenly heavy on her shoulder. He raised himself.

> An old man, Elias Caldwell, death already smothering his breast, tries to tell a child something of all he has learned, something of what he would have her live by—and hears only incoherent words come out. Yet the thoughts revolve, revolve and whirl, a scorching nebula in his breast, sending forth flaming suns that only shatter against the walls and return to chaos. How can it be said? Once I lived in softness and ease and sickened. Once I chose a stern life, turning to people hard, bitter and strong—obscure people, the smell of soil and sweat about them—the smell of life . . . But I failed. I brought them nothing. To die, how bitter when nothing was done with my life. And the nebula whirls and revolves, sending its scorching suns that break in a chaos of inarticulateness about this child with a sound of fear. Nothing of it said.

His voice goes on. "Whatever happens, remember, everything, the nourishment, the roots you need, are where you are now."

The voice falters, dies; *no, none of it can be said when I myself do . . . not . . . know.*

Mazie sits with a sense of non-being over her—of it being someone other than she sitting there timeless, suspended in a dusky room, feeling a voice gathering around her, kind still hands of sound flaring into words meaningless and strange, meaningless when one tries to understand, but meaningful for a fleeting second. And she creeps her hand over the hand that lies on her shoulder. He laughs. A musical grieving sound. Calling, "Bess, see she gets some of the books. Those fairy tales, Wilde's, and the Dickens and Blake, and that book of Greek myths. Someday she will read them.

"Goodbye, my wonder-gazer companion."

Whimpering, running down the road, each step pain, the shadows were long and clutched at her, the corn by the wayside, some fallen, some shorn, was desolate and terrible, a flesh of her flesh.

Coming to the kitchen, she heard her father's angry voice: "They're taking all of it, every damn thing. The whole year slaved to nothing. I owe them—some joke if it wasnt so bloody—I owin *them* after workin like a team of mules for a year. They're wantin the cow and Nellie . . . takin Fred Benson's farm and Eldridge's. Batten on us like hogs. The bastards. A whole year—now I'm owin them."

The wind started a laughter in the fallen dried leaves, stirred them round and round senselessly in a mocking mimicry of being alive, rose in mocking laughter through the trees that beat up over the sky.

Caldwell died a week later. Mazie never got the books—Jim sold them for half a dollar when he got to town, though Anna cursed him for it. As for Mazie's slashed feet, it was weeks before she could do without rag bandages, could bear the wearing of shoes.

Overnight in late October, the ground grew hard and unyielding. Mazie and Will, trudging to school, felt their blood draw into little lumps under their skin and congeal under the touch of the wind. Tears would be frozen down their faces by the time they reached the schoolhouse, and Willie's feet, in their torn shoes, insensible. The snow came and fastened itself upon the earth. Finally it lay in too high waves of white over the fields, so that Mazie and Will had to stay home. Then the school itself closed.

Days were dim and short. Snow lay on the earth continually—blinding white at noon, yellow and old at dusk, ghost white at night. Life ceased beyond the kitchen. In the circle of warmth around the stove, everything moved and revolved. Distance was enormously magnified by the cold. Far and far it seemed to the woodpile; to the henhouse, where the hens gathered in drooping ovals of dejection, their cheeps coming out in little frozen spears; to the stable, where the sweet rotting smell of hay and the great cloud of warm breath from the cow stained the air. They scarcely moved from the stove. All day they sat around, Will's staccato cough mingling with Baby Jim's ceaseless sniffling. Anna was pregnant again—caught in the drowse of it, drugged by the warmth, she let things be. In the yellow kerosene light at night, she sewed or thumbed over the pages of a catalogue. But the other work she left. Dirty clothes gathered into a waiting pile, bacon drippings coiled greasy in the bottom of the pans, bread went unmade, and the smell of drying diapers layered over the room. Meals were quick, slapped together, half burned. It drove Jim crazy. The untidiness, the closeness, the inaction. The querulous children, half sick, always hungry—thinning, while Anna grew monstrous fat as if she were feeding on them.

"A woman's goddam life," he would shout, "sittin around huggin a stove." Then contrite, jerk out long fiery stories to the kids, sometimes stopping abruptly in the middle to brood. He whittled toys for them—blocks, dolls, animals, and gentle with Anna, straightened up for her, kneaded the bread. But when it was time for the chores, for the first time he would be eager, alert.

Quarrels flared up. Sometimes he beat up on the kids. Anna, the dream paralysis on her, unlike her old self, scarcely seemed to hear or care. "Snowed in like this leaves a man too much with himself," Jim would explain. "He starts askin why, and what for, like a kid."

One day through the sad sifting sound of snow came the high cheep of newborn chicks. Jim ran out. "Some fool hen hiding her eggs and settin. Wonder she didn't pick out the ice on the crick to set on. C'mon, Mazie." He piled them into her apron. Very alive and vital she felt in all the frozen world, but inside the house again, with a tiny oval of fluff against her cheek, barely moving, a shadow of sorrow fell on her heart. They put the chicks in the oven to warm, and Jim disappeared—probably to plow through the snow to a neighbor's for drink and talk.

The afternoon was a short gray blur; whirring of white against the windows, and stillness, except for the crackling of icicles and the short quick *spfft* of wood in the stove. Nobody noticed when the cheep became hysterical and finally ceased. Mazie and Ben peopled a city with things cut out of a catalogue, while Will watched them, his head a tangle of fever, remembering how the snow had soaked through his shoddy shoes and he could not be out till spring. Anna sat unmoving by the stove, her hands over her belly, a half smile of wisdom on her mouth, coming out of her dream to say, "Wipe Jim's nose, Mazie. I see the grease didn't do no good to drive that cough out, Will." And then sinking back into the dream again.

Jim came in. He stood at the door a moment, blind. For the first time, they noticed the smell of burning. "Crissake." He swung to the oven in one step and opened it. "The chicks, sure enough. Roasted to death. Have I got a bunch of dummies in here that can't even smell?"

No one answered. With shocked eyes, they stared. "Dumb, too? Your mouths stuffed up like your noses with crap? But you'll smell 'em." He grabbed Anna and forced her down by the open oven. "You'll fill your eyes with 'em."

She flung herself free. "Don't you touch me."

"Don't touch ya, huh. You don't always talk like that. No wonder I never got anywhere. No wonder nothing ever comes right. Lots of help I get from my woman."

"You get plenty. Kitchen help, farm help, milkin help, washwoman help. And motherin too."

"Who asked for your goddam brats?"

"Who? I'll never have another, to starve to death with you."

"No wonder we're starvin. Look at the woman I got."

"Poppa, stop, Momma, don't," Ben was screaming. Mazie held Jim scooped in her arms, her head buried in his baby body to stifle the sounds. Only Will moved. He was pulling on his father's pants leg, shouting, "Don't, don't, don't."

"Oh, fine bargains you make, fine bargains," Anna taunted. "Anybody can cheat you out of anything. Can't even make a livin. Fine bargains—how to starve your wife and kids quickest."

"Shut up."

"Oh sure, it was all goin to be fine. A new life, and you made one all right. A new way to keep us cold and wantin."

"Shut up." His fist crashed against her shoulder; she sagged under it. For a moment he stared at her, at the crying children, at Will beating him with small fists, at the diapers flapping over the stove, then he went out the door, closing it behind him, dark.

The worst storm in years arose that night. Over the torn and scattered sky, a wild hungry darkness came, then snow, driving in the wind like steel whips. The window in the bedroom shattered on the floor before it, and neither the chair bottom pounded over, or the quilts stuffed around, kept the bitterness out. For three nights they all slept on a mattress on the kitchen floor, Mazie and Anna venturing out only once a day with a bucket of hot coals to warm their hands over when they milked the cow or fed the horse and hog. The chickens they brought to the cellar and bedded in straw.

Outside, the charred bodies of the chicks lay where Anna had thrown them. That night, the snow covered them. Four days later, the sun rose at last over a vast white world, pure and unmoving.

It was ten days before Jim returned. Where he went or what he did, he never told.

Early in March, Mazie and Will wandered to a high wood where hidden wild violets with tears in their eyes carpeted the ground. Restless, Mazie pressed herself into the earth, but the soft dankness brought a faint remembrance of a face like jelly pushed against hers. Shuddering, she got up again. "Butterflies live behind your eyes, Will, butterflies. Their wings all colored. You dont believe me? Go ahead and try it—push your finger in your eye and you'll see 'em, butterfly wings."

Ugly and ugly the earth. Patches of soiled snow oozing away, leaving the ground like great dirty sores between, scabs of old leaves that like a bruise hid the violets underneath. Trees, fat with oily buds, and the swollen breasts of prairie. Ugly. She turned her eyes to the sky for oblivion, but it was bellies, swollen bellies, black and corpse gray, puffing out baggier and baggier, cloud belly on cloud belly till at the zenith they pushed vast and swollen. Her mother. Night, sweating bodies. The blood and pain of birth. Nausea groveled. "Think I'm lyin, just push your finger in your eyes and you'll see. Butterflies." She could feel words swollen big within her, words coming out with pain, bloody, all clothed in red. She began to hit Will, hard, ferocious. Then a weakness of tears—"Wouldja live in a room all breath, all winter breath?" He was raining small futile blows on her, blows unfelt. "Oh Will, Oh were I a Lum Ti Tum Tum." Ugly. Swollen like bellies.

She wakened that night to a nightmare of Jim's savage hand on her shoulder. "Wake up now. Your mother's goin to have a baby, and you've got to help her. I'm drivin over to Ellis's and takin Will and Ben. You put on water for me, now, right away."

The nausea came again. In the kitchen her mother was sitting, on her face a look of not seeing, although the black gates of her eyes opened on something too far to see to.

"Momma," Mazie cried, frightened, pressing her head in her mother's knees. "Momma."

For a moment Anna turned her eyes to her, with

a look compassionate and troubled. "It's all right, Mazie. I'm beginnin to have the baby. It's my time. I told Poppa not to leave you." Her face masked into a stranger's again, and her body stiffened, her hand clutching the chair back. Spacing her words, she said, "Better fire up the stove. Then come in the bedroom and help me fix up the bed."

The blackened fire leaped under her touch to embers and later to flame. Cheerlessly the water fled into the bucket and teakettle. But there was still the bedroom to be faced. She found her mother quietly kneeling before a drawer, holding a sheet. "Here," she said in a remote voice, "we'll put this one on. Then get out those newspapers."

"Yes, Momma." A nausea was gathering into her breast, clotting there. "Yes."

They came at last so that she could flee into the night. But the clatter of their voices came after. Uneven words. She clutched herself and sank into the soft dust. A forlorn wind fingered her hair and went gently over her body. But the nausea contested there, unmoving. Yes, Momma. The face set like a mask, purified, austere. To fix her mind to a time of dancing when laughter rose like froth; but the face curtained over everything. Yes, Momma. Miss Burgum was saying something about a dry birth, the waters broke. She crept into the henhouse, not to hear. Full and quiet in the darkness the house lay and the fields beyond.

Then, strangely, hunger came. Trickles of it in her mouth, battling under the nausea. Food—the smell of it yearned in her nostrils. She found an egg, warm. It slipped down her throat, then it was washing up again, spurting over the ground. Yes, Momma. I'm sick, Momma. Butterflies live behind your eyes. Perhaps there were stars above, known stars. Light, weightless, she walked out to the yard, the earth under her feet like air, and turned her face to the heavens. Pale, half drowned, blurred like through tears, the stars. Where was the belted man Caldwell had told her of, lifting his shield against a horn of stars? Where was the bright one she had run after into the sunset? A strange face, the sky grieved above her, gone suddenly strange like her mother's.

After a long while she felt a drenching mist. Rain, she thought without thinking. A shadow of rain. Back in the henhouse, she heard it descend upon the earth, gentle and grieving. Perhaps after a while she slept. A half sleep into which voices came. "Now. Push hard now, Anna. Did you boil the spoon? I have to use it. Hard, Anna."

Then a cry, ecstatic, profound, shattered the night, and a thin wail wove it under. It was dawn. Her father's arms were carrying her into the house through the gray and lonely light, his voice saying, "looked . . . so long . . . you tired? Big-eyes . . . I had to leave you in the rain. . . ."

The sleep still lay on her eyes, or was it sleeplessness? Yellow light flowered before her eyes in the warmth of the kitchen. "Her breasts cracked, so it'll be no fun feedin the youngun," someone was saying, and "Where'd you find her, Jim?"

Bess cradled her. "You really set on leaving, Jim?"

"You know it's no use to stay."

"But what if you cant get on at the slaughterhouse?"

"I'm goin anyhow. Soon as Anna's fit to. We cant stay here."

"You really think things'll be better there, Jim? . . . Go to sleep now, Mazie. Everythin's all right."

"They cant be worse. Anyway, I've got to try."

"Life," heavily from Ellen Burgum. "Life's no bottle of perfume. I'm tired enough to die."

Two figures moving with pain in the dawn darkness, in the vapor mist. Two voices lashed by a dry and savage wind, bringing strangely the scent of lilac.

"Almost time now, Anna. We'd better go."

"Yes, it's so quiet now, Jim."

"Mr. Burgum's waiting."

"You'd think you could hear somebody's rooster.

Doesnt seem like other mornin's we woke up to work in."

"No. C'mon, Anna. Let's go. Now."

"Funny how Will cried all last night, and Mazie wouldn't sleep but in the hay. You'd think children wouldn't care."

"Anna—they're waiting."

"This hay smells good. I'd like to breathe it in so's not ever to forget."

"Right away now, or we'll miss the train."

"Right away now Jim. . . . What's the matter, life never lets anything be? Just a year ago . . . I tried for us to have a good life."

One word, austere. "Anna."

The two figures blur into one, gnarled and lonely. Very low he says: "You're shivering. Cold?"

"Awful cold. Lets go. Now."

"But you cant take it lyin down—like a dawg. You cant, Anna."

FIVE

Myriad and drumming, the feet of sound move always through these crooked streets, trembling the shoddy houses, jerking the skeleton children who scream and laugh so senselessly to uneven rhythms they themselves know not of. Monster trucks shake by, streetcars plunge, machinery rasps and shrieks. Far underneath thinly quiver the human noises—weeping and scolding and tired words that slip out in monosyllables and are as if never spoken; sighs of lust, and guttural, the sigh of weariness; laughter sometimes, but this sound can scarcely be called human, not even in the mouths of children. A fog of stink smothers down over it all—so solid, so impenetrable, no other smell lives beside it. Human smells, crotch and underarm sweat, the smell of cooking or of burning, all are drowned under, merged into the vast unmoving stench.

That stench is a reminder—a proclamation—*I rule here.* It speaks for the packing houses, heart of all that moves in these streets; gigantic heart—pumping over the artery of viaducts the men and women who are the streets' lifeblood, nourishing the taverns and brothels and rheumy-eyed stores, bulging out the soiled and exhausted houses, and multiplying into these children playing so mirthlessly in their street yards where flower only lampposts. (They say this heart pumps lifeblood far and far—thin and blue the vein—to nourish a rare and cherished few in purest air where scents flower under glass and in hundred-dollar perfume bottles.)

A man's face, heavy and sullen (strange and bright the blue of his eyes) moves here awhile and is gone: *Jim;* a woman's face, thinning, skin tightening over the broad cheekbones, the great dark eyes down a terrace of sunken flesh, fading until the eyelids shut over forever *Anna.* A child's thin face looks up a moment, wondering dazed eyes *Mazie;* a boy's face, scowl over the mouth, eyes hurt with the hurt of not understanding, then insane with anger *Will.* On this face, half baby's, half child's, the breath of fever glows, closing the sober eyes; a tiny boy running along croons a song that is silenced; a tiny girl's fists beat the air, stiffening, stiffened *Ben, Jimmie, Baby Bess.*

Yes, it is here Jim and Anna Holbrook have come to live. (Old and familiar the streets to them, the scenery of their childhood, rearranged.) Over the cobbled streets, past the two blocks of dump and straggling grass, past the human dump heap where the nameless FrankLloydWrights of the proletariat have wrought their wondrous futuristic structures out of flat battered tin cans, fruit boxes and gunny sacks, cardboard and mother earth. In this ancient battered house that leans to the river. What matter the second story, windowless and roofless, the paper-thin boards, the dirt which has eaten into and become a part of the walls? It has a space that might be called a yard, and when the wind blows hard to the west, you can smell river and dump instead of packing house.

(And beauty? Until the mammoth stone beauty of the city has carved itself into their blood, the children can lie on their bellies near the edge of the cliff and watch the trains and freights, the glittering railroad tracks, the broken bottles dumped below, the rubbish moving on the littered belly of the river.)

"See, Anna," says Jim. "It's got a yard for the kids. They wont be runnin out in the streets to play, anyhow. And just think, runnin water with a faucet and a toilet inside the house. We never had that before."

"No" (trying not to see or smell).

"And electric lights. Hey, over there, kids—you ever see electric lights in the house? And electric lights if we want."

"If we want?"

"You know what I mean, if we can fork over. We'll have 'em too, quickern a hen could lay an egg."

"Yes. Lets go inside, Jim." (Holding Baby Bess to her nostrils, holding Bess against the corrosive eating into her heart.)

"Sure—and four rooms. Say, what's the matter with you? Lookin as if you're seein a corpse. I know this aint no palace, but you ought to see what other folks are livin in for what we're payin."

"Sure, Jim, I know it's a real find. Guess I'm tired, that's all."

"Ma," said Ben, running up, "what smells so awful funny? It makes me sick to my tummy, Ma. It smell like this all the time?"

When Anna made Will and Mazie ready for school that first morning, she stood them up against the wall and said fiercely, "You two got a chance to really learn something now; you're goin to a good school, not a country one. I catch you not doin good and I'll knock the livin daylights out of you, you hear?"

But Mazie hated it. The first day: "MazieandWill-Holbrookhavecomefromthecountrywheretheygrowthecornandwheatandallourmilkcomesfromsayhello toMazieandWillchildren." Her palm held in Will's moist with fear. A big room, biggern the whole country school, squirming with faces, staring. (Whatcha shiverin for, you scairt? Me? Scared?) Faces mad and tired and scared and hungry and dead and their eyes like they want to eat you up. No, dont look at the faces, look out the window—but it is greasy, like drippings was smeared all over, and stink comes in from the top, comes in and fills the room. All the faces (if her heart wouldn't beat so fast) . . . Dont look, read the funny words on the blackboard —Na-tion-al-it-ies American Armenian Bohemian Chinese Croatian (Croatian—that was what ol' man Kvaternick was, ol' man Kvaternick in the mine and he was dead now, dead. Worms . . . no, dont think of ol' man Kvaternick) Irish French Italian Jewish Lith . . . A face was black, black like when the men come up from the mine, blacker; lots of faces were black. Maybe the mine was here too, maybe kids had to live in the mine here like they had to live in gunnysack houses, maybe the whistle would be again, but the whistle was all the time now. Mexican Negro Polish Portuguese. If her heart beat any faster she would have to scream and all the faces would turn and look, . . . One face was honey color—honey like on the farm. The farm. It is just a dream, a bad dream, and it really is the farm, really the farm, in a minute now you will get awake, and it will be the farm again.

At recess, her heart quieting, telling two girls, Annamae and Ellie, about riding a horse, somebody hissed: "So ya come from the country where our milk comes from; ya learn about bulls?" and smack, a head butted her in the stomach. Bewildered, gasping for breath, swaying, she heard Annamae laugh, "Oh, Smoky, didja put that one over," and in a darkness of rage and hatred she lunged at him, but already he was across the playground, his too big shirt flapping in the wind, his angular face jeering. And then she turned to Ellie and shoved her down, and turned to Annamae to shove her down, but the teacher was holding her shoulder, steering her inside the school. "Perhaps you indulged in rough play of this nature where you came from, but we do not permit it here, nor does it go unpunished." Mazie could still see Smoky's jeering face. "Lemme alone," she cried and, making her body a hard ball of force, wrenched herself free. Then, paralyzed at what she had done, she stood in front of them all and began to cry. Hearing Will savagely whisper to someone next to him, "That aint my sister, that aint my sister," she cried louder and louder, uncontrollably.

That night they went to the Bedners, old friends Jim and Anna hadn't seen for seven years. Alex was doing well—he was a tool and die maker now. They lived in a five-room house with a piano and a stained-glass window, and it didn't smell around there, except when the wind blew strong from the south. They went on a streetcar, the kids' first ride, but only Will seemed jubilant. Jimmie and Bess slept, Ben was sick all the way, and Mazie kept looking out the window with her eyes shut tight. Anna, kept smoothing her hair and passing her hand over the lines in her face.

Else let out a cry of pain when she saw her: "Why, Anna, honey, you've changed so, I wouldn't hardly've known you."

"But a lot happens in seven years," Anna reminded her.

"So it does, so it does," Else agreed and began to cry. She was fat and smelled too sweet and had on a tight yellow dress. "So you're Anna's little man," she said to Will, tears still on her face. "Give an old friend a kiss." But Will wouldn't. He ran over to the piano and banged it, and Jim had to slap him before he would kiss her.

Everything was strained and shaken. Jimmie and Will ran into the other rooms to watch the electric lights on the ceiling and turn them on and off. Alex cleared his throat, then Jim cleared his, and then they smoked cigars in silence. In a low voice Else was saying to Anna, "So stuck up around here . . . So lonesome I could die . . . such a brood . . . and we cant even manage to get one . . . been to all the doctors . . . just breaks my heart . . ."

On a little table there were a lot of magazines. *Screen Star* and *True Confession*. Mazie turned the pages—there were pictures in them of men and ladies smiling, or kissing. Alex, his thumb in his lapel, his voice suddenly loud and important, said, "Now if you still cant get on by the end of the week at the yards, you go on down and see Mulcahey; he's the biggest contractor in town for road and sewer work —and he dont hire niggers or furriners when there's white men begging."

"O.K.," said Jim, but he looked awfully funny.

"Well, believe me," Alex said, noting that look, "a man cant pick and choose nowadays."

"He cant pick and choose," said Jim, "but he can sure pick and shovel."

Nobody laughed but Else, who laughed and laughed for a long time. "You grow up with your papa's sense of humor," she said to Ben, curled up in her lap, "and you'll have them in the aisles. My, but he's a cute tyke, Annie. Who woulda thought Mazie would grow up to be so homely? She was such a cunning baby. But they do say a homely kid makes a pretty girl."

Mazie pretended not to hear. "Who plays the piano?" she asked as loud as she could.

"Me, honey, if you can stand plunking. Your ma used to play real good by ear. Why dont you play something for us now, honey?"

Mazie thought her mother was going to have another sinking spell, she looked so awful. But her voice sounded all right. "I haven't touched the piano since I don't know when," she said. "*You* play, Else."

Else sat down on the piano bench. As she played she swayed her body. Underneath her dress you could see her flesh ripple. But when she began to sing, Jimmie came from the other room and put his head up against her lap, and Will came in too and stood listening. Alex began to sing, and then Jim and Anna. One after another they sang old songs, some Jim or sometimes Anna had sung in old times of happiness; some the children had never heard before. "Red River Valley," "Sweet Genevieve," "When It's Lamplighting Time," "In the Gloaming," "When You and I Were Young, Maggie," "The Wreck of the Old '91," "Down in the Valley," "Roamin' So Far," "Shenandoah," "Nelly Gray," Foster songs, "I Saw a Ship A-Sailing."

From the opened window, the sweet intoxicating smell of spring floated in; the lamplight made soft lakes of light, shadows bending over, gentle. They sang and sang, and a longing, a want undefined, for something lost, for something never known, troubled them all. The separate voices chorded into one great full one, their faces into beauty. Oh, singin is like . . . Mazie, broken, searched for the word, feeling tears stand behind her eyelids. Singin is like . . . But no right words would form. Bess, quietly sleeping, wore an eternal dream look. Singing Anna's favorite song:

Throw your arms round me, 'fore it's too late
Throw your arms round me, feel my heart break

a fifth voice, pure, ethereal, veiled over the rest. Mazie saw it was Jimmie, crouched at the pedals of the piano. "Ma," she said after the song was done, "it's Jimmie, JimJim was singin too." Incredulous, they made him sing it over with them and over and over. His words were a blur, a shadow of the real words, but the melody came true and clear.

And then it was over. Else, the same chirp, the dearie and honey, the perspiration rings under her arm, Alex laughing too loud, and Jim trying too hard to laugh, and Anna sitting shrunken and ill, her arm tenderly around Jimmie.

The weariness. The ghastly nausea in her belly (in all their bellies) from the stench. Ben feverish in bed with it. And her banner of defiance—up the first day —the clean cheesecloth curtains, yellowing, browning. All that scrubbing to make a whiteness inside—and the stubborn walls and floors only a deeper smoke color. Even the cardboard tacked for a carpet in the front room so Jimmie crawling around would cease to be a graveyard for splinters—even that was damp and soggy and would have to be ripped up again. How the house resisted her.

Anna sat in the armless chair, Bess tugging at her breast and pulling away and tugging again and giving out small frantic cries. "Guzzle, kitten, guzzle, dont make such a fuss." All that scrubbing and she was always so tired nowadays. So awfully tired. "C'mon, Bessie, hold still and eat." Well, she'd try washing soda in the scrubbing water next time. Maybe that might do the trick.

A fine joke on Jim to be back in the earth again, sewering. He should've known the stockyards job couldn't pan out in spring when they were laying off. How they'd manage on what he was getting with the rent high as it was and the children needin this and that. Awful to be sendin them to school looking like they did. And Will wouldn't mind anymore, as if he knew . . .

A familiar faintness dizzied her. With Bess still crying and tugging she sank to the bed, thinking: I oughta see what Jimmie's doin and set him down on the hopper. But she was wandering through old childhood streets. Bess lay in the scrub pail, under water. And Jim was fleeing, shrinking to a tiny dot on the lurid sky. A speck of dust floated from where he had gone, growing larger. And now the gaunt haggard house towered above. Where were the children? MazieWillBen she cried, but a smell was filling her mouth so no words could come. "It'll fall," she tried desperately to warn, beating it away with her broom. Right in front of her, right to the house, Will danced. "It'll crash," she screamed. It crashed. "Momma, Momma," someone was calling. "Yes, Ben," she managed to answer, "I'm coming." She had to steady herself against the wall, her body drenched with sweat and fear. The dizziness was still there. Funny how Bess was sleeping, still sucking away as if she had the nipple in her mouth.

Outside a wan sunshine lay over the grimy streets, the streets of her dream. She pulled the blinds down. Will was sitting in the kitchen morose, just home from school, chewing bread with drippings on it. "Didnt you hear your brother callin?" Anna asked. "Dont you know he's sick?" He just looked back at her, not answering. "All right, git in there with this drink of water afore I skin you alive." There, her head felt better now, the splashing water cooling her cheeks.

The little stream on the farm glinted in the sun of her memory, and Mazie was spraying her with water, laughing. That was gone, it was long ago, it was forgotten.

"Well, you little horntoad, now what's the matter, wakin your momma up first chance today she's had to get a little rest."

"I can't breav, Momma." (You'd think he'd get used to the smell in two weeks.)

"Sure you can, see you're breathin now, you've been breathin all the time; here, we'll make a bundle and prop it under your head."

"No, Momma, cant breav . . . Let's go home, Momma. It smells of vomit here. I had a dream and Shep was barkin for me, tellin me not to smell vomit no more, and come back to the farm. It's so hard to breav. It smells so hot, so awful hot."

(The farm—why couldnt the kids leave her alone about it?) And what was the matter with Will? Looking at her face like that and now hitting Ben, shouting, "Shut up, you crybaby, you big crybaby, shut up or I'll kill ya." And she was holding Will and hitting him. "What did you do that for?" beating him till she sank to her knees, still drenched in sweat, trembling from nervousness and crying, and Ben was out of bed with great sober eyes, stroking her cheek, begging, "Dont cry, Momma, don't cry," and outside Will was shouting to Mazie, "Does too smell like vomit, worse'n vomit, worse'n dead dogs and garbage, worse'n the crap can. I'm gonna run away to the farm, you come too, Mazie," and Mazie was yelling back, "Shut up, we are on the farm, we are on the farm," and Will was quiet suddenly, asking of the sky, "What's the matter with everything anyhow?" and running, running down the street. And in the front room, Jimmie pounding on the wall was yelling, "Out, out. Lemme out. Out."

Into her great physical pain and weariness Anna stumbled and lost herself. Remote, she fed and clothed the children, scrubbed, gave herself to Jim, clenching her fists against a pain she had no strength to feel. In the front room Jimmie played and sang to himself, falling asleep when she didn't come for him, wetting his overalls when she forgot. Else worried over her: "Land sake, Anna, what's the matter with you anyhow? You useta be strong as a bull, and look at you now. You aint even ornery with the kids. You take this here tonic now, you hear? It'll do you good. It says for all female complaints."

"All female complaints, huh?" Anna answered. "Well, I guess I got all of them. But I never was much of a hand at patent medicines." On the kitchen shelf, the bottle mantled in dust.

Bess shrank and yellowed. Anna fussed with food.

"You really think Eagle Brand is good, Mis' Kryckszi? It oughta be the way they soak you for it, but you never can tell. And Bess needs perkin up bad. When it's tomato season, I'll try juice, they say that's awful good. But when I gave her some of what I had canned from the farm, she spit it right back. And just look how she's gettin blue around the mouth and squalls all the time now."

But she could not really care. Only sometimes, nursing the baby, chafing the little hands to warm them, old songs would start from her lips and tears well from her eyes, tears she did not even know she was weeping, till Ben would come in, standing lacerated till she would notice him and ask, "What's the matter, Benjy, did you hurt yourself?" and he could come over to her and say gently, "Mommy, you're crying."

The money going drove Jim crazy. "Jesus Christ, woman," he would shout, "where does it all go to? God knows we're eatin worse'n animals, and Bess eatin off you dont cost no more. You useta be so smart with money—make it stretch like rubber. Now it's rent week and not a red cent in the house. I tell you we gotta make what I'm gettin do—they're takin off for my waterproofs."

But she could not heed—the old Anna of sharp words and bitter exaction, and fierce attempt to make security for her children was gone, lost in a fog of pain that seemed the only reality. Will was the only one that really saw—but a lust for the streets was on him, a lust to hit back, a lust not to care. He had learned how to scramble up and down the cliff, hanging onto roots and digging his toes into the crumbling clay; he knew the railroad tracks and the walk and talk of the bindle stiffs hightailing it down the roadbed; he knew the dump and the kids on his block and strange wild games to play. And in these, in the quick movements of his body, for a while he anesthetized himself.

Ben saw too—but in the confused, entangled way of a small child whose mind is a prism through which the light shatters into a thousand gleams and shadows that can never come whole. Say rather, a weight, an oppression dragged always in his chest; a darkening shadow hovered over his days that in moments descended and pierced sharp claws on his heart. Only he did not know why or how—he but knew there was a darkening where had been light, he but felt there was a weight where had been lightness.

And Jim? Ah, he knew, but in a half way. He was padded about with weariness, he was blinded with despair. Coming home with the smell of liquor on his breath, thinking the remote look reproach, bristling up to say, "All right, havent I got no right to spend two bits once in a while to make me feel good? If *you* was workin under icy water all day with your head bustin from bein so far underground, dancin round like a monkey to keep your footin till your can's draggin and every nerve shootin like lightnin" (and, he did not say, come home to disorder and anguish) "you'd be achin for a snifter too once in a while. Aw hell, *hell.*" Kicking the table leg. "Where's that Will? Runnin off with my jackknife. I'll knock the s--t out of him. And playin with all the furrin scum and niggers around. C'mon over here JimJim and sing your old pa a song. Sing 'For I'm a Poor Cowboy and I Know I Done Wrong.' "

Only Mazie did not see. Still she lived on the farm in June, in early June, when a voluptuous fragrance lay over the earth. Wooden she moved about, lifting and washing and eating, and always a scarcely perceptible smile about her mouth. Mazie, a voice came shrill, you see that tub of diapers? Git to that tub of diapers. Yes, Ma. You will recite, Mazie. A hushed voice, faltering, that was she. We will have a test. And her pencil would move over the paper, separate from her guidance and her body. Sometimes a dingy sky was overhead and a graveled playground underfoot, and her body made a circle with other bodies. Then the schoolroom or the walls of home would encase her again. Noise ceaselessly rained blows upon her, the stink smothered down into her lungs. Enveloped in the full soft dream of the farm, she was secure. Hollow and unreal the dirty buildings and swarming people revolved about her, flat like a picture that her hand could smash through and see the rolling fields and roads of home just beyond.

But terrible moments of waking would come when the world that was about her would crash into her dream with terrible discordant music. Fear held her limbs there in the streets where the flats rose a tumble of ruins, and a voice would cry: Run, run, the next shake the houses'll fall, run, run.

And every step was pain, every look was pain, those moments of awareness when the people streamed by her in the streets with their hideous faces that knew her not. Suddenly she would see before her a monster thing with blind eyes and shaking body that gave out great guttural sobs, a truck, she would tell herself, just a truck, but her eyes would try to close and her feet to run; suddenly she would see before her a woman with her mother's face grown gaunter, holding a skeleton baby whose stomach was pushed out like a ball, and behind was a wall like darkness and misshapen furniture. These had no reality, only the reality of nightmares, for only there had she seen such grotesqueness and crooked vision. And it would seem that her limbs were crooked in sleep and a nightmare sweat was on her, that it would be useless to resist, to cry out, because it all was a voiceless dream to be endured.

"Just see," Tracy promised, "just see. I'll make a kick with that bastard today. Twelve foot he wants out of us, when ten's all anything on two legs can manage."

"All right," said Jim wearily, tugging off his soggy work pants. "All right."

"And calling this a dry house," Tracy muttered. "Give me a cloudburst anytime."

"Hell, the Mississipp's a road of concrete and the ocean's a dry bed."

"How you two can beef after the day's work you put in is beyond me," old man Albright butted in. "Even my tongue's laid out."

"Well, this goddam business of hangin up my work clothes in what they call a dry house and puttin em on the next morning twice as wet is just gettin under my skin."

"All right, son, wait'll you get the rheumatiz. Then you *will* have something under your skin to beef about."

"You wont see me doin any waitin," said Tracy. (I guess not, Jim thought, not till you got a woman and kids hangin around your neck.) "Look at those puckers—" pointing to his bare feet—"bigger'n on a washboard. Waterproof boots, hell. How you guys take it is beyond me."

"O.K.," said Jim, "put on the low needle and give our ears a vacation. Maybe we got somethin besides gettin canned up and steppin out a chippie to think about."

They dressed in silence. "Hey," Jim warned, "here comes the workingman's friend."

The contractor came in, puffed up like a balloon, with a smaller red balloon of a face wobbling on top. He spat his tobacco juice square into Jim's empty boot.

"So ten foot is all you women made today, huh? What I want to know is what the hell you do when you're on the job, suck titty?"

"Now, boss," Albright said hurriedly, "we're doin the best we can. We went like a redball all day."

"Ya mean a standstill, dont you? Well, ten's the footage all right from now on, but for two of you to manage."

"Two?" came from all their startled throats.

"Two! A miner and a mucker to a job. Miller's tried it with his monkeys and they're doin it. My crews can do as good."

"Not and stay human," Jim said.

Tracy sputtered, "It cant be done."

"Shut up—I'm the one who says what can and cant get done. Tracy and Holbrook, Marello and Albright, that's the lineup."

"But say—"

"You heard me. There's plenty good concrete men and muckers with their tongues hangin out for a job. You'll make ten or you're out."

"Not me," exploded Tracy. "I'm throwin up this sh---y job."

"O.K. by me," the contractor said, "but dont come panhandlin when you're up against it . . . Anybody else feel like the breadline?"

Nobody said anything. Jim clenched his fists. "Dirty rat," he said in his teeth, "I hope his guts wither. I hope . . ." He flung his boots and mackinaw into the locker and walked out into the dwindling light. There was a darkness in him, a heavy darkness that wound into a hardness. When the slaughter-house workers got on before the viaduct, he pushed his way viciously out of the packed streetcar and walked into a "soft drink" parlor. "A straight," he ordered. To himself, "All right for Tracy to talk, he doesnt have a wife and brats. But no man has any business having 'em that wants to stay a man. Having to take all that crap. . . . Not that they aren't worth it though," thinking of Jimmy, "And what else you got?"

The sound of the two bits clamped down on the counter brought harshly the picture of Anna counting his pay money. "Goddam woman—what's the matter with her anyhow? Dont even have a wife that's a wife anymore—just let her say one word to me and I'll bash her head in."

He thought he saw Mazie across the street, but he was not sure. No one greeted him at the gate—the dark walls of the kitchen enclosed him like a smothering grave. Anna did not raise her head.

In the other room Bess kept squalling and squalling, and Ben was piping an out-of-tune song to quiet her. There was a sour smell of wet diapers and burned pots in the air.

"Dinner ready?" he asked heavily.

"No, not yet."

Silence. Not a word from either.

"Say, cant you stop that damn brat's squallin? A guy wants a little rest once in a while."

No answer.

"Aw, this kitchen stinks. I'm going out on the porch. And shut that brat up, she's drivin me nuts, you hear?" You hear, he reiterated to himself, stumbling down the steps, you hear, you hear. Driving me nuts.

All right for Tracy to talk, all right, he didn't have a wife and kids hangin round his neck like an anchor. All right for him to talk, all right with nothin more important to worry about than gettin canned up and steppin out a floosie.

And Tracy was young, just twenty, still wet behind the ears, and the old blinders were on him so he couldn't really see what was around and he believed the bull about freedomofopportunity and a chancetorise and ifyoureallywanttoworkyoucanalwaysfindajob and ruggedindividualism and something about a pursuitofhappiness.

He didn't know, so the big sap threw it up, he threw up his job, thinking he was flinging his challenge into the teeth of life, proclaiming I'm a man, and I'm not taking crap offn anybody, I'm goin to live like a man. There's more to life than workin everything you got to live with outa you in order to keep a job, taking things no man should stand for to keep a job. So he threw it up, the big sap, not yet knowing a job was a straw and every man (having nothing to sell but his labor power) was the drowning man who had no choice but to hang onto it for notsodear life.

So he threw it up, not yet knowing a job was God, and praying wasn't enough, you had to live for It, produce for It, prostrate yourself, take anything from It, for was it not God and what came was it not by Its Divine Providence, and nothing to do but bow to It and thank It for Its mercifulness to you, a poor sinner who has nothing to sell but your labor power. So he threw it up, the big sap (not knowing), he renounced God, he became an atheist and suffered the tortures of the damned, and God Job (being full up that generation) never took him back into the fold only a few days at a time, and he learned all right what it meant to be an infidel, he learned:

the little things gone: shoeshine and tailor-mades, tickets to a baseball game, and a girl, a girl to love up, whiskey down your gullet, and laughter, the happy belch of a full stomach, and walking with your shoulders back, tall and proud.

He learned all right, the tortures of the damned:

feet slapping the pavement, digging humbly into carpets, squatting wide apart in front of chairs and the nojobnojob nothingdointoday buzzing in his ears; eking out the coffee—and shuffling along, buddy (they made a song out of it) can you spare a dime, and the freights north east south west, getting vagged, keep movin, keep movin (the bulls dont need to tell ya, your own belly yells it out, your own idle hands), sing a song of hunger the weather four below holes in your pockets and nowhere to go, the flophouses, the slophouses, a bowl of misery and a last month's cruller and the crabs having a good time spreading and spreading (you didnt know hell would be this bad, did you?).

Oh he learned all right. He never even got a chance to have a wife and kids hang round his neck like an anchor and make him grovel to God Job. (And I guess it's just as well, Jim Tracy, because even among the pious who heed and prostrate themselves It's wrath is visited, for Many Are Called but Few Are Chosen, and are not the Sins of the Fathers (having nothing to sell but their labor power) Visited on the Sons, and it's no fun to see the old lady nag and worry her life away, no fun to see the younguns pulpy with charity starches drowse and chant the lesson after the teacher: we-are-the-rich-est-country-in-the-worr-uld).

So (not knowing) he threw it up, the big sap, thinking, the big sap, jobs grew on trees and (believing the old bull) a man didn't hafta take crap off'n anybody, he renounced God Job—and the tortures of the damned were visited upon him in full measure, he learned all right, all right that last hour writhing in the "piano" in the chain gang down in Florida.

And there's nothing to say, Jim Tracy, I'm

sorry, Jim Tracy, sorry as hell we weren't stronger and could get to you in time and show you that kind of individual revolt was no good, kid, no good at all, you had to bide your time and take it till there were enough of you to fight it all together on the job, and bide your time, and take it, till the day millions of fists clamped in yours, and you could wipe out the whole thing, the whole goddam thing, and a human could be a human for the first time on earth.

Momma was asleep again, falling asleep right in her chair like she was always doin now, with her mouth open, and cryin as if somebody was hitting her, turnin her head and cryin. Ben stood looking at the little worm of water on the floor from the leaking washtub. "Ma," he called, trying not to cry, "ma." She moaned and her hands twitched at him. "Ma," he called again, louder.

She didn't wake up. Ben pushed open the kitchen door and ran out; the clothes flapping on the line slapped in his face with a crackling noise, but the wind felt good on his hot cheeks. His finger hurt awful there in the tip, like a heart was beating in it. He put it in his mouth and tried to suck the pain away.

Jimmie, stirring the ashes on the dump heap with an old broomstick, singing, "Pudding wiv kithes, pudding wiv kithes," saw him and stood up. "Go bye?" he asked, "Ji go go go bye?"

"No," said Ben, "Momma said no." His finger throbbed and throbbed. He felt so empty inside, like when he was hungry, but the idea of food made him shudder.

"See car?" begged Jimmie. "Go bye bye, see street-car?"

"No, go on play." He pushed Jimmie down and kicked the piece of stick out of his reach.

"Go bye?" quivered Jimmie again.

"No." The yelling of it made him feel good. "No," he yelled, "no, no, no."

Near the ashes there was a tuft of fur like part of a tail of a cat. "All right, c'mon," said Ben suddenly, "we'll go bye-bye, Jimmie, far away bye."

"Go go go," sang Jimmie, collecting his broken bits of wood, "go go go."

Up at the corner big men were standing around laughing. Through their legs Ben could see a dog, a dog like Shep. One held him by the collar, and another was sticking nails all over a piece of meat. "The funniest sight you ever did see," he chortled, "the way a dawg tries to get at the meat."

"Shep," called Ben, "here, Shep, here, Shep."

The man in front turned around. "That aint your dog. Scram!"

"Maybe it is," faltered Ben. "Shep, here, Shep."

"Say, I said beat it, you and your shadow. Go on home and get some titty."

"No, I wanna see."

"Scram now." The man pushed his shoe into Ben's back and gave him a shove. "Go on."

Ben ran. But Jimmie tugged back. "See streetcar," he wept, "see car." In vain Ben pulled and pulled, finally Jimmie gave. Then tears came, and in the middle of the tears an anger lashing. Ben picked up a rock and smashed it against the telephone pole, he pounded, pounded the pavement. Frightened, Jimmie began to cry too.

"Aw hush up," Ben savagely commanded. "Hush up, nuffin to cry about, nuffin. You heard me," pushing him down. "You heard me." Then, "I'm sorry, Jimmie, please dont cry, JimJim, we'll go see a streetcar, we'll go see a car, we'll go see a car. Please dont cry." Seeing Mazie come down the street, slowly, dreamily, a paper clutched in her hand: "See, Mazie'll take us bye-bye." But she walked past.

Bess was wailing. "Ma," said Mazie, shaking her, "wake up, baby's cryin, she wants to nurse."

With her mouth open (so far in some sharp livid place), Anna slept on, drawing deep hoarse breaths.

"*Ma,*" yelled Mazie again, "baby's cryin, wake up, wake up."

Anna's body became rigid, then convulsed. She

sprang out of her chair with a cry, trembling. "What?" she asked in a voice not her own, "What? . . . Oh." The kitchen, the half-done wash, a glimmering face like Mazie's. She pushed her hand hard over her brow. "Must've been asleep. Now . . . what did you say, Mazie?"

"Bess's cryin, Momma."

"Yes, Bess's cryin." It seemed Mazie's face dipped and swayed like a sea. All that heaviness . . . to batter through. "Better bring her in here." Sinking again. Then with a start: "My land, you home already? I musta been asleep a long time. And dinner to get, and still clothes to get out on the line. I'm gettin up right now" (but she sank right back in the chair). "Will home yet?"

"No'm." An absent smile. "He said he was gonna play ball."

The room would not come clear. Such a burning somewhere, such a swimming and a haze. Bess's cry was lost and struggling somewhere. "Hush, baby," she said automatically, pulling out her breast. "Hush now." Calling, "Mazie."

With such an effort she managed to find the thought and push it out steady. "Better go get a pail of lard down at the store and tell him to put it on the bill. Say please. Best bring a diaper first."

The room swimming, swimming, or was it she?

Bess did not seem to be at her breast at all. Soaked, soaked through to the bone, she thought, but her fingers felt no wet. She tried to rise. A great wave of giddiness and illness rose and waited to engulf her; she sank back down. "Them clothes, I guess. Leavin me tired enough not to move for a thousand years."

Cleanly, suddenly, she arose and stumbled to the table. There, it was all right now. She lay Bess down and took off her wet diaper and put on another. The paper Mazie had laid there danced before her eyes, so she could not read it. A long while before she made out the words.

It would have struck her like a blow on the naked heart once, this failure report from school, but now she folded it carefully and put it into her pocket. "You bring another one and I'll beat you to a pulp," she said to the empty room. To Bess, "Dont you know learnin's the only hope a body's got in this world?" And her lips curved in a smile, remembering the remote dream look in Mazie's eyes as if she were not there at all. "I aim to see any kids we have happy, Jim, not like we were brought up. Happy and with learnin." Her hand lifted to caress his cheek.

Shuddering, she clutched the table edge. "Hold on, Anna old girl," she said to herself. "Hold on. Gettin a little teched in the head from the heat, I guess," she explained carefully. The wave of pain gathered her up, engulfed her, so that she swayed. Where

. . . was . . . that . . . chair? God she *was* sick. Sick enough to die. The quivering in her back and the pounding in her head. "Will," she called faintly, "Mazie. Oughta know they wouldn't be around when you want them," she reminded herself scornfully, "and it was you sent Mazie to the store."

A terrible sobbing anguished her ears. Stop it, Anna, she begged, stop it, dont be such a baby. But it was only Bess crying. "Only . . . Bess, what's the matter with you anyhow?" There, it was going to happen again, the dizziness and pain. She sank down to the chair, down, down as far as she could go, and the pounding of her heart filled the world.

After a while she lifted her head. "I'd better jest set here a while yet," she said out loud, "but not for long. I cant let Jim find me like this."

Ben's face was so red and funny. Could he have been listening or watching there at the kitchen door? "It's about time," she managed to say as loud as she could. "I thought I told you not to go away."

"Didnt, didnt, dont care." He turned around to go.

"C'mon back here, you . . . Oh." It was a cry of anguish. Trying to rise, the waters of pain had closed over her head again, and a terrible something, hovering, had sunk its claws in her back.

"Oh, Momma," begged Ben, running back, "dont be sick."

"No, Ben, Momma's not sick." Faintly, "But can

you hold Bess and not—" it was better now—"drop her? Just put her down . . . in the basket."

Jimmie here too. But best dont get up. Sit here and let your strength gather up. (The main thing, not to wander off, not to let the fever bear her away.) "Ben, you and Jimmie want to help Momma make dinner now? You bring me the pan over there and a knife, first, Ben, and you and Jimmie take the potatoes out of the sack, and bring them to me till I tell you to stop. Thats right. Thats right."

Clutching a pail of lard, dreaming a sweet dream of twilight on the farm and darkening over a fragrant world, her face not shadowed by the buildings above, her nostrils not twitching with the stink in the air, her eyes not bewildered by the seething of people about her, dreaming the sweet dream unutterable, a hard body crashed into her and a voice thundered: "Whynt you look where you're going, stinking little bitch," and she was pushed in the stomach, punched down sprawling, a drunken breath in her nostrils. (Fear remembered such a breath. It seemed a mass pressed itself into her face, wet earth, or something she did not remember. In a minute she would be lifted and carried through a blackness of terror.) A wet was on her cheek, not blood, but a blob of spit she had fallen into. Feeling it, shuddering awoke her veins. She struggled to get up. Harsh, the pavement grated against her. It was real then. She moved her hand over the walk. Yes, it was real.

A streetcar plunged shrieking down the street, scraping over a naked nerve. Set, intent faces passed by. Terrible faces, masked in weariness and hate and lust, faces that knew her not, that saw her not.

The long street stretched infinite, a space that could never be finished traveling over, distorted buildings blocking each side. There was no sky, only a slab of one, draining color, vanishing into darkness.

She put her arm around the lamppost. Its solidity was fearful to her. As for the first time she saw the street and people, and it entered into her like death. A woman was sitting in the basement window in front of her, a great black around her eyes, teeth bared in a terrible smile. A man in a soldier's uniform, seeing her, staggered down the steps. The window blind went down. Real then, real.

The trembling, vibrating sound in the lamppost like a wild imprisoned heart. She sprang away. A shriek from behind. Slowly, slowly, with such laboriousness she turned her head. A bum was hurtling out of an eating joint, hitting the sidewalk, and the man coming after, roaring: "Dont ever try that again, you rat, or you wont have a face left or a belly." He gave him a kick, the body stopped sliding, he kicked him again and again. Faces distorted into laughter, and from the street around a fearful sound of hoarse joy went up into the sky.

Mazie ran. She fell. Here near the top of the street, she could see the shattered sun die in a sky of bruises over the decayed line of houses and buildings. Way down, like a hog, a great hulk of building wallowed. A-R-M-O-U-R-S gray letters shrieked. Armours, said Mazie over and over: Armoursarmoursarmours. Beautiful, suspended, the farm, softened by twilight floated an instant before her eyes. A new bulk, "C'mon, hand it over," shattered it forever. It passed her, and Mazie could see it was two people, and the man was twisting the woman's arm. Armoursar-mours. Every step was pain, every look was pain. The spit felt on her face again and the terrible face of the soldier as he ran down the stairs thickened her in horror that over it held the shadow of something mushy, opening in the middle, pressed hard against her cheeks.

Only a block to home. She began to run, running, trying to run away from the stink, away from the street, back, back, to something that had never been. Mr. Kryckszi held her arm. He was all stink, all stink, he helped kill cows, cows like Brindle, and Annamae said he washed blood off himself. "Come, little one," he said in his funny English (he was a furriner), "do not hasten so. Life will catch up with you soon enough. Let us walk together."

There was a man with him, something wrong with his shoulders, so he hunched over, misshapen. They walked along in silence. But their shoes made an awful sound. Long shadows lay over the street; the wind—flinging the arc lamp—twitched them as if they were alive. Mazie was glad for Kryckszi's hand, and she held it tight, tight.

There was no light in the house, as if nobody was home. But her father sat on the steps, weariness riding his shoulders like despair. Kryckszi called through the windy dark: "You not try to get on at the yards any more, Holbrook?"

"Naw."

"Today they hire."

"Damn shame you aint a nigger," the other man interrupted. "If you was you could get on in a minute."

"Today they hire," Kryckszi said again. "They think you are scissors bill maybe they take you too—that is why they taking blacks—they think they scab if there is strike—have to scab, how else they get job?"

Mazie went up to her father. He did not even look at her. Flat, inflectionless, he spoke: "Git in there and help your ma git dinner on the table. You might tell her Bess aint the only one in the house that wants to eat."

There was something she wanted to say, but she could not remember it. "Go on," her father harshly ordered, "get in there."

The light was not on. In the dirty light of dusk her mother sat motionless, her eyes large and feverish, the baby at her breast asleep. The lifeless hair hung in two black braids, framing her like a coffin, and above a spiral of fire foamed, reflected from the open damper. "Momma," said Mazie for no reason and went up and kissed her. The cheek was burning to her lips.

Armoursarmours, her lips said soundlessly, and she slipped to her knees and buried her face in her mother's lap.

Her mother did not move. Mazie clutched her closer. The limbs began to tremble. "Yes," her mother spoke, "I never was much of a hand for tonics, but when it gets you like this, Else . . ."

Mazie pushed herself away. The nightmare feeling came back. But the table felt solid against her back (the pavement grated her hand, harsh). In the darkness she brought out the dishes and put them on the table. She opened the oven and fed it wood.

Up above her mother's head the swirl of color foamed larger and larger. Suddenly it brought a nausea of fear (the jelly mass pushing against her face, the breath stinking, the shuddering laugh). She ran for the lamp and turned it up and stood there in the sudden light, trembling. There, it was gone now.

"What?" a hoarse, startled, fear-stricken sound from Anna. "What?" then realizing. "Oh . . . the light. Musta startled me. Where you been so long, Missy? Better get the table set and the bread cut. Poppa'll be home any minute now."

"Poppa *is* home," stubbornly, "he is. The table's set and Poppa *is* home."

"Yes. Poppa is home. I'll put Bess to bed and we'll eat." Falling on her knees in front of the oven as if she were praying, "I guess nothin burned. You can take the bean pot out and turn the potatoes into a dish. And call your dad. . . . Why, baby," sensing her vibrating body, "dont tremble so. You didnt think I was goin to hit you, did you? What made you think that? I wasnt goin to touch you."

And Will coming in—Will? This stranger with the dirt on his cheek like a bruise and the sullen gray eyes? "Oh boy, are you goin to get it for flunkin. Oh boy, you'll be so raw you wont be able to sit down for a millyun years," without zest. "Oh boy, wait till Ma tells Pa . . . Who you sayin shut up to," pushing her against the wall.

Perhaps it frightens you as you walk by, the travail

of the trees against the dark crouched house, the weak tipsy light in the window, the man sitting on the porch, menacing weariness riding his flesh like despair. And you hurry along, afraid of the black forsaken streets, the crooked streets, and look no more. But there are those who have looked too much through such windows, seeing the pain on everything, the darkening pain twisting and writhing over the faces, over and about the lamp like a wind to blow the flame out.

The pain, the darkening pain on everything. And it seemed to Mazie that her limbs were crooked in sleep and a nightmare sweat were on her, for only there had she seen such grotesqueness and crooked vision. And Anna struggling to keep her head clear and far above. They sat there at the meal in silence, only Jimmie chattering away, Will choking his food down as if he never expected to eat again. Once Jim pushed his plate away and said clearly, distinctly (against the darkening pain), "Any time I want sewage to eat I can get it on the job," but it seemed no one heard, and hastily he pulled the plate back and shoved the food down.

The stink of burning bacon in the air. Reaching for the frying pan, for the burning handle, with a bellow Jim dropped it, and with one kick sent it flying to the door, with another out into the yard, then turned (is the burn in his hand? it seems to be burning far inside, a scorch that will not let him be), facing Anna, facing Will, who laughs louder and louder, facing Mazie, who stares (useless to resist, to cry out, because it all is a voiceless dream to be endured), and Ben, who pales. "So ya think it's funny, do ya?" not knowing it is a chair he holds in his hand and is crashing toward Will, ducking under the table. She wrenches herself free from the battering pain. "You crazy?" slapping his face savagely. "You gone crazy? You coulda crippled that kid. Set down and finish eatin. It's all right, kids, everything's all right. If you hold out your hand—I'll smear oleo on so it wont blister. Jim? Set down, you hear! Please?" And he sinks down, the madness ebbing. Fearful what it leaves behind, the shame.

And perhaps it all would have been all right, that night anyhow, but after supper Ben (so wanting love) buried his face in his father's big shoulders and proffered his finger for sympathy. Shocked, righteous, Jim told Anna (not seeing how she clutched the sink rim between dishes), "Dont you pay no attention to these kids? You do something right away about Ben's finger. It's swoll up like a tire. What do you mean lettin it go like that? Better soak it, draw the splinter out."

She put on the water to heat, poured Purex into a

glass, but after she'd mixed the boiling water (pain's hand in hers, and all else fled) she forgot that hot was hot and plunged Ben's finger in. And still held it against Ben's scream and writhing till Jim knocked the glass out from under. "You crazy" was all he could say. "You crazy—this madhouse. I'm clearin out."

She managed through the nursing, she managed through the loving till Ben was comforted and through the sharp commands till the others quieted, and then she fainted. Now she should have called WillMazieBen, for they were fled into a terror which nothing could reach. When Mis' Kryckszi came, gleaning only from Ben's skirt tugging and incoherent mommamomma, something terrible had happened, Anna lay peacefully as if she were drowned, in a pool of water, and Will was pouring over more, and Mazie was shaking her and begging, "Wake up, wake up."

Vinegar on her nostrils and wrist-chafing, and Anna cleft back from the tranquility and the quietness. Lucky the pain that bore her into its own world, so she could not see her children's faces; lucky the numbness of sleep that came after.

Mis' Kryckszi said nothing, carrying sleeping Jimmie from the front-room floor onto his cot, mopping up the floor, bathing the children's hot faces, but after it all was done she took Ben on her lap and sang to them not lullabies but songs of her own country in which her fierce anger flashed.

Lurching down the streets, his face lifted to the stars, singing out his great crude singing, feeling the wind like a flame against him, singing against the night and the wind—so that the little Negro boy, Jeff, on the corner, waking smiled and hummed softly to himself, and heard a humming in his head like a thousand telegraph wires, a thousand messages of sound that would blend into music—singing his wide crude singing (I hear America singing, the varied carols I hear) so that the vast night throbbed about him, Jim came home.

Mazie, her head under the bedclothes, trying to stifle the fear and horror that retched within her, heard the singing; heard the door slammed shut, the thudding steps, the toilet flushed, the drunken talk her father had with himself that the rising wind enclosed, swept away.

No use to tell him, not a bit of use, stiffly repeated itself and marched round and round her head. No use, no use.

What was happening? It seemed the darkness bristled with blood, with horror. The shaking of the bed as if someone were sobbing in it, the wind burrowing through the leaves filling the night with a shaken sound. And the words, the words leaping.

"Dont, Jim, dont. It hurts too much. No, Jim, no."

"Cant screw my own wife. Expect me to go to a whore? Hold still."

The merciful blood pounding in Mazie's ears, battering away the sounds. Oh Will. Crawl up close, put your arms around.

As if in sleep (pretend sleep?): "Get away from me, ya damn girl." He hears too? The hoarse breathing—the moan? Will, Will.

Ben in his sleep, sucking in his breath sharp and wounded, Jimmie in his sleep, blowing out a soft bubble of sound.

"Will." All right, act like you're asleep. I'll be like asleep too. Lay down heart, go to sleep. Poppa, quit shakin me. No Poppa here—you shakin yourself. All right, I'll go.

Oh, Ma, Ma. The blood on the floor, the two lifeless braids of hair framing her face like a corpse, the wall like darkness behind. Be away, Mazie, be away. "Poppa, come in the kitchen, Momma went dead again, Poppa, come on." The drunken breath. (Fear remembered such a breath.) So cruel the way he pushes her away, uncomprehending. "Lemme sleep." "Oh, Poppa," crying now, "Momma's dead again. Please, Poppa, please come."

Running to the kitchen (so ugly, Momma, all the hair, the blood), running back with water, calling "Poppa" again till he somehow comprehends and comes. How clumsily he lifts Anna and carries her to the bed and brings the lamp. And remembering something of what Bess Ellis had done after the baby was born; with tremor hands he kneads the flesh above her womb till the blood stops pouring and stillness comes.

What does Bess have to wake up again and cry for? Poppa gone, and I dont know what to do. Dont cry, baby, dont cry. The lamp dancin, dancin. Whats the matter with you, lamp, what you see so funny you hafta dance about? Daddy singin when he comes home like the world is all strong and singin; and the wind—hear the wind in the trees, cryin for people that cant cry no more, cryin for people that want to cry and cant. Oh Momma, dont talk like that. ("So sweet Jim, a little oyster, a little pearl, a-growin . . . No, Bess . . . not bad, only I wish the bearin-down pains would start. Oh." Such a shriek. "Elma, be careful . . . All Elma's fingers gone, Ma, just a stump a bleedin left. I didnt know so much blood was in the world. And the damn forelady yelling, go on back to work . . .") No, Momma, no, Bess, dont cry. I'll hold ya and love ya, Bess, I'll tell ya a story, see, I'll diaper you and I'll tell you a story, onct upon a time the night was quiet, and the river, a cool river, Bess, was goin along, goin along, talkin to itself so happy, and it said maybe Bess would like to come and Mazie too and it dont go by no cities, Bess. Stop cryin, Bess, even baby's cryin (so ugly the naked thigh, the coarse hair, all the blood), please, somebody, oh Momma, stop talkin.

And the lamp in the wind from the open windows and the twitching shadows, the writhing of the trees, the waiting and words in fever and delirium.

He is back. He sits there immolated, a frieze, holding Anna's hand, and Mazie, so cold, clutches Bess, frightened of going back into the night of the bedroom *(get away from me, ya damn girl).* And they wait till the doctor comes.

"Miscarriage. You didn't know she was pregnant—again?" And Mazie runs; on the kitchen floor, the blood; runs, runs outside.

"How old's the baby?" (Damn fools, they ought to sterilize the whole lot of them after the second kid.)

"Four months, mm. You remember how long your wife's been feeling sick?" Of course not. These animals never notice but when they're hungry or want a drink or a woman.

"Hmmmm. Yes." She took the ergot down quietly, but moaned at the hypo. "So it was intercourse before as well as the fall?" Pigsty, the way these people live. "And she's been nursing all along? We'll have a look at the baby." Rickets, thrush, dehydrated; don't blame it trying to die. "Viosterol is what it needs—and a dextri-maltose formula.

"Your wife's a sick woman. Needs all the rest she can get, fresh fruits, vegetables, and liver. And medical attention. So does the baby. Unless you can afford a private doctor, see she gets to the clinic—Thursday, anyhow, for a curettage—a cleaning out. And the baby's to be weaned right away—I'm writing it all down here—wait a minute, there's a change. Karo syrup and canned milk for the formula; try to get some cod-liver oil—the baby really needs it—or at least all the sun it can stand with most of its skin exposed."

Running, so much ugliness, the coarse hair, the night bristling, the blood and the drunken breath and the blob of spit, something soft, mushy, pressed against her face, never the farm, dont cry, even baby's cryin, get away from me, ya damn girl, the faint gray vapor of river, run, run, but it scares you so, the shadows the lamp throws in the wind.

The cold, the world was so cold, she was wearing her slip and barefoot, and seeing the lamppost, she clutched it, trying to press the trembling vibrating thing inside her, back into where she had first heard it. And her eyes lifted in horror . . . lifted in horror that wavered and broke.

Globed and golden in the green light of early

dawn, the street lamps stretched far and far. Beside them crouched the solid rows of buildings, little weak lights in their windows, and down in the valley, solid and quiet, the great mass of packing house and stockyard. The viaduct was laced in fairy lines, and against the sky four great smoke stacks reared, so strong, so beautiful in the glowing light with the fading smoke from their throats, she could not help it, her arms reached out as if to touch and embrace them. A shudder went over her body, a shudder of quietness, and then tears, through which the beautiful street shimmered and was diamonded, the street lamps rayed and haloed.

He lifted her and carried her toward home, her father. "Were you scared, were you scared? Momma's sick, awful sick, Big-eyes. Awfully sick, and the doctor says she needs everything she cant get, tells me everything she needs, but not how to get it" (cry from a million swollen throats), "everything she needs but not how to get it. You're so cold, kiddie. Why do you want to go back to the top of the street for? Kiss Poppa and we'll go home and I'll make a fire and warm you, a nice fire, and you can fall asleep on Daddy's lap . . .

"And Bess's pretty sick, me not noticing, blind as a bat. And medicine, he says. Everything, but not how to get it. Stop shiverin, baby. We'll make a big fire and warm you up."

No, he could speak no more. Watching the flame catch and sputter and die and leap up again. Covering up Anna and the baby. No, he could speak no more. And as he sat there in the kitchen with Mazie against his heart, and dawn beat up like a drum, the things in his mind so vast and formless, so terrible and bitter, cannot be spoken, will never be spoken—till the day that hands will find a way to speak this; hands.

SIX

Two days she lay there quietly, in a merciful numbness that was half sleep, half coma, emerging out of it once to say: I'll be getting up now, Else, but making no move to, just lying there, tracing with her eyes the stains on the ceiling, sinking back into the twilight dimness again. Once Bess's fretful piping pierced into her dream, and with trembling fingers she pulled her breast out, trying to rise to the baby. Ben, playing by the bed, saw and ran for Else. She came in time to hold the struggling woman down, saying over and over, Lie still, honey, go on back to sleep, lie still, till Anna gave way and turned on her pillow and closed her eyes. After that, Bess was kept daytimes out in the yard, beyond hearing.

Wild with the exultance of the first vacation days, Mazie and Will were off somewhere. Quarrels flared in the kitchen when they came in on their forays for food.

"I declare, I dont know whats the matter with you," Else would say, "carryin on so with your ma sick in bed in the next room, needin every bit of rest she can get. Aint you shamed pickin on your sister, Will? And you, Mazie, you oughta be home lookin after Jimmie and Ben, you're the little mother now. Come back here, where you runnin off to again, *come back,"* the last yelled to figures vanishing with their loot of bread and shortening. And then the house would stand empty and quiet again, save for Else's padding about and the shuffle of Ben's pieces of cloth as he arranged and rearranged them in pattern play on the floor by Anna's bed.

And at five when Else left, the stillness deepened and darkened, the late-afternoon sunlight filling the rooms with a haze golden and tranquil, gilding the face of Will as he crept in to look at his mother, flickering over Mazie taking up Bess to see if she needed changing, haloing little Jimmie's head as he crept in, weary and dirty. And in the stillness, Will and Mazie would lift down the heavy pots and Mazie fill the plates and together bring them out on the back stoop, where they sat, Mazie and Will and Ben and Jimmie, watching the sun fire up the sky, burst and fade, while they ate their supper.

And at seven Mrs. Kryczski would come, quieting Bess till her bottle was ready, crooning softly while she fed her, washing up Ben and Jim for the night; and last with the last darkening—Jim—to eat his solitary meal in silence, to tend Ben's finger and round up the older children, and sit there in the soft dark, whittling, trying to figure a way out on the money, prodding himself to stay awake, fumbling through another feeding for Bess so he could go to bed at last; and the house stand there in its curious empty stillness till dawn and the same day begin again.

The third day, Jim's Sunday off, began a tossing. Whenever Jim came in she would be lying with her head turned toward the window, asleep, he would have thought, except for the staring eyes and the hand that quivered at her throat. Go back to sleep, he would say, best sleep again, but she never answered, answered or looked at him or questioned why it was that she was lying there, or what had happened. Once he heard her whimper: Oh my breasts, they sting so, they're so full, but hearing him approach, she turned her face sharply away, asking in a voice not hers: "Is Bess eating all right?" But before he could answer, her eyes were closed and she was lying in a semblance of sleep he did not disturb.

Helped up, supported by Else, still in the seeming quietude, she went to the clinic, clutching the doctor's slip of paper Jim had put in her purse to give.

Else, by her side, could not get a word out of her. But sitting in the clinic, waiting in the smell of corroding and the faces of pain, she lifted Bess out of Else's lap, shielded her close and rasped out fiercely: "We shouldn'ta brought baby here, we shouldn'ta brought her." And all the way home she hugged the squalling child to her—against the frowsy houses and streets of filth the streetcar jolted past.

Home, clutching the pillow to her inflamed breasts as if she still held Bess, she sank into exhausted sleep into which the distorted faces of pain marched round and round in endlessly dragging regiments of themselves.

In the kitchen Jim was saying to Mrs. Kryczski, stitching at a canvas: "One way to swell up the paycheck anyhow. No more soakin me for the waterproofs and boots every week. But do you think I'm gettin one cent back of all I been payin in? Not one cent. They said did I think they was in the equipment rentin business?" Then he saw Anna in the doorway.

"Anna! You aint supposed to be up. Was you needin somethin?"

". . . The house . . . It needs cleanin."

"And you're in fine shape to do it. Get back to bed."

In a mesmerized voice. "Dirt, the poster said. Dirt Breeds Disease."

"C'mon now. You ain't supposed to be up." At her side but hesitant to touch her. "C'mon. You been awful sick."

"Disease . . ." She recoiled from his touch, said, "Why, Mis' Kryczski" cordially, naturally, relapsed again into the automaton voice: "Disease . . . Your children . . . The posters . . ."

"Outa her mind," he explained to Mrs. Kryczski. "I said c'mon. You lost a lot of blood."

"Germs spread . . . The house . . . The posters . . ."

"I said come on. Easy now."

"At the clinic, they scare . . . And all the poor sick people settin . . ."

"Dont worry your head. Cover up good now."

"So many ways of bein sick . . ." Wringing her hands, "We shouldnta brought baby there! We shouldnta brought her!"

"I said: dont worry your head. Sleep now, you hear?"

She looked at him sharply, bitterly; mutely turned her head away.

"You want anything, just holler. Sleep. Try." He did not leave her till it seemed she slept.

Back in the kitchen, miserable, he watched the needle glitter in and out of the stiff poncho. He yearned to ask Mrs. Kryckszi about Anna but could form neither words nor thoughts.

"It fit now, I think," she said at last, folding up the canvas and handing it to him. "Try on." Then, with a nod toward the bedroom: "She begin to get better now. She begin to feel things again. You be careful with her now."

She is stirring in the night, in the great black and blue bruise of night, waking and creeping out of bed, groping along the wall, past Bess's basket to the open window where she kneels down and lays her hot forehead on the cool windowsill. Her fists are clenched, and behind her eyes the unshed tears stand in knots of pain. Money, she is thinking, sicknesses. Streets. Dirt. The children, my children. What is happening to them, what will be? My babies, my children. Outside no answer. Only the smell of earth, expectant of rain, the mysterious blue light that is on everything, the trees moving palsied against the sky, and strident, strained, breaking, the sound of a freight starting up. My children, the children.

Heavy to take up again, being poor and a mother.

She lay there a long while after she awoke, trying to make out what time it could be. If there had been rain, it was over now. Dust motes were gleaming in the shaft of light that slanted in through the window. The house seemed empty. "Else, Ben," she called softly. No one answered. Slowly she pulled herself up and edging along the wall, pushed open the door into the front room. It lay in shadow, and out of an old enlarged photo, a very young Anna with a baby Will in her arms smiled down upon her. Her face contorted. Quickly she closed the door.

She had not wanted to go through the bathroom but there was no other way now. High up in a dirty brown corner, a cobweb spangled. Unsteadily she picked up the plunger and swept it down. One fly, still alive, moved an iridescent wing and buzzed. The kitchen stood blank and empty in glaring afternoon sun. It was a long while before she could make out the potato peels turning black in the sink, the dirty dishes, the souring bottle of milk about which flies droned. Flies, the poster said, Spread Germs. Germs Breed Disease. Cleaving to the table for support, disregarding the flame of agony in her engorged breasts, she swatted feverishly. The flies lifted and evaded. Disease . . . Your children . . . Protect . . . The soap was gone, the water spluttered malevolently at her. She rinsed the dishes, scooped the garbage up into a pot, and went out into the yard. It was deserted but for Bess sleeping in her basket, covered with an old curtain for netting.

Someone had forgotten to put the cover on the garbage pail, and below the solid droning mass of flies gray things slithered and struggled. The stench steamed up and hit her in the nostrils. Gasping for breath, she threw the garbage in, pot and all, and jammed the cover on, then stumbled over to the stoop and sat down. The vomit kept rising and rising, but none came. Didnt know I was so delicate, she whispered. Whew. Whew. And jest garbage smell mixed in with a little packin'house.

All the time it kept nagging, the pot still there, the pot she could not replace. Scarcely realizing that she was doing so, she pulled herself erect by the screen-door handle and, half falling, got back to the pail. The flies sprang to her face as before and the stench retched up, but she stood there stubbornly, with head averted and nostrils stiffened, clutching for the slippery surface of the pot.

This time she barely managed to reach the stoop. Her limbs were trembling, her bones seemed water, her heavy breasts burned, burned. All she could do was sit there, her head against the screen door, her eyes closed, waiting for the trembling and faintness to cease. Slowly, slowly, her fingers loosened, and the pot slipped from her hand to the ground.

It was very quiet. The sun lay warm on her shoulders, and far off through the muted voices of the street a peddler was calling, his voice reminding of an old song. Softly, she began to sing. Now a train puffed by, and the long wail dissolved in distance. The wind just lifted against her cheek. Ben came from nowhere and nuzzled against her. Momma, he said. She held him warm into her singing.

"Momma." She opened her eyes and saw his eyelashes fluttering over the patches of rash on his cheek; the dirty sore on his unbandaged finger; the stubble ground, the harsh curtain that made the netting on Bess's basket, and beyond, far beyond, white foam of bridal wreath on the sea blue sky.

White bridal wreath. When she was a girl . . . Oh when she was a girl . . . The life she had dreamed and the life that had come to be . . . The scabby sore on Ben's finger scratched against her arm, and the vagrant wind retched the garbage smell. She closed her eyes again, but this time when she opened them, her fists were clenched, and Ben she had held so close to her was pushed away. Whether or not she said it aloud, a cry throbbed in the air: *No. No.*

She had wrapped a rag around the broom and swept down the walls, and swept the floors, and scrubbed the toilet bowl, and put the diapers to soak, and was filling a tub with water preparatory to scrubbing the floor, when Mrs. Kryckszi came in with Mazie and Jimmie.

"You been cleanin, Anna?" Mrs. Kryckszi asked,

incredulous. "You go to bed." Then, seeing the stubborn face flaring white behind its fury, in harder tones: "What the matter? You want to stay sick? Cleanin goin to wait for you, it not going noplace. You go lay down."

"I *been* layin down. As for you, Missy," seeing Mazie, "where have *you* been? Git in here. There's work for you to do."

"Annamae's waitin." Defiantly: "I gotta play." Then with sullen averted face: "Poppa says you'll get . . . that way again if you don't stay in bed."

"Poppa says! Annamae's got a long wait, sister. Git in now and git started. You hear me? Now if you'll excuse us, Mis' Kryckszi, and I want to thank you for all you been doin, I'll get back to my work."

But the tub would not lift, though she heaved and heaved, and when it finally did, it was because of Mis' Kryckszi's hands at the side of hers.

"You see you not so strong yet, Anna," her neighbor said softly. "You lay down again, you find how you feel."

"Mazie and me got this floor and wash to do."

"All right, I start the floor for you and tell Annamae to call Willie. You make him and Mazie do heavy work. Now time to feed baby; she beginning to fuss. Sit down, I fix bottle and you give her. Then you clean."

But Bess seemed so heavy in her arms, and the feel of her made her breasts sting, sting. (The frenzy was ebbing, ebbing.) And her head was faint, and the hand that held the bottle beginning to tremor.

"I need some air, I guess . . . Feed baby, Will." Remembering to say like they told her in the clinic, "Hold the bottle up so's there's always milk in the neck or it gives baby colic bubbles. That's right."

But it was not outside she went, but into the children's bedroom. Mazie was there, changing her clothes. "Just look at this mess," her mother said. "I was holdin off cleanin it till you came. Dont you know if you cant keep your own things out of a mess, you'll never keep your life out of one? You clean up Jimmie and put clean rompers on him and then get back here. Go on." Mazie just looked at her with her great eyes. "Go on. I'll find him clean things . . . Well?"

"Nothing." She was gone. Well? Well? re-echoed in the air. Well? Such a mess, said Anna. I never asked her: Is that Ben or is it Will is wettin the bed again? Yes, get things back to regular and start takin in laundering.

Mazie's dress was crumpled in the corner. Anna picked it up and stuffed it into the dirty-clothes bag. Then she smoothed out Will's jacket that had fallen on the floor and hung it on a nail. It was worn thin on the unpatched elbow and the buttons were off again. "Mend jacket," she said to herself and passed her hand caressingly over the few other garments that dangled there.

"Mend tomorrow, dont forget now," starting over to the chest of drawers with its crust of stuff to be mended. But she stumbled over the children's shoes, left in a tangle in the middle of the floor. Crouching down beside them, she whispered, "Ben. Needs soles, well, maybe a cardboard inside will do. Will's: holes, holes. He always wears them down on the side like that." Smiling. "I would know Will's shoes outa anywhere in the world. But no soles or new heels or stitchin, even if there was money, going to fix these. Too far gone." She stood up abruptly and the shoes dropped with a clatter. *Too far gone.*

Jimmie did not seem to have a single whole sock in the drawer. Ben's hand-me-downs, no wonder; and only one pair of rompers. She began going through the sock pile for a pair that could be most easily mended. Bess's baby socks, Jimmie's, Ben's, Will's, Mazie's, they passed through her hands, and with each one inspected, her head ballooned lighter and lighter. "Barefoot season, I forgot. Socks can just wait."

The rompers. There was a tear in them, too, right across the seat. She had not noticed. "Mend," she said loudly and stopped there and stood in the middle of the bedroom, holding the rompers.

The strength and fury she had felt an hour ago were all gone now, and she stood there swaying in the middle of the bedroom with its swayback bed and the mattress on the floor with its acrid urine smell, and the trickle of light coming in through the thin high window—and she thought that she would suffocate of the tears strangling in her throat that would not ascend to her dry eyes.

It was not that the clothes were beyond or almost beyond mending and that there were none others and no money to buy more; not that four children slept here in this closet bedroom, three on a mattress on the floor; not that in the corners dust curled in feathers, dust that was Dirt That Breeds Disease You Make Your Children Sick; not that one of her children had stood a few minutes ago (ah, which hurt more, the earlier averted face or this?) looking at her with pain and fear and pity in her eyes.

It was not any and it was all of these things that brought her now to swaying in the middle of the floor, twisting and twisting the rompers in soundless anguish. It was that she felt so worn, so helpless; that it loomed gigantic beyond her, impossible ever to achieve, beyond any effort or doing of hers: that task of making a better life for her children to which her being was bound.

Oh, what was the matter with Momma when Poppa said she had to stay in bed, acting and looking so funny, and that ol' Jimmie having to say (cheerfully), "Madie hurt me, Momma, she hurt me in the baf."

"Tattleliar! I didnt hurt him, he's slippery, Momma. Poppa said you got to stay in bed, got to. Momma, can I have JimJim's rompers?" Coming closer, but wanting to run. "Oh Momma, what's the matter?"

"Nothing, Mazie." Kneeling down on the floor alongside to reassure her; smiling a tormented smile. "I've got to . . ." her throat constricting, "do something."

"What, Momma?"

"I dont know," twisting and twisting the rompers, "I . . . dont . . . know."

When Jim came home she was sitting on the back stoop, directing Will to hoe up the stubbly ground.

"Hey, what are you doin up?" he asked gently, coming up to her. "Forget them take-it-easy, stay-in-bed orders?"

She clenched her teeth and fists and huddled farther back into the twilight shadow.

"You feelin that much better, honey? Then let's go in," hesitantly touching her arm, "and you can set up and tell us how to fix supper so it tastes better . . . C'mon, Anna, the kids'll be waitin."

"Maybe they'll be waiting for supper someday and there'll be none to give. You ever think of that? We're puttin in a garden like you promised and never done, that's what I'm doin up. And I'm startin launderin work again if I can get it . . . Go on in yourself."

"Don't get me mad now, Anna." Beseechingly: "Anna, you been so sick. You know you shouldn't be up."

"And shouldn't I?" pulling herself erect, "and shouldn't I? Let the dirt stay, let the kids run wild and not a decent stitch on 'em, let there be no makin do on the money, I shouldn't be up. Don't touch me! And who's to cook and clean and look after the kids if I'm in bed? Who? The servants? The fine servants we keep on the big wages you're makin?"

"Stop it, Anna, stop it. You're makin yourself sick . . . Oh Anna, honey, dont."

"Dont sweet Anna me. Who's to do it if I'm not up? Answer. *Who?* Who's to . . . look out for . . ." Gasping hoarsely. "Who's to care about 'em if we dont? Who?"

Fighting off his attempt to enfold her, to quiet; his broken: "Anna, dont, please dont."

"*Who?* Answer me. Oh Jim." Giving in, collapsing into his reaching embrace. "The children." Over and over, broken, "The children. What's going to happen with them? How we going to look out for them in this damn world? Oh Jim, the children. Seems like we cant do nothing for them."

Oh Will, hoe in hand chopping viciously the air, running down the block away from his father's stricken face, his mother's convulsed words; oh Ben, clutching first his mother's legs and then his father's legs, trying vainly to still them, curling up now close to Mazie, heaving his asthma breaths; oh Mazie, stopping up her ears so as not to hear, yelling out a song to Jimmie and to clinging Ben so they will not hear —it is all right, it is over now.

It is over. There is reconciliation in the house where your mother lies weeping; not hearing *I'll spade up your garden and tomorrow, payday, we'll get seeds. We'll work things out, you'll see, dont take on so.* Hearing only the attempt at comfort. And now your father lies beside her, stroking and kissing her hair, silently making old vows again, vows that life will never let him keep.

SEVEN

Always while Jim worked—*down underground the dripping water diamonds his hair, trickles down his neck, makes a gay sound on his canvas poncho: no mackinaw and boots, but it means a buck more a week dont it, it means stuff for the baby, dont it?*—heavy and sore in his breast would lie the torment of the questions Anna had asked, and such a sad baffled flame of tenderness flicker above.

Work through, with a heart that ran far ahead of his feet, he would hurry, hurry home, a nameless fear on him, and his hello be almost a sob of joy as he flung open the door and saw that all seemed as it had been.

A gaunt Anna who could not understand this body of hers that tired so quickly and quivered like a naked nerve; this stranger self. One minute her old competence and strength; the next: addled, nervous, brutal, lost. Not managing, having to give under, to let things go. Any effort wearing her out; everything an effort.

Seeing her so, with the look of exhaustion on him, Jim would ask: "Is there anything I can do to help?"

Sometimes she did not answer at all, sometimes say: "You look right tired. Go ahead and set." But once she blazed: "If you cant see what *needs* doin, just dont trouble to ask, you hear, just dont trouble to ask." And another time, in the most chilling of voices: "Why dont you go set like you always do; done." Adding: "'Cept that one wintertime on the farm I was carryin Bess. And that didn't last long."

Now, in her slow mending, she began to ask him to chase the kids down, or to chide, or distract them. "They're runnin me crazy. I declare I dont know what's got into 'em, seems like the devil hisself."

Ben whining or wanting to be babied, afraid to let his mother out of sight, always underfoot with questions. Go out, she would force him, go out and play. Go on. But he huddled close to the kitchen door, his only playmate Jeff and sometimes Jimmie. Jimmie at an age where he was always having to be watched, likely to get into any manner of mischief. Will defiant; Mazie contrary—too exhausting to force their help (and the feeling: they're kids, let them play and feel good while they can).

Troubled, she saw them running, shrilling out

laughter, playing their frantic games wildly, disappearing to come back hours later; flushed, hostile, excited, secretive. A lust for sensation, for the new was on them, a lust for the streets, for looking into store windows; for moving over the dump, the stretches of weed and alley. They clamored for pennies she did not have for licorice, shoestrings, blackjacks, jawbreakers, Juicy Fruit gum—litany of wonders endless at the corner store; on Saturdays, for nickels to go to the movie show. No, she had to say over and over, we dont have it, no—but sometimes if she had it set aside for another purpose, she gave them what they asked.

She began to neglect the already neglected house to go out and weed and work in the garden. The washtubs and wringer sat out in the yard now, beside Bess's basket. She would have liked to range the stove alongside too, even cook over an open fire. Inside suffocated her (outside too when there was packing-house stench) but a need was in her to be out under a boundless sky, in unconfined air, not between walls, under the roof of a house.

The cumulating vision of overwhelming, hostile forces surrounding which had come to Anna that week of the clinic, never left her. But she was not strong enough to contend with it now. Only sporadically could she try to order, do something about their lives. And a separation, a distance—something broken and new and tremulous—had been born in her, lying by herself those long unaccustomed hours free of task.

One dusktime, when Jim got home, she and Mazie were still wringing and hanging clothes. "Get in and see to supper, Mazie, while I finish up out here," Anna said, seeing him. Cheerfully: "I got my first launderin job today."

"I see that." Sinking down heavily onto the stoop as the light drained. Bitterly: "You aint well enough to keep us 'uns clean, or get your other work done like you used to, let alone do for other folks."

"What's well enough or other work got to do with —have to?" she asked, and went on hanging up what was left in the basket; took down blouses, shirts, dresses from another line.

"I said you aint well enough for what you got to do for us 'uns now," he repeated. "We never lived in such a mess."

"It's a dollar every time." Dreamily: "That looks nice across the river, dont it? The mist comin up like way away soft laundry blowin on a line. White."

"You fixin to get sick on me again? . . . Ferget that launderin, Anna. We'll get by. We ain't starved yet."

She looked at him with an expression that, in the

uncertain light, he thought might be anger or bitterness, but her voice came humble: "I'm helpin, Jim." She came over, her arms heaped; sagged beside him. "Feels good to sit, dont it? You look mighty weary." Carefully she smoothed and rolled the garments, arranged them in the basket.

"That's pretty how you do that," said Ben, rising from the shadows. "Are you making it a sunflower? Can I try tree and branches?"

"You touch that wash with your dirty hands, and you'll never touch another thing. How long since you washed up?"

"Bess was laughin and laughin today, Poppa," Ben reported. "Lookin cross-eyed at her hands, so *we* got laughin. When I say, 'Bessie, Bess, Bonny Bess,' she turns and looks for me, dont she, Momma? Do you have a penny for Will? Your hair's still wet, Poppa."

"How's yourself, old tricks?" drawing Ben close. "I got a penny for *you*, all right."

"Jim, a man came by today and for a quarter a week if we start now, a kid gets three hundred dollars when he's sixteen. For a sure edjication."

Jim jabbed at Ben's arm, shadow-punched at his face. "Dont you know how to duck yet?"

Holding his father's hand: "Guess what, Poppa? We blewed soap bubbles today with green onions. Momma showed us how. All shiny. Mine was the biggest, then Mazie's. Where do bubbles go with your breath when they bust, Poppa? Where's gone? What does nothing look like, Poppa?"

"I want it for Will, then he can help the others. Finish high school sure. A good job, Jim."

"You think I dont want it? Even to be sneakin timekeepers and office people that treats you like dirt? But you dont know nothing about it. Miss one week pay'n' and you lose it all."

"I asked him. He said the plan allows. He said . . ."

"It's a buck a month. A buck a month. Ferget it, Anna. Ferget that launderin, too."

Voices of children around the corner lamppost. *"Alley, alley 'ats in free"* came shrill and sweet. Mist tendrils curled closer over the river bluff, heavier fog behind already blotting out the farthest line of clothes.

"Momma, Poppa, why do peoples talk and dogs cant, but last night Shep came back and talked words, but I couldn't any more, just in 'woof, woof.' What did I say in woof woof that made Shep mad? He bit me, Poppa, bites all over. Do you see bites on my neck, Poppa?"

"That was a dream, Benjy." Anna said. "Dont you remember Momma came in? I held you and showed you there wasn't no bites and sang you back to sleep?"

"But I *saw* Shep. Poppa, Momma, for why do mens give dogs nails in meat, laugh and the dog is bleedin, shakin? A big boy, Antsy down the block, if he sees me he says, 'Hey, shit, come here,' bad words like that. 'I'm going to have me your birdie.' I dont like that big boy, Poppa. For why is he that way? For why is . . . ?"

"You need a muzzle, kid," said Jim, spreading his hand gently over Ben's face to hold it still. "For why'n and for why, huh. How'm *I* supposed to know? Yeah, get eddicated, you get a little respect; know better than to ask fool questions that get lies or nothin for answers . . . Like always happened." Rising: "What's it all for, anyhow? . . . A buck a month. Ferget it, Anna." Sharply: "You goin to leave this kid out all night in this damp?" taking up Bess and her basket. "Let's eat. Now."

In the square of lemon light from the kitchen window, Anna picked up the laundry basket. The moistness and dimness were all around now. Mazie, slipping out to fetch Anna and Ben, stood transfixed in wonder and fear. Her mother was walking dreamlike round and round the yard, laundry basket on her head, disappearing in and out of the clutching mists; emerging, disappearing; an enchanted Ben following her. Her voice came dreamy and disembodied.

"Yes that's how they carries clothes there, Benjy, basket on their heads, hands on their hips like I cant do. Walking like queens, hoop earrings big as bracelets in their ears. Parrot birds that talk, and flowers bigger than washtubs, all colors and smells."

"Where is it, Momma, where is that place?"

"I dont rightly know. I aint ever been, Benjy. I only saw it in a picture book." She put the basket down, bent to him fiercely: "You read books, you'll know all that. That's what books is: places your body aint ever been, cant ever get to go. Inside people's heads you wouldn't ever know. There's a place here, a library where I've been fixin for us to go, where Else gets her reading. They let you borrow books, picture ones if you cant read yet."

"I want to go see the earrings, talk to the parrot birds that talk. Will the streetcar take us?"

"It's a far place, Benjy. You have to be rich to go, take trains and boats. Or when you grow up you can go, like your Uncle Ralphie, the one you never did see, the one that ships. Boys get to do that," her voice was wistful, "not girls. Ralph's been everyplace. Wonders of the world."

She picked up the basket, set it back on her head, moved back into the dimness. "Wonders of the world." Her voice was dreamy again. "Everything's gone. You cant see 'ary a light. Yes one, so weak and pitiful. You cant see where is our house, where does the bluff end. A body could end right in the river, not knowin; drift; not fall. As if the world ending right here, we all closed in; just me and the basket and you, Benjy. No, we're not going to fall over the edge, silly . . . Dont it breathe good . . . fresh? Let's not go in. I declare I feel like a gypsy, wanderin and campin, doing everything outdoors, rolling up in the night too, sleepin out, never goin in."

"Let's go in, Momma," pulling at her in sudden fright. "We got to go in. Its suppertime. Don't talk goofy, Momma. Mommas always goes in."

Rent week—little in the house to eat besides potatoes and flour—Anna left the baby with Mrs. Kryckszi and wandered the streets with Mazie and Ben and Jimmie, looking for empty lots where dandelions grew. *(The Wheel of Nutrition: One Serving: Green Leafy Vegetable Daily.)* "I hanker for greens," she told them. "We been without a far time now."

She showed Mazie how to look for plants with fresh yellow flowers or just-opening buds, how to select only young, juicy leaves, telling them by their glossy green and tender feel. But the lots were mostly weed, the dandelion heads seedy white, their leaves woody. Though Ben helped too, their paper bags held scarcely a layer.

They wandered on and on. It was a gentle morning; light and warmth flowed in ripples. "I dont remember since when I been out just walkin like this," Anna said. Her lips were parted, her face uplifted to the blue seamless air. Mazie felt the strangeness rising in her mother, not like the sickness strange, something else.

One lot Anna gathered a handful of the seedy puffs and, without warning, in one great breath, filled the air with white fluff. "You blew a hundred wishes," crowed Ben, impressed. "You blew a hundred wishes. What did you wished, Momma?"

"You know if I tell, it cant come true." She bent to her paper bag, blew it full, with a sudden sharp blow popped it; laughed. Jimmie, startled, began to cry. "I'm sorry, Jimmie, I didnt think. We got more paper bags than greens," she explained. "That was to even it up. I guess. You want Momma to carry you awhile? No, dont you dare bust that bag, Ben. Give it here. We're goin to need it, you'll see. Three bags full."

Another lot, she fell to braiding the stems, while Mazie stood disdainful. "We'll make a chain a block long. Clover's better, but where's any clover?" Ben and even Jimmie ran to get chain makings, carefully running their fingers down the flower stems to the bottom like she showed them to get the longest stems. "Is it a block long yet? Is it a block long yet?" But, abruptly, she stopped, threw the unfinished chain at Mazie, who threw it back, wrapped Jimmie round and round with it.

They were in a different kind of street now. Lawns, flower beds and borders, children on bikes. Jimmie kept having to be chased after by Mazie and dragged away from other children or things that fascinated him. "This would be a good neighborhood to ask for launderin work," Anna said. A vague shame, a weedy sense of not belonging, of something being wrong about them, stirred uneasy through Mazie. "Momma, I have to pee," Ben said. Anna walked on carelessly, dreamily, ignoring Ben, who gripped tight her skirt with his free hand, his other clutching himself, ignoring Jimmie, who was now petulantly complaining that he was tired tired tired and Mazie was bad and he didn't want to walk any more.

Two girls walking toward them stared and snickered, turned their heads to look after them. "Ben, get your hand away from yourself," Mazie hissed, and savagely to Jimmie, "If you'll just shut up I'll carry you." For some reason it came out in a hushed whisper.

"Piggyback?"

"If you'll just shut up. *Ma, this isn't the way.*"

"Why dont I have a tricycle?" Ben asked. "Will I get one ever?" and he slowed to stare longingly after an empty one on a lawn, still clinging to Anna's skirt so that, walking on obliviously, her thigh came bared. A woman putting on white gloves came out of a house and smiled at the four of them. Quickly Mazie moved between her and Anna, as if to protect her mother against something.

"Just you keep your face to yourself, lady," Mazie muttered furiously in her head. "Old crummy Nicey Nice. Ben!" she ordered in her mother's voice, "dont drag on Momma, walk straight. *Ma, this isn't the way.*"

"That's a fine horse you've got there," the lady said to Jimmie. "Pretty big load, though, aren't you? Are you lost?" she asked Anna.

"Giddyap, Horsie," yelled Jimmie. Mazie galloped ahead, round the corner, out of sight. She shifted Jimmie into her arms, glared at him, said in the earlier savage whisper: "You're a big boy. Big boys walk."

"No, JimJim tired," patting her face lovingly, luxuriously abandoning his body against her. "Swing and sway some more, Madie, swing and sway. Good horsie."

At the end of a cobbly street that had no houses, only high wire fences, they came to a stretch along the river bluff, yellow and green and white with flowers and grass and dandelion glory. A strange heavy fragrance drenched the air. "There's millions here," exulted Ben after he and Jimmie had relieved themselves. Mazie was already gathering at the river bluff edge, as far away from them as she could get. "This was somebody's good yard," Anna said, bending and inspecting. She put Ben to picking nasturtium leaves —"only the little ones, Ben, no bigger'n a penny"— then set to work herself in a swift, practiced rhythm, bending, loosening, gathering. Bees drowsed there; they had to be careful. White trumpet-shaped flowers were scattered in the green.

"Catalpa," Anna said suddenly, scooping up a handful of the blooms, "that best smell." She stood up, pointing to the great tree above. "Mazie, come over. See you suck honey syrup out of the little end. Taste, Benjy. Taste, Mazie. Look inside. There's black and gold and blue markings, beautiful. And the tiny glass threads standing up as if they was flowers themselves. Yes, Benjy, they feel velvet inside. Rub it on your cheek."

She bent to gather again, went on talking. "One year when I was high as you, Mazie, we lived a place where was a tree like that. The leaves aren't rightly out yet, but when they are, they get the biggest leaves ever you saw, heart-shaped, and then that tree gets cigars. We'll come back fall time, you'll see."

Her rhythm had slowed. In between gathering she sucked the blooms, and Mazie saw that each time before, she drew her breath in deep to smell, deep as if she had to blow off dandelion heads or pop a paper bag. A remote, shining look was on her face, as if she had forgotten them, as if she had become someone else, was not their mother any more. "Ma, come back," Mazie felt like yelling, in rancor, in fear; jumping up, snapping her fingers into that dreaming face to bring attention, consciousness of them back, make it the old known face again. *Snap my fingers.* But her fingers were moving deftly, happily; cool slim mindless tracing down the notched leaves to the roots, the responsive tug, the tiny spurt of juice spilling its spicy smell.

A peace and content began to drowse through her. Bees sounden, she whispered. Sweet smellin. Lady bugs. Butterflies like your dizzy. Unbidden: If you dont look no place, just down, if you dont listen, pretend the trucks and freight noise is 'quipment, it's the farm. Stupid, she chastised herself grievingly, stupid. Who cares about the farm? Who wants to pick stupid weeds? *Snap my fingers in her face.* Loudly: "Ma, dont we have enough yet? *Ma!*"

"Three bags full," said Ben, inspecting. "I can 'cite that," Jimmie said. "Baa, baa, black ship, three bags full. Watch how I jump," jumping over and over from a wide step of what had been a house, burned down how long ago.

"Dont we have enough yet?" Mazie repeated.

"You know greens boil down to just nothin," her mother answered. "Yes, I guess that's enough. We'll set awhile. My head is balloony, balloony. Balloony." She staggered, put her arms around Mazie, sang:

"O Shenandoah, I love thy daughter,
I'll bring her safe through stormy water"

smiled so radiantly, Mazie's heart leapt. Arm and arm, they sat down under the catalpa. That look was on her mother's face again, her eyes so shining and remote. She began stroking Mazie's hair in a kind of languor, a swoon. Gently and absently she stroked.

"Around the springs of gray my wild root weaves,
Traveler repose and dream among my leaves"

her mother sang. A fragile old remembered comfort streamed from the stroking fingers into Mazie, gathered to some shy bliss that shone despairingly over suppurating hurt and want and fear and shamings—the harm of years. River wind shimmered and burnished the bright grasses, her mother's hand stroked, stroked. Young catalpa leaves overhead quivered and glistened. Bright reflected light flowed over, 'lumined their faces. A bee rested on Mazie's leg—

magic!—flew away, and a butterfly wavered near, settled, folded its wings, flew again.

"I saw a ship a sailing "

her mother sang.

"A sailing on the sea "

Mazie felt the strange happiness in her mother's body, happiness that had nought to do with them, with her; happiness and farness and selfness.

"I saw a ship a sailing,
And on that ship was me."

The fingers stroked, spun a web, cocooned Mazie into happiness and intactness and selfness. Soft wove the bliss round hurt and fear and want and shame—the old worn fragile bliss, a new frail selfness bliss, healing, transforming. Up from the grasses, from the earth, from the broad tree trunk at their back, latent life streamed and seeded. The air and self shone boundless. Absently, her mother stroked; stroked unfolding, wingedness, boundlessness.

"I'm hungry," Ben said.

"Watch me jump," Jimmie called imperiously. "Momma, Mazie, watch. You're not watching!"

The wind shifted, blew packing house. A tremble of complicity ran through Mazie's body; with both hands she tethered her mother's hand, to keep it, stroking, stroking. Too late. Something whirred, severed, sank. *Between a breath, between a heartbeat, the weight settled, the bounds reclaimed.*

"I'm watching," Anna called. The mother look was back on her face, the mother alertness, attunement, in her bounded body.

"I didn't think to bring a bite for us, Ben. Wherever is my head these late days? Balloony. Catalpa." She laughed. "Holy Meroly," using an expression they had never heard before, "there's nary a shadow. Noontime. And I promised Mis' Kryckszi we'd be back."

Never again, but once, did Mazie see that look—the other look—on her mother's face.

EIGHT

Easeful and huge, the hot July goes through the barefoot weather, the idleness weather. The cramp the clamp of school released enough, the children of packingtown turn from June wildnesses to deeper, more ancient play.

On the dump, territory is established, shifted, abandoned, fought over, combined. Peerers, combers and excavators go treasure hunting. (They compete with old men and women looking for covering, furnishings, sustenance—anything usable, transformable, barterable, salable.) Children—already stratified as dummies in school, condemned as unfit for the worlds of learning, art, imagination, invention—plan, measure, figure, design, invent, construct, costume themselves, stage dramas; endlessly—between tasks, errands, smaller children to be looked after, jobs, dailinesses—live in passionate absorbed activity, in rapt make-believe.

On the inexhaustible dump strange structures rise: lookout towers, sets, ships, tents, forts, lean-tos, clubhouses, cities and stores and train tracks, cabooses, pretend palaces—singularly fitted with once furnishings, never furnishings, or nothing at all.

On the streets, strange vehicles move: a barrel in which one rolls; cars of apple boxes on wobbling wheels, steered by broomsticks; axles triumphantly balanced on between bare tires; Pet milk cans strung, rafted together, used as rollers on which one bellyflops and with swimming motions pushes along; and favorite mover of all—ridden dreamily or madly to who knows what fabled destination by the commander at its steering wheel—sunken rusted Ford front end that never moves at all.

In the long dusk evenings, the hiding games, the whirling games begin. Round the lampposts, thick like the winged things above, children circle and flitter. On the dump, watch fires burn. And on porches and stoops, secrets are whispered, songs sung, stories told, make-believe selves expanded, and dreams float in the dim enchanted light like iridescent bubbles in the sifting sad sweet peace.

July—surcease, release, month.

He stands in the doorway and, smiling faintly, says, "I'm on, Anna. Feeder and utility man; when the run starts—splitter. Forty-five cents an hour."

"Pritcher up maybe," corrects Kryckszi behind him. "Long way to splitter."

"No wood-burnin stove for you *this* summer. We're gettin the gas connected. No launderin someone else's duds, either. Didn't I tell you we'd manage? Good times comin, honey, good times."

"Drunk with the job," says Kryckszi, smiling with his eyes. "Few pennies more pay an hour. You see how little it takes to make a man happy."

The fireworks go up from their yard too, that Fourth of July. Mid-afternoon Jim and Will tramp into the kitchen, their arms bulging triumphantly with packages.

"Bangers and fireworks, rockets and bangers," exults Will.

"Jim, you didn't!" says Anna, paling. "And when Alec said he'd bring some. . . . That's like burning money, money we aint got. The rent money?"

"Now, honey, I'm earnin, aint I? Independence Day, isn't it, honey? Grand and glorious. We got to celebrate, dont we?"

"What independence *we* got to celebrate?"

"Independent of property, aint we? Got me a woman too independent to kiss her old man, aint I?"

"Will says I'm not getting any firecrackers," burst in Mazie, Annamae trailing behind. "I want my firecrackers. Where's my bangers?"

"Girls don't get firecrackers, do they, Poppa," said

Will smugly, rummaging through the packages. "They burn theyselves. Girls and little kids get sparklers."

"Sparklers comin out of your ears tonight, Bigeyes," says Jim expansively, grabbing her as she starts by. "Roman candles, fountains, pinwheels. We're celebratin tonight. Give Poppa a kiss."

"But thats tonight. Poppa, they been scarin the little kids all morning. We got to get them back, dont we, Annamae? Antsie popped a cracker right on Ben's ear, and Annamae's leg is burned. *Let me go, Poppa.* Will's taking them all, dont you take them all, Poppa, he took them all."

"He's just havin fun. Celebration. Hold still, squirmy. You're not going noplace. Not till daddy gets his kiss. Holiday day."

"Will!"

"If I hear another scream like that outen you, Mazie," said Anna, "you'll have something to scream about. Isn't there enough noise round here already? Get Ben out from under that table and make yourself useful. I could stand a little helpin. Else and Alec are due any minute. There ought to be a law against them bangers anyway."

A strange sweat of tension is on Anna, her lips moving, trying to remind herself of what is next to do for the holiday dinner. She does not notice Ben huddling back under the kitchen table, holding his ears, rocking and rocking. Up on the roof, Mazie and Annamae throw ineffectual lit matches down when the boys hove into sight, Jimmie shadowing Will and Smoky and Antsie in delighted terror. Out in the back yard, where Jim and Kryckszi and Alec pitch horseshoes, Else soothes Bess, who starts at every bang.

Now at last, in the warm darkness, plumes of light arise. Children run with sparklers, Jimmie darting after, cupping his hands to catch the spray. Alex and Jim and Will in glory select, set up, light fireworks. Puffs and bursts and sprays.

"Look, we makin stars," Ben greets each fountain, skyrocket, roman candle, "we makin stars. What's next, Poppa?" Jeff makes a chant of it, moving his body in time. "Look, look! We makin stars. Dance till you out, stars, dance till you out."

"Fallin and dancing," Ben chants back, "Fallin and dancing. Poppa, what's next? Dance till you out." Annamae and Jimmie chorus along: "Stars. Stars. Fallin and dancin. Dance till you out. You out. You out. You out."

All over the sky, echoings, flowerings. Sizzles. Stems of flame, tendrils coiling, climbing. Anna—gratefully off her feet for the first time in that long day—sitting and watching, forgets the grudging rankle at the needed money thrown away, folds herself into the beauty and singing and everyone's happiness. But her heart yearns over Mazie, sullenly apart on the roof, refusing to touch the fireworks, to be part of the celebration.

(Only it excites Mazie so, the stems and jettings of light, the momentary lit faces, the chanting. And now the great pure ball of light rising over the dark shoulders of bluff.)

"Stars. Stars. Dance till you out."

Kryckszi takes his violin and in the moon dappled darkness makes a tune of it. Else and Jim, Alex and Mis' Kryckszi dance.

"Fallin and dancin. Dance till you out." The headlight of a train weaves and flickers through the dark bluffs across the silvered river, is lost in distance with its high forlorn flickering whistle.

"Stars. Stars."

Oh it's us again, thinks Mazie, it's us. Then in clenching fear: Now something bad's going to have to happen. Again.

But it is easier for a while. The old Anna back in command, reclaimed, wholly given over; the house once more orderly. Secretly the first insurance payments are made; secretly Jim looks for a secondhand sewing machine for Anna. The garden spews forth puny and pale, gains confidence, begins to garnish the table. Expeditions are for berry picking now as well as for greens, one lot where the brambles grow.

One afternoon Anna cleans up the kids and brings them to her Temple of Learning. A squat dirty converted storefront (good enough for packingtown, they said) shelved with opiates and trash and marvels (from which most of the children are already turned in outraged self-respect, for is it not through books, the printed word, or so it seemed, that they had been judged poor learners, dumb dumb dumb? Told: what is in us has nothing to do with you).

But marvels to Anna *(places your body aint ever been, cant ever get to go; inside people's heads; things you wouldn't never know);* keys, too, in that door to a better life on which opportunity would knock some day. She took out a library card for each. Only Ben pored over his (picture) books. Mazie's and Will's lay untouched. For how onceuponatime and theylivedveryhappyeverafter fairy tales which the librarian had selected for Mazie? How adventure and magic books she had picked for Will, when there was the adventure and fairy ground of dump and city; the conjurer magic of a shining screen in darkness Saturdays.

(*Already the conjurer is working spells on Anna's children. Subtly into waking and dreaming, into imagination and everyday doings and play, shaping, altering them. Even outwardly: Will's eyes are narrowed now, his mouth drawn up at the corner, his walk—when he remembers—loose; for the rest of his life he will grin crooked:* Bill Hart.)

Sometimes Will or Mazie bring home finds from the dump. A rusted waffle iron, clothespins, blackened forks and spoons, coils from a crystal radio set, a solderable pot. Once a fought-over chair—rung and leg gone. On the high window sill in the kitchen, along with a fragment of prism, is an indigo-blue ink bottle soaked and scrubbed a dozen times to get the glass clear—beautiful to Anna for the light shining through. A saucer—its cracks adding a ghost mysteriousness to its landscape—snowy mountain, fir trees, clouds, tiny burdened Japanese figures toiling across a red curved bridge—is kept in the center of the kitchen table for all to marvel at.

Stealthily Mazie and Will stalk the ice trucks and wagons for falling slivers to trickle down their throats; for handfuls that can be scooped up while the iceman delivers his ice. Lithe and graceful, they learn to hitch onto the moving trucks, shove over chips, sometimes a whole ice block onto waiting hands. (But Mazie is not long among them. Once a chant starts up:

Girl go to London, go to France
Evrybody sees your pants.
Girl shimmy shimmy shimmyhigh
Evrybody sees your pie.

and after that shame and self consciousness make her body awkward. Twice she misses, almost goes under the wheels. No more for her that lithe joy, that sense of power.)

On the dump there is Ginella's tent, Ginella's mansion, Ginella's roadhouse, Ginella's pagan island, Ginella's palace, whatever Ginella wills it to be that day. Flattened tin cans, the labels torn off to show the flashing silver, are strung between beads and buttons to make the shimmering, showy entrance curtains. Here sometimes, in humble capacity, Mazie is admitted—*if* she brings something for the gunny sack. The gunny sack into which the curtains and tent themselves go when Ginella must go and which is stuffed with "properties": blond wood-shaving curls, moldering hats, raggy teddies, torn lace curtains (for trains and wedding dresses), fringes, tassels, stubs of lipstick, wrecks of high-heeled shoes and boots, lavish jewelry Tiffany would never recognize: greening curtain rings, feathers, fish lures, dress beadings, glass bits, shiny coils and machinery parts. Anything that dangles, jangles, bangles, spangles.

Twelve-year-old Ginella's text: the movies, selected. Ones Mazie, the late-come country novice, has never seen. *Sheik of Araby. Broken Blossoms. Slave of Love. She Stopped at Nothing. The Fast Life. The Easiest Way.*

Luxuriously on her rug, pretend silk slinking and slithering on her body, turbanned, puffing her long pretend cigarette: Say vamp me, vamp me. I'm Nazimova. Take me to the roadhouse, I want to make whoopee. Hotcha. Never never never. O my gigolo, my gigolo. A moment of ecstasy, a lifetime of regret.

And once alone, smelling sweet of Blue Waltz and moist flesh, her arms tight around Mazie, passionately: Whisper to me: Jeannine my queen of lilac time. Jeannine, I dream of lilac time. Whisper it. Kiss me. Forever, forever never to part, my pagan love.

On the stoop, evenings Ben imparts his terrible texts to Jimmie:

Skinny, skinny, run for your life,
Here comes fatty with a butcher knife.

Ladybug, ladybug, fly away home,
Your house is on fire, your children all gone.

You're it and got a fit,
Never, never get over it.

Never know how to get over it.

Plaintively, as if he understands its meaning:

Ol' clothes to sell, ol' clothes to sell,
If I had as much money as I could tell
I never would cry ol' clothes to sell.

And desolately:

Mother, Mother, I am sick.
Call the doctor quick, quick, quick.
Doctor, Doctor, will I die?
Yes. You will. And so shall I.

Mazie, slackly sitting, suddenly *listens*, shudders and gathers them both to her, saying firmly: We're going to sing "Hoopde Dooden Do Barney Google with the Googlygoogly Eyes, I'm Dreamin Now of Hally;" Pop, tell Ben and Jimmie when you were little. But the day at Cudahy's has thieved Pop's text—his mouth open, he sleeps the sleep of exhaustion. And when Anna comes out, her apron front still wet from doing dishes, it is already too late for texts—the children's eyes droop.

In the dim enchanted light, in the sifting sad sweet peace of summer evening.

And now the dog days are here, the white fierce heat throbbing, when breathing is the drawing in of a scorching flame and the pavement on the bare feet of the children is a sear; when the very young and the very old sicken and die, and the stench cooking down into the pavements and the oven houses throbs like a great wave of vomit on the air.

There in the packing houses the men and women somehow toil through. Standing there, the one motion all day, their clothes salty with sweat, or walking in and out of the cooler till the cold is a fever and the heat a chill, and the stink bellying up from the blood house and casings forces the beginning of a vomit, even on those who boasted they hadn't a smeller any more.

Oh yes, the heavy air clamps down like a coffin lid over the throbbing streets, on the thin cries of babies and the querulous voices of the old, and a sound of breathing hoarse and strained, of breathing feeble and labored goes up; and from beneath the glisten of sweat on a thousand brows, a mocking bitterness in old old words: Is it hot enough for you? In a dozen dialects, is it hot enough, hot enough, hot enough for you?

Nights, sleepless nights. Sad rustle of trees in the unmoving trees and the creak of bedsprings as the sleepless ones toss.

"How much longer can it last, Jim?" asks Anna. "Six days not down to a hundred *once*. The kids cant stand it."

"Just the kids? . . . Whew, if I could get just one cool breath. You'd think we'd get a little wind out the window."

"Momma, why cant I sleep?"

Will is sleeping. Will is lying out on his mattress in the yard, under the bleared stars and the unmoving trees, dreaming of movies, of the shining screen in the darkness and the gallop, gallop of cowboy horses. Waking to a whining mosquito sting, he stares into the sky and tries to breathe and feels as if a lasso is looped tight around his chest a hundred times. Only the trees so high and the cool far stars make him remember his horde of findings he will sell to Curly tomorrow who will sell it to the junkman, and the worms he and Smoky will dig by the river to sell; and his hand curves to the imaginary ball he will buy with his money, and he smiles, tosses restlessly awhile and sleeps.

"Momma, why cant I sleep?"

In the little room the heat is entombed deathly still and unmoving, sweat almost breaks out on the walls, and the slit of window is like a hungry mouth that stifled, opens to suck in the air. Jimmie is moaning, scratching his mosquito bites, doing a dance on the mattress with his body, waking and sleeping again, waking and sleeping; and Mazie wakes from terrible lands of dream to feel the heavy heat still there.

Outside it is better, dragging her quilt out besides Will, but the dark mysterious night scares her and the mosquitos bite worse and worse and lying there awake she is thinking of the smoke and fires curling up around the lady in that movie tied there to the stake, she can hear in her ears the crackling, hot hot, and she is thinking of Erina, Erina of the twisted jerking body and the fits who dragged away Mazie's findings from the dump and moaned Suffer little children the Bible says Children suffer suffer. Her body is becoming Erina's. She is Erina, stump arm ending with a little knob, the spasm walk, the drool. Slapping at a mosquito, missing, then it splotching squishy under her hand, a lot of blood, she could see it in the vague light, blood; dragging her quilt back in again.

"Momma, why cant I sleep?"

Ben is sick, Ben cant sleep, Ben is saying, Momma, why cant I sleep, Momma, only he can't remember whether he is saying it or not and the air chokes thick in his nostrils, sits humping up and down on his chest. Fast fast fast goes his heart, where is it going, it will run out of him, run away. There is a big fire somewhere, that is what is making it hot, somebody making a fire or it was a fire and he is in the stove, black all around like something burned.

"Momma, why cant I sleep?"

Down the street they are all lying together, Jeff and Buford and B.G. and Ellis on one great tick, and they sleep with delicate sharp breaths; and farther down old lady Dykstra is breathing hoarse and strained, her mouth open, her heart flaying and jumping, and faint and far are babies crying, well babies, sick babies.

The ice is melting in the iceboxes faster and faster, the melting that is the women's despair. Cattle trucks are rattling on the spoke roads to the slaughter houses, thick-packed lambs and calves and hogs snuffling and swaying and stamping, cattle lowing plaintively. Far off the freight trains make a sleepy sound; then faster louder faster.

Gurgle gurgle, the river quiet and secret, the weak soiled vapor shawl, a few men standing and fishing. And for miles and miles the corn in white gold stillness stiff and parched in black baked earth in the black baked night.

"Momma, why cant I sleep?"

Thoughts of death, in this still heat Mazie waking again and thinking thoughts of death, doctor doctor will I die yes you *will* and so shall I, the sad rustle of the leaves in the trees with drier sound of coming fall.

"Momma." Crying. And momma is coming and wrings out a towel; Ben, Benjy; will she have to take him to the clinic? Thank God Bessie is a baby and sleeps, Bessie is all right. There, Ben, momma has helped the rash, if I hold and fan you and we set outside, will it help you catch your breath?

"Momma, I wish it was mornin."

The fire is coming into the sky, the still still fire, and suddenly it has blazed up, the fetid sun, the red red sun. And the dew which is the tears the sweat of the night is vanished.

Jim and Anna are up, then Jimmie and Bess. Ben is sleeping now and Mazie is sleeping, no need to wake them, and Will is up, secretly shuffling things under his bed.

"Will you get it for me today, my 'monica?" begs Jimmie as he trundles down the street with his father. "Tonight will you bring it, tonight?"

"You going to have a harp, make music for us all maybe?" asks Mr. Kryckszi, joining Jim. "Stay out of the sun today, little Jim." Looking at its festering orange straight ahead. "Not good. A hundred and ten in kill room, more in casings today, you see. Oven. Maybe already. Afraid for Marsalek, for Mary. I talk to Misho, to Huff, to Slim. We have to slow it, I tell them, get break too. Misho talk for us to Wild Man Ed." Shaking his head: "No good."

"That prick Ed," says Jim. "How else'd he make straw boss?"

"Wild Man Ed say Bull Young tell him is no sweat. We bunch lazies."

"Lazies! That pusher. Beedo* hisself, in person." They are over the viaduct now.

"You see, a hundred and ten—maybe hotter."

"Be hell," says Jim, looking down at the plant. "Be hell."

Hell.

Choreographed by Beedo, the B system, speed-up stopwatch, convey. Music by rasp crash screech knock steamhiss thud machinedrum. Abandon self, all ye who enter here. Become component part, geared, meshed, timed, controlled.

Hell. Half-seen figures through hissing cloud vapor, the live steam from great scalding vats. Hogs dangling, dancing along the convey, 300, 350 an hour; Mary running running along the rickety platform to keep up, stamping, stamping the hides. To the shuddering drum of the skull crush machine, in the spectral vapor clouds, everyone the same motion all the hours through: Kryckszi lifting his cleaver, the one powerful stroke; long continuous arm swirl of the rippers, gut pullers; Marsalek pulling leaf lard, already faint in the sweated heat, breathing with open mouth.

*Beedo: A speed-up system of the 1920's.

Breathing with open mouth, the young girls and women in casings, where men will not work. Year-round breathing with open mouth, learning to pant shallow to endure the excrement reek of offal, the smothering stench from the blood house below. Windowless: bleared dank light. Clawing dinning jutting gnashing noises, so overweening that only at scream pitch can the human voice be heard. Heat of hell year round, for low on their heads from the lowering ceiling, the plants' steam machinery. Incessant slobber down of its oil and scalding water onto their rubber caps, into their rubber galoshes. Oh feet always doubly in water—inside boots, outside boots. Running water overflow from casings wash. Spurting steam geysers. Slippery uncertain footing on the slimy platform. Treacherous sudden torrents swirling (the strong hose trying to wash down the blood, the oil, the offal, the slime). And over and over, the one constant motion—ruffle fat pullers, pluck separators, bladder, kidney, bung, small and middle gut cutters, cleaners, trimmers, slimers, flooders, inflators—*meshed, geared.*

Geared, meshed: the kill room: knockers, shacklers, pritcher-uppers, stickers, headers, rippers, leg breakers, breast and aitch sawyers, caul pullers, fell cutters, rumpers, splitters, vat dippers, skinners, gutters, pluckers.

Ice hell. Coolers; freezers. Pork trim: bone chill

damp even in sweaters and overshoes; hands always in icy water, slippery knives, the beedo piece work speed—safety signs a mockery.

—All through the jumble of buildings old and buildings new; of pens, walkways, slippery stairs, overhead chutes, conveys, steam pipes; of death, dismemberment and vanishing entire for harmless creatures meek and mild, frisky, wild—Hell.

Today—the fifth day of hell-heat added—104° outside, 112° in casings. Seven o'clock.

Ooh it's so hot, Mazie waking up feeling charred and smoldering, and going into the kitchen, her legs scabby and blood-splotched with open mosquito sores scratched too much, and Bess cooing at her, Ben up and in a chair, his eyes looking too big and too sick.

Not hungry. Her head hurting and hurting. Having to help pit and peel the canning apples and peaches.

"Havent I done enough, Ma? Cant I go out and play? It's too hot in here."

"If you get back 'fore noon," Anna says, thinking: Better now before the sun's really up. "This cannin's got to get done today."

But it was even hotter outside. The sun burned on her back, but her head didnt hurt so much, only the light seemed fire.

Annamae ran out when she saw her. "What we gonna do today?" Mazie asked listlessly.

"The findins! There was new things dumped yestidday. Maybe we'll pass a ice truck or wagon."

No trucks; the streets glittered empty like in a dream. And there was nothing really new on the dump. It smelled sewer, smelled garbage, smelled crap 'cept right at the river-bluff edge. Grubbing, Mazie found a torn magazine with funny words—a furrin language, painting pictures, different colors and patterns. "Wallpaper for our dollhouse, it'll make wallpaper." But out of one of the pages, a little girl's eyes stared at her, big eyes, black, almost holes, from her face lots and lots of lines going all kinds of ways, so much lines you couldn't look at them all but you had to try while your head got dizzier and dizzier. And scareder. It was something like you, like something . . .

Mazie tore the little girl and the scary lines into teeny kite bits but didn't have any breath to blow them; lay down on her belly looking down over the bluff and fluttered them away instead. No cool wind came up. The tracks and trains flashed hot; the river flashed too though a dirty haze lay on it as if it were too lazy to move.

"My momma don't let me go down by the river," she told Annamae. "Will your momma? She says bad people's there that hurts girls." She grubbed with one hand for what turned out to be an old doorknob to throw down to where she couldn't go. It landed right on the open gondola of a sluggish freight train. All the way to California, she thought.

There was Will, going down the road with Smoky. "Where you going?" she hailed, scrambling after though getting up so fast made her head pound and be dizzier.

"No place."

"Then I'm going too."

"Oh no you aint. We dont want no tattletale girls."

"I am too goin."

"Oh no you aint. Run, Smoke, run," scooping a handful of pebbles and dirt to fling at her.

She chased them a block, but then fell and skinned her knee and they were out of sight. Where the pebbles hit, it stung and prickled like the mosquito bites. She scratched them all open again, sucked at one on her arm, for she was so thirsty, so thirsty.

The sun seemed to have a big tongue that was licking her back and her head hurted worse and worse and the lines going in all directions round and round. Everything looked glassy and wavy in the heat.

Ginella was in her tent. Mazie stood outside the glittering curtains. Katie and Char were fanning her;

Ginella was Queen Tut or Nazimova, lying on her rug, pretend smoking. "Googly," she said languidly, seeing Mazie. "Gwan and melt. We dont want any Miss Uglys around . . . Unless you got ice." Yesterday she had passed their house when Mazie was holding Ben. "Fishface," she had said coolly, cruelly to Ben, "Whyn't you close your mouth, Fishface?"

Miss Ugly!

Annamae was still scrabbling in the pile for stuff. Ellie was there, eating a huge peach. "My grandma gave it so I wouldnt make noise. She's sick, maybe she'll die." Proffering a bite.

"My little brother's real sick too," said Mazie, wishing she could add self-importantly: he may get dead too. (I dont mean it, Benjy.) "Let's go look for a ice truck."

"No, it's lucky here," objected Annamae. Her face was flushed. "See?" Holding up a tiny round mirror.

"That's mine," lied Mazie, thinking of Ginella. "I put it there and now you took it. Give it back."

"It's not either yours. I took it out of a compact, didnt I, Ellie? It was all moldy and greeny, ughy ughy, and I had to clean it, didn't I?"

"Give it to me," swiping for Annamae's hand. "All right, dont. I dont want to play anyway."

Erina was coming. Wavering in the heat waves, dragging along, jerking funny; skinny with her bones sticking out like great knobs and the tiny arm stub that hung down and ended in a knob. Coming closer, coming right to them. Flickering out her faded tongue and the spit slobbering down. "Pennies," she said. "Little girls, do you have any pennies? For ice cream. It hurts. Pennies."

"I dont have none," faltered Mazie, backing toward Ellie and Annamae, who shook their heads mutely to signify that they didn't have any either, unable to look away from the running sores on her legs and her pitiful arm.

"What you think you're staring at?" advancing ferociously as they kept backing. "Pfeh," she spit.

Ellie surrendered what was left of the peach to Erina. There was no place but the river-cliff edge behind.

"I'll go home and ask a penny," said Annamae.

"Me too," said Ellie.

"Payday my papa buys us Eskimo pies," said Mazie faintly. "I'll give you mine, Erina."

"Now," said Erina. "I'm burnin. God is looking at you. That is his burning eye up there."

She will push me over the cliff, thought Mazie. I have to run quick like Annamae, like Ellie. But it was a bad dream where you couldn't move. The lines going dizzy.

"The devil is roasting us today; the devil is frying

us, like in hell. For our sins." Erina's breath was in Mazie's face; Mazie saw how the pus oozed from her eyes, stuck on her eyelashes; weed stickers—maybe lice—in her hair. *Go away, Erina; it's so hot and you are wavy like everything else. Last night I was your body, I was you. Go away.* "Maybe my momma will give a penny."

"It hurts inside," Erina said, crying and slobbering. "Hold me so it dont hurt." She put her one arm around Mazie, who shuddered violently. "I'm ugly," Erina sobbed. "God made me like this." Crouching down at Mazie's feet.

(Miss Ugly) Mazie sank resistless down on the cracked earth beside her; its heat came up in waves too, like the glassy wave she could see in the air. "Shall I go look for a ice truck and steal you some ice, Erina?"

"Shall we pray?" asked Erina. "I pray but God dont make me better and Pa and Tammysue socks me 'cause it means I was sinnin too bad to get forgiven. Do you sin, little girl?"

"I'm big," said Mazie. "I'm going to be nine, almost as old as you, Erina," and began to grub in the hot stiff soil at the half-decayed rags in it.

"Watch for my bird," said Erina, "Watch for its little bones. It was deaded and I put it in the ground there and blessed it, but when I got back it was on top half et with worms and crawly things and stinky and I had to cover it back. Bones now. When you die your soul goes to hell or heaven but your body gets et and stinks." Swallowing thirstily and slobbering.

"That's a song," said Mazie, a sick-happy feeling to be with Erina, to listen to Erina, rising in her. "The worms go in and the worms go out and they eat up all of your chin and mouth."

"Watch for the little ants," said Erina. "Dont hurt their houses. They have to hurry and work so hard and carry heavy things and I sees them carry each other sometime."

Erina looked really sick; her eyes were like that little girl's in the painting-picture, black holes. What Mazie had thought was dirt on her cheek was bad bruises. Was she going to get a fit? "Erina," she said gently, "Ginella has lemon cream soda in her tent. I'll ask will she give some."

"Ginella!" said Erina. She smoothed and gentled her little stub arm and it tried to rise up as if to gentle her back. "When she sees me she says here comes freak show, stink show, Miss Sewer from shantylice-town." Her face quivered. "Suffer little children the Bible says."

"Rest, Erina. I'll get you some ice quick, or ice cream or another peach or lemon cream."

Ginella and Katie and Char were gone; the tent

and the clinky glittery curtains and the dress-up bag, gone. Erina was gone too, weaving toward the viaduct under where shantytown was. Mazie wanted to fall and push herself along on her belly after her. Flat like a caterpillar, not wavy like a worm or jumpy like a grasshopper. Crawl flat on her belly. Not have to walk. Her head throbbed biggern the whole world and like all her blood was percolating, boiling up into it, piercing up into it. She walked slow as she could, but fell. It was the sole of her shoe come loose and flapping made her stumble. *I told you I didnt want to have to wear shoes today, Ma,* taking them off. But the ground frizzled and she put her shoes back on.

She wanted to cry but she did not know what about. She wanted to hear Erina talk—but not have to look at her. She felt sick and mean and screamy, and sad and mad and bad. Her throat swallowed and swallowed with nothing in it to swallow, so dry, sticking together, hurting. Last night she dreamed she swung the Big Dipper round and round and drank the night with the ice stars in it. She could have told Erina that, Erina would have listened. Stars are fire, not ice—stars are suns, she reminded herself scornfully. Old Man Caldwell. Tied to the stake, flames curling round her feet and up toward her belly, everybody laughing, Miss Ugly. Yes, she was. She sat down on the curb and looked at her burning feet. She wanted to go to the catalpa place and sit under that tree; or down to the river where she had never been and Will got to go; it would be cool with ice like night in God's Dipper.

A lady in a car stopping at the corner held a handkerchief to her nose, real delicate. Mazie picked up a corncob from the gutter and threw it hard at the car.

Right by the house, in the shade, Jimmie and Jeff and Ben were playing. Jeff held a strange stringed instrument his brothers had made for him, a cigarbox body with a long slab of wood jutting out; strung on it a dozen kinds of strings and wires. With it he made a jangling and sang in an unearthly voice. Jimmie sang too, rocking a half of a Quaker Oats round cereal box cut the long way; in it was a stick wrapped round with rags in the semblance of a doll. Ben, for all the heat swathed in a blanket, sat gravely watching and rocking himself in time.

"Fishface," she heard herself saying in Ginella's inflections, "why don't you close your mouth, Fishface? My cradle," swooping down, "my own cradle I made."

"It's to rock baby," pleaded Jimmy. "We're rocking baby to sleep."

". . . playing . . . house," Ben explained, breathing loud between each word.

"You never asked could you have it. And there goes your baby," swinging it out far as she could into the yard.

"You . . . hurted . . . her," Ben said accusingly, his eyes, bigger than ever with their illness, filling with tears.

But she was in the kitchen, tears and meanness fighting in her, banging the door after her right into wailing Jimmie's face.

"Now what's the matter?" Anna asked, her head bobbing over the steaming kettles. "Oh its you. Now what trouble you been up to?"

"She tooked it away, she threw it away," wailed Jimmie louder and louder.

"Hush, you, hush. Don't you know Bess is finally sleepin and you mustnt make noise?" Opening the door to let him in. "*What* did she take away?"

"*My* cradle," defended Mazie, "the one I made."

"She took our baby too. She tooked it and threw it far away."

"By . . . the cliff." Ben toiled in. Reproachfully: "You're bad, Sistie."

"Did you go hunt for it, Ben?" Anna splashed her spoon in the kettle she was stirring, "when you knew you arent to move at all, and I just let you out if you'd set still?" To Mazie: "Miserable child! Look what you've done. He wasnt to move."

"I didnt know he would go lookin for it," Mazie said. "And it was my cradle, wasnt it, my very own I made?"

"Wash your hands—it wouldnt hurt your face none either—and get a apron on," Anna commanded, wringing a cloth for Ben's head, taking him on her lap and fanning him. "You knowed we have to get this cannin done, and I'm gettin no place fast between watchin Jimmie and tendin Ben and baby. We got to get lunch too."

"Why is it always me that has to help? How come Will gets to play?"

"Will's a boy."

"Why couldn't *I* get borned a boy?"

"You get to play enough," Anna said shortly. *(Just seems the devil's got into her.)* "Don't you move now," settling Ben on the couch; shaving the paraffin into a pan to melt; and going back to stirring the bubbling mass of jelly. If this heat keeps up, I'll just melt, she thought, drop and melt all over. They wont know which is paraffin and which is me. . . . If only Benjy dont get so bad I have to fetch him to the clinic.

Mazie was yanking her skirt, her face white, in her hand an empty bottle. "Somebody spillded it," she shrieked, "somebody spillded my perfume I made. My very own perfume."

"Shhhhh. It was me. How should I a-known it was supposed to be perfume you wanted to save? It was dirty-smelly stuff stuck in the cupboard where it didn't belong."

"It was perfume. I made it out of flower leaves. You put them in a bottle and cork it and leave it. It was for Ginella and I never get a nickel to buy her Blue Waltz and now I haven't any perfume."

"Well there's more makings where that came from. And next time dont keep it where it dont belong."

Shrieking again: "I don't *have* no place. If I'd kept it in the bedroom Jimmie woulda been into it, or maybe Will." Violently: *"Why dont I have no place?"*

"Hush, I said. That's enough outen you. You wake baby and see what you'll get. Start to stirrin now . . . Maybe I can make a place for you on a shelf somewhere soon as I get some time. Dont see why not."

But Mazie was gone.

"Come back," yelled Anna out the screen door, "come back right this minute or you'll get a whoppin." Now who's wakin baby? she asked herself. Uncomfortably: She oughtn't to be out in that sun without a hat . . . And she *doesn't* have a place.

"Ben!" She hears the loud rattling of his breath, turns. He points at the opening door. Mazie crawls in, puts her arms around her mother's legs and howls.

"What's the matter, sweetheart?" Helping her upright.

"I dont know. My head, Momma. I dont know."

Falling. Fainting.

"Sistie! Maaaaaaa!" begs Ben, baaing like a sheep. He runs with his fan and water.

Overhead the inflamed sun glares in an inflamed sky. Twelve o'clock noon. 106°.

"Slow it," Kryckszi sends the message to Misho, to Huff, to Ella. "We got to slow it."

The fifteen-minute lunch break goes like nothing. Those who (against the rules) had crowded into the cooler or the chill damp of pork trim to eat their lunch find their names up on the bulletin board with fines posted against them. *(Who ratted?)* Those who had sluiced themselves down with the hoses in the yards for momentary relief (also against the rules) suffer other punishment. Their clothes will not dry; cling; tighten; become portable sweat baths as they work. Aitch-sawyer Crowley, the venerable, faints. Prostration. By word or gesture or look of the eye, the message goes out in each department: spell Marsalek; spell Lena; spell Laurett; spell Salvatore: however possible, spell, protect those known near their limit of endurance.

In casings it is 110°. A steam kettle, thinks Ella, who has a need to put things into words, a steam kettle, and in a litany: *steamed, boiled, broiled, fried, cooked; steamed, boiled, broiled, fried, cooked.* Tony, Smoky's older brother, lugging his hand truck from fire to chill to fire (casings to cooler to casings), fans the cooler door open for the women as long as he dares. Each time (the hands never ceasing their motions) even those too far away for relief turn their heads in unison toward the second's different air, flare their nostrils, gulp with open mouths. The stench is vomit-making as never before. The fat and plucks, the bladders and kidneys and bungs and guts, gone soft and spongy in the heat, perversely resist being trimmed, separated, deslimed; demand closer concentration than ever, extra speed. A hysterical, helpless laughter starts up. Indeed they are in hell; indeed they are the damned. *Steamed boiled broiled fried cooked. Geared, meshed.*

In the hog room, 108°. Kerchiefs, bound around foreheads to keep the salt sweat from running down into eyes and blinding, become saturated; each works in a rain of stinging sweat. Almost the steam from the vats seems cloud-cool, pure, by contrast. Marsalek falls. A heart attack. (Is carried away, docked, charged for the company ambulance.) Other hearts pound near to bursting. Relentless, the convey paces on.

Slow it, we got to slow it.

Is it a dream, is it delirium? Arms lifted to their motion *(geared, meshed)* have nothing to move for. The hog has been split, has been stamped—yet still dangles; the leaf lard, the guts, have been pulled, yet no new carcass is instantly in place to be worked on. Has life suspended, are they dead? The skull-crush machine still stomping down, sprays out its bone bits in answer. "Fined, fined for carelessness," yells Bull Young. "What jammed the convey?"—turning instinctively toward Kryckszi.

At that moment in casings, as if to demonstrate that there is a mightier heat, a higher superior heat, the main steam pipe breaks open, and hissing live steam in a magnificent plume, in a great boiling roll, takes over. Peg and Andra and Philomena and Cleola directly underneath fall and writhe in their crinkling skins, their sudden juices. Lena, pregnant, faints. Laurett, trying to run, slips on the slimy platform. Others tangle over her, try to rise, to help each other up. Ella, already at the work of calming, of rescue, thinks through her own pain: steamed boiled broiled cooked *scalded,* I forgot *scalded.*

When the door to the hog room, always kept closed against the casings stench, the casings heat, is flung open, the steam boils in so triumphantly, weds with the hog-vat vapors to create such vast clouds, such condensation, the running scalded figures of horror (human? women?) seem disembodied flickering shadows gesturing mutely back to whence they have fled. "Stay where you are," yells Bull. "Carelessness. Nobody's gettin away with nothin. You'll be docked for every second you aint workin. And fined for carelessness."

Already some are in casings, helping. Carrying Lena out of the scalding fog, Jim sees plastered onto her swollen belly the SAFETY sign torn from the wall by the first steam gust.

Three o'clock. 107°.

Old Mrs. Dykstra cries out once into the heavy air, gasps and breathes no more. Overhead, blown egg-shell doves she has made old-country style with wings and tail of white pleated paper, bob three times—and still.

Will and Smoky turn from the river for the steep climb toward home, their dream of pockets of jingle money from juicy fishing worms, defeated by the impermeable armor of the sun-hardened shore. Outside the Palace, they stare at movie stills. "A crook picture," Will says longingly. But nowhere, nowhere that nickel.

On her way home—where she will be beaten for having been gone, for having been born, for having been born crippled and epileptic, for being one more mouth to feed and because out of sheer nervousness and exhaustion there is a need for someone to beat —Erina no longer feels heat or thirst or the gnawing in her belly. On a tin-can roof of one of the shacks someone has set a pan of shining water where cat and dog cannot reach it, and a bird is bathing itself, fluttering its wings in delight. In its tiny spray that the sun rainbows, Erina stands motionless, feeling in herself the shining, the fluttering happiness. The thigh-high weeds are powdered white with dust. When the bird is done, she climbs to drink of the water in which feathers float, takes and holds one to dry in the furnace air, turns and smoothes it over and over against her bruised cheek. The vast winds of fit may blow any minute; the shameful trembling and great darkness begin, but she walks now in the fluttering shining and the peace.

In her secret place, the shelter under the porch stoop, Ginella hides and is ill. "Too hot," she whispers, "too hot," turning her head from side to side as if that would fan coolness. How rosy she is from the heat, how creamy. Droplets of sweat glow like moonstones on her flawless skin.

"Gertrude," her mother calls, "Gertrude. I seen you come." Ugly, the Polish, the foreigner sound of her mother's voice. Ugly what waits upstairs. Spiders of heat waver through the splintered steps onto her red knuckled hands with their broken fingernails. Spasmodically Ginella folds their shame into her skirt. Ugly. Slender white fingers with talon fingernails float unattainable in the dust mote air. Ugly, I'm ugly.

"Gertrude," her mother calls again, "work waiting. You do before you have to go Mirkas or you get whipping. You be late Mirkas, you get whipping. Gertrude!" In an hour she must go to her aunt's diner, be among thick crowded, guttural-voiced, sweating working men; plunge her hands into scalding reddening water, be the slavey, scrub greasy pots and dishes and counter tops. "Hot, it's so hot," fanning her head from side to side. "I'm sick, Ma. I cant do nothin." Sick with the feverish heat; sick with an older feverish longing, unutterable, to be other than she is; to be otherwhere than she is—places spacious and elegant, idle and served and cool. *Slave of Desire. Forbidden Paradise.* Not shamed and shameful, not judged and condemned. "Classy, I want to be classy," she whispers.

"Gertrude," her mother yells, "Gertrude Skolnick. *Wstawach!* Now!" *Human Wreckage.* She starts up the stairs.

In the humid kitchen, Anna works on alone. Mazie lies swathed in sweated sleep in the baking bedroom.

Jimmie and Jeff sleep under the kitchen table, their exhausted bodies, their hair damp and clinging to their perspiring heads, giving them the look of drowned children. Ben lies in sleep or in a sleep of swoon, his poor heaving chest laboring on at its breathing. Bess has subsided in her basket on a chair where, if she frets, Anna can sprinkle her with water or try to ease the heat rash by sponging. The last batch of jelly is on the stove. Between stirring and skimming, and changing the wet packs on Ben, Anna peels and cuts the canning peaches—two more lugs to go. If only all will sleep awhile. She begins to sing softly—*I saw a ship a-sailing, a-sailing on the sea*—it clears her head. The drone of fruit flies and Ben's rusty breathing are very loud in the unmoving, heavy air. Bess begins to fuss again. *There, there, Bessie, there, there,* stopping to sponge down the oozing sores on the tiny body. *There.* Skim, stir; sprinkle Bess; pit, peel and cut; sponge; skim, stir. Any second the jelly will be right and must not wait. Shall she wake up Jimmie and ask him to blow a feather to keep Bess quiet? No, he'll wake cranky, he's just a baby hisself, let him sleep. Skim, stir; sprinkle; change the wet packs on Ben; pit, peel and cut; sponge. This time it does not soothe—Bess stiffens her body, flails her fists, begins to scream in misery, just as the jelly begins to boil. There is nothing for it but to take Bess up, jounce her on a hip *(there, there)* and with her one free hand frantically skim and ladle. *There, there.* The batch is poured and capped and sealed, all one-handed, jiggling-hipped. There, there, it is done.

Anna's knees begin to tremble. No, she dare not sit. *You know if you set down you'll never make yourself get up again.* One of the jelly glasses has burst; the amber drips onto the floor, has to be mopped; and Bess still to be hushed. *Hush you, hush, you'll wake every sleeping one, there, there,* transferring her to the other hip and one-handed sponging her again and her own sweating face as well. *There, there, poor baby.* The tenderness mixes with a compulsion of exhaustion to have done, to put Bess outside in the yard where she can scream and scream outside of hearing and Anna can be free to splash herself with running water, forget the canning and the kids and sink into a chair, lay her forehead on the table and do nothing. *There, there, Bessie, there, there, we'll go out a spell, see what's outside,* fixing a sun shade for the baby out of a soaked dish towel.

The stink, the stink. What glares so? The air is feverish; it lies in a stagnant swill of heat haze over the river and tracks below. Anna gags, turns to go back in from the stench and swelter, but Bess has quieted, is reaching her arms to the air. Giant cracks have opened in the earth. At her feet she sees her garden is dying; each plant in its own manner, each plant known and dear to her, blackening or curling or shriveling or blotching. "I aint had time, I'm sorry," she whispered. "The water's savin for sundown waterin time. And maybe nothin coulda helped. *There, there, Bessie.* I cant stand here and be shade for you neither," thinking with bowed head of the dying crops—corn and wheat and tomatoes and beans—and farmers' families drooping in the miles and miles of baking prairie. "Burning all over, Bessie," she said, "Kansas and Dakota and Ioway too," and went to fetch the saved water. The first pail ran off as if off clay, the earth refusing to absorb. The second pail she sloshed slowly, still one-handed *(there, there, Bessie),* breaking the flow over her grateful feet, red and swollen from the all-day standing. The water sinking into the dried earth seemed to sink into something parched and drought-eaten in her as well. "We have to go in, baby," she said, "we'll scorch," but stood there in the mud-feet coolness and the blister air, making the slenderest shade over the tomato plants. Stinging dust, spitting up suddenly from a quick hot wind, took her by surprise. She covered Bess's face, saw that great columns of dust-wraiths were swirling across the river and down the street. *There, there;* Bess's body relaxed into sleep.

The furnace wind was gone as suddenly as it came, though dust still moved through the again stagnant air. Washing her feet in the kitchen, she saw in astonishment a thick dust frosting on the caked mud; dust pitted in every visible pore of her legs and arms. All had settled outside; inside her sleepers slept. She started back on the peaches.

Five o'clock. Still 107°.

Mazie half wakes from her sweated sleep; her mother is sponging her, calling her name urgently over and over. "You been sleepin so long I got worried; everytime I looked in on you, you was sleepin. Are you all right? I cant tell is it fever or this heat? Tell me, where is it hurts? . . ."

Still the need to slither along the floor; douse, rid herself of her vast billowing head.

Somehow on the couch in the kitchen beside Ben, head to his feet, feet to his head. The sun is slanting its long last rays through the window. An iridescence floats on her hand, rainbows the wall, shifts in scales of hue here and there in the room. What is it, what is it? The hanging prism? One of the rays, touching it, has cracked open; burst; unfolded the radiance. The others still slant unbroken—straight shafts of light, clear threads of glass. Are the rainbows, the floating pools, the radiance folded into each one of them too? Where kept? How hidden? The wonder dazes her head and she turns her hand to hold the stammering light, unlock its magic, but she grasps shadows, and the iridescence glides onto Ben's unconscious face.

Not knowing an every-hued radiance floats on her hair, her mother stands at the sink; her knife seems flying. Fruit flies rise and settle and rise.

"Momma."

"It's the last batch," she answers. "Are you all right?" Smiling with the happiness of the worst not having happened. "Benjy's better too. Wait, soon I can sponge you. . . Can you drink something or try a little sugar bread?"

Jim does not stagger nor waddle coming in; it is more a hitching, straight for the sink—turns the water on full force, gulping great draughts, submerging his face, dousing himself. Red, boiled; under the faucet blowing his walrusy spray. Grabbing the watering bucket and splashing it over himself, filling and refilling it, pouring it over his body.

Running for a towel to wipe him, a pitcher she can fill and a glass to drink from, some relief she can give him. "Jimmie run to Kryckszis quick and ask ice for poppa." Anna thinks: The water, the water; hating herself for thinking: The money, the waiting garden, the mess to be cleaned, will it be one more, Jim bad-sick too? and begs: "What happened, Jim? What's the matter?"

But Jim lies as if he were drunk, out by the stoop in the evening shadow, sousing himself with sponge and the pail water, and will not speak.

Seven o'clock. Heat lightning. 106°.

Jim still lies on his water-soaked pallet below the stoop, but he sleeps now, snoring, twitching his hands.

Ben shifts around to lie in Mazie's arms—not too close, for it is so hot. "'Splain to me about bad dreams," he whispers into her ear, "tell me about boogie mans and scaredies and ghosts and hell."

Flies bumble and fry in the lamp; peach and amber jars of jelly and fruit cover every surface. Anna sits at last, holding Bess at the kitchen table, singing with heat-cracked lips "I Saw a Ship a-Sailing," waiting for Will to come home so that the lights can go out and the trying-to-sleep time can begin again. *I Saw a Ship* . . . It is all heat delirium and near suffocation now.

Bang!

Bess who has been fingering a fruit-jar lid—absently, heedlessly drops it—aimlessly groping across the table, reclaims it again. Lightning in her brain. She releases, grabs, releases, grabs. I can do. Bang! I did that. I can do. I! A look of neanderthal concentration is on her face. That noise! In triumphant, astounded joy she clashes the lid down. Bang, slam, whack. Release, grab, slam, bang, bang. Centuries of human drive work in her; human ecstasy of achievment, satisfaction deep and fundamental as sex: *I can do, I use my powers; I! I!* Wilder, madder, happier the bangs. The fetid fevered air rings with Anna's, Mazie's, Ben's laughter; Bess's toothless, triumphant crow. Heat misery, rash misery transcended.

And Will comes in to the laughter with coils and boxes and a long, long wire. One by one, on the Metzes borrowed crystal set, they hear for the first time the radio sound. From where, from where, thinks Mazie, floating on her pain; like the spectrum in the ray, the magic concealed; and hears in her ear the veering transparent meshes of sound, far sound, human and stellar, pulsing, pulsing. . . .

Dust blows up and, stinging, flings itself against the house. Anna imagines the great dust wraiths swirling again, goes to wake Jim and urge him in. Trees move in the furnace wind, in the lightning quiver. She yearns to be out into it.

"Jim, wake up. Come in, come in; this dust. . . . Bess . . . Mazie . . . The cannin' . . . The crystal set."

He is too dazed to listen.

"Here, I'll help you. The air's changin, Jim. I see for it to end tomorrow, at least get tolerable. Come in and get freshened up.

Reader, it was not to have ended here, but it is nearly forty years since this book had to be set aside, never to come to completion.

These pages you have read are all that is deemed publishable of it. Only fragments, rough drafts, outlines, scraps remain—to tell what might have been, and never will be now.

Yonnondio! Yonnondio! —unlimn'd they disappear.